THE JAGUAR STONES

Book Three

THE RIVER OF NO RETURN

J&P VOELKEL

EGMONT
USA
New York

AUTHORS' NOTE

The Jaguar Stones are fictional, as are all the characters in this book except for Friar Diego de Landa, the true-life Spanish priest who made one big bonfire of ancient Maya books and artworks. San Xavier is a fictional country based on present-day Belize.

EGMONT

We bring stories to life

First published by Egmont USA, 2012
443 Park Avenue South, Suite 806
New York, NY 10016

Copyright © J&P Voelkel, 2005, 2012
All rights reserved

1 3 5 7 9 8 6 4 2

www.egmontusa.com
www.jaguarstones.com

Library of Congress Cataloging-in-Publication Data
Voelkel, Jon.
The river of no return / J&P Voelkel.
p. cm. — (The Jaguar Stones ; bk. 3)
Summary: "Deep in the jungle, Max and Lola battle a zombie army, mutant cave spiders, and even the ancient Maya Lords of Death"—Provided by publisher.
ISBN 978-1-60684-073-3 (hardcover) — ISBN 978-1-60684-270-6 (e-book) [1. Adventure and adventurers--Fiction. 2. Supernatural—Fiction. 3. Mayas—Fiction. 4. Indians of Central America—Fiction.] I. Voelkel, Pamela. II. Title.
PZ7.V861Ri 2012
[Fic]—dc23
2012007093

Book design by Becky Terhune
Illustrations by Jon Voelkel

Printed in the United States of America

To Harry, Charly, and Loulou

k yahkume'ex

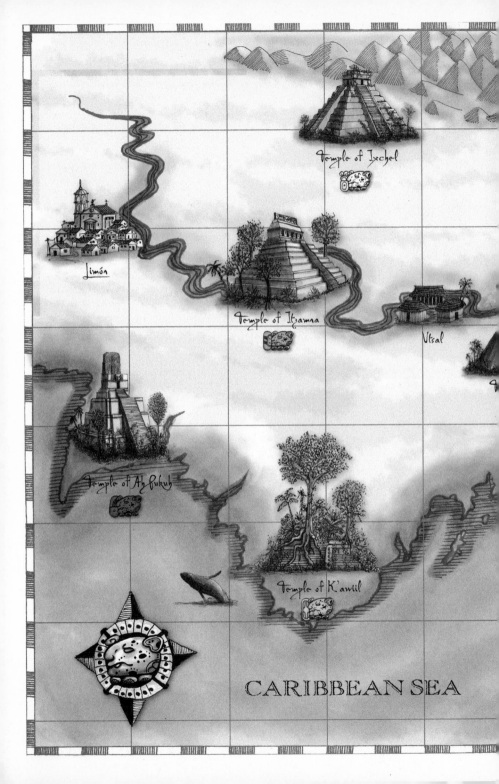

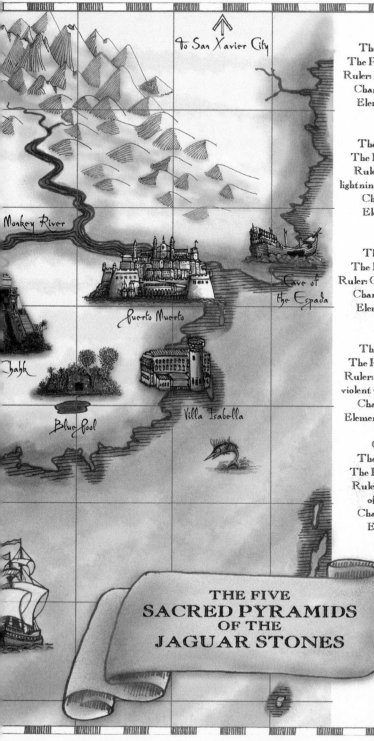

To San Xavier City

Monkey River

Cave of
the Espada

Puerto Muerto

Chahk

Blue Pool

Villa Isabella

NORTH:
The White Jaguar
The Pyramid of Visions
Ruler: Ixchel, moon goddess
Channels: Creativity
Element: Alabaster

SOUTH:
The Yellow Jaguar
The Pyramid of Blood
Ruler: K'awiil, god of
lightning, lineage & kingship
Channels: Truth
Element: Amber

EAST:
The Red Jaguar
The Pyramid of Rain
Ruler: Chahk, god of storms
Channels: Prosperity
Element: Fire Opal

WEST:
The Black Jaguar
The Pyramid of Death
Ruler: Ah Pukuh, god of
violent & unnatural death
Channels: Courage
Element: Black Obsidian

CENTER:
The Green Jaguar
The Pyramid of Time
Ruler: Itzamna, lord
of the heavens
Channels: Wisdom
Element: Jade

THE FIVE
SACRED PYRAMIDS
OF THE
JAGUAR STONES

CONTENTS

	CAST OF CHARACTERS	10
	PREFACE: THE DREAM	14
I.	ROGUE OCTOPUS	21
II.	PIZZA GELATO	30
III.	MASQUERADE	44
IV.	THE BLACK PYRAMID	66
V.	WAKING THE DEAD	72
VI.	MIDNIGHT MEETING	80
VII.	CLAUSTROPHOBIA	91
VIII.	A NEW PLAN	104
IX.	CRASH LANDING	116
X.	CHANGES	130
XI.	HURRICANE HOTEL	142
XII.	IN THE DARK	158
XIII.	TERMITE TAMALE	169
XIV.	THE LAST JAGUAR	178
XV.	THE VAMPIRE'S KISS	185

XVI.	PYRAMID OF PERIL 3-D	194
XVII.	SHAMPOOS, TATTOOS, BAD NEWS	205
XVIII.	SHOWTIME	218
XIX.	THE SUPERHERO TWINS	229
XX.	THE TAPIR'S REVENGE	247
XXI.	ACROSS THE ABYSS	261
XXII.	THE VISION SERPENT	280
XXIII.	ATTACK OF THE ZOMBIES	298
XXIV.	FACING THE MUSIC	306
XXV.	NO MORE SECRETS	320
	GLOSSARY	338
	A MIDDLEWORLD BESTIARY	342
	A SIDE TRIP TO VENICE	344
	MAYA BEAUTY SECRETS	346
	MAYA CALENDAR	347
	RECIPE—PIZZA GELATO	348
	ACKNOWLEDGMENTS	349

CHARACTERS
In order of appearance

MAX (Massimo Francis Sylvanus) MURPHY: fourteen years old, only child, video gamer, drummer, pizza connoisseur

LOLA (Ix Sak Lol—*each sock loll*): Maya girl about Max's age

DEMON OF FILTH: one of the twelve ancient Maya Death Lords—along with his colleagues ONE DEATH, SEVEN DEATH, BLOOD GATHERER, WING, PACKSTRAP, BONE SCEPTER, SKULL SCEPTER, SCAB STRIPPER, DEMON OF WOE, DEMON OF PUS, and DEMON OF JAUNDICE

NASTY (Anastasia) SMITH-JONES: Max's friend, music blogger

FABIO: Venetian gondolier

FRANK and CARLA MURPHY: Max's parents, archaeologists and Harvard professors

LORD KUY (*coo-ee*): messenger of the Lords of Death

AH PUKUH (*awe pooh coo*): Maya god of violent and unnatural death

EEK' KITAM, aka BLACK PECCARY aka SKUNK PIG aka STINK PIG: zombie warrior from the Undead Army

OCH and his brother, LITTLE OCH: village children from Utsal

UNCLE TED: Max's uncle, banana exporter and reformed smuggler

LORD 6-DOG (Ahaw Wak Ok—*uh how walk oak*): ancient Maya king

EUSEBIO: chili farmer and boatman

CHAN KAN: Maya wise man, Lola's adoptive grandfather

CONCIERGE: head of Guest Services at the Grand Hotel Xibalba

BAHLAM: one of the last wild jaguars of the Monkey River area

RAY LOVE, aka LOVERBOY: movie star famous for his vampire roles

KOO: stylist at the hotel beauty salon

ANTONIO DE LANDA, aka TOTO: Spanish aristocrat and descendant of Diego de Landa, the priest who burned Maya books

PUNAK HA: ancient Maya king, Lord 6-Dog's father

IXCHEL (*eesh shell*): ancient Maya moon goddess

PRINCESS INEZ: Maya princess, wife of Max's conquistador ancestor

SYLVANUS GRISWOLD MORLEY: archaeologist most famous for his excavations at Chichen Itza and his work as an American spy in World War I

LADY COCO (Ix Kan Kakaw—*each con caw caw*): Lord 6-Dog's mother

HERMANJILIO (*herman-kee-leo*) BOL: San Xavier archaeologist, university professor, Lola's mentor

RAUL: Uncle Ted's butler

JAIME BEN aka LUCKY JIM: Uncle Ted's former foreman and bodyguard

ZIA: the Murphy family's mysterious housekeeper

The continuing
adventures of
a city boy and a jungle girl
who are about to discover
that in life,
unlike in video games,
you can never, *ever* go back.

(Unless, of course, you happen
to be a zombie, a vampire,
or an ancient Maya
Lord of Death.)

THE DREAM

"**O**ne last mission," Max pleaded. "Just help me rescue the White Jaguar, and I promise I'll never ask you for another thing." He gave Lola what he hoped was an irresistible smile. "It'll be fun. You and me, working together again. Like old times."

Lola curled her lip at him. "There is no you and me."

"How can you say that," protested Max, "after everything we've been through together? Underground rivers, haunted temples . . . we're a team, remember?"

"I will *never* be on your team!"

She tried to run, but he blocked her way.

"Please, Monkey Girl, I'm begging you."

"Don't call me Monkey Girl."

"But it's our thing. I call you Monkey Girl because you hang around with howler monkeys. And you call me Hoop because . . . um . . . what was it again?"

"It's from the Mayan word for matchstick."

"Matchstick?"

"Red hair, white body—it's a joke."

He looked unconvinced. "So you'll do this one little thing for . . . for Hoop?"

"You're not Hoop."

He pulled the brim of his Red Sox cap lower. "Yes, I am."

"No, you're not."

"Why would you say that?"

"Oh, let me think," said Lola, looking him up and down. "Well, for one thing, Hoop keeps his intestines on the *inside* of his body."

The boy followed her eyes down until they came to rest on a loop of squirming purple intestine that was hanging out from under his shirt.

"Oops," he said.

"So which one are you?" asked Lola, folding her arms. "From the trailing innards, I'm guessing the Demon of Filth?"

The boy smirked and nodded.

Lola rolled her eyes. "Every night it's the same. One of you Death Lords appears in my dreams in some stupid disguise and tries to persuade me to bring you the White Jaguar."

"Hold that thought," said Filth, "while I change into something a little more comfortable." With a disgusting array of squelching, slurping, and popping noises as his body parts freed themselves from their disguise, the Demon of Filth shed his outer persona of a fourteen-year-old Boston teenager and emerged as his true self: a moldering corpse in a rat-skin loincloth, dragging his diseased guts behind him. A cloud of flies instantly formed over his head. "That's better," he said, stretching his waxy limbs. "Now where were we?"

"You were just leaving," replied Lola.

"I'm not going anywhere, Ix Sak Lol." (He called Lola by her Mayan name, meaning Lady White Flower.) "I'm under orders to torment you until you give in."

"Whose orders? Ah Pukuh's? I'm not afraid of him."

"You should be afraid of him. He is the god of violent and unnatural death, and he blames you for everything. As he sees it, you are all that stands between him and the power he seeks. He expects you to put things right."

"Why me?"

"It was *your* friend who stole the White Jaguar. So *you* need to bring it back. Or else."

"Or else what?"

"Or else Ah Pukuh will personally extract your heart."

Lola shrugged. "I can't win. If I *do* bring it back, Ah Pukuh will have all five Jaguar Stones—and I'll be doomed along with everyone else in Middleworld."

"Then join us, Ix Sak Lol. Come over to the winning side. We'd be like family." Filth glanced at her slyly. "Isn't that what you've always wanted—a family?"

Lola looked flustered. "I have a family," she answered defensively. "Chan Kan calls me Granddaughter."

Filth laughed so hard that his intestines danced pinkly on

the ground. "Chan Kan? That lying snake! You bad-mouth Ah Pukuh, but you praise Chan Kan?"

"He adopted me; he gave me a home."

"He has deceived you."

Lola's skin prickled. "What do you mean?"

"Ask him yourself"—Filth snickered—"if you live that long. You have until the next new moon to return the White Jaguar or . . ." He mimed open-heart surgery.

"Never." Lola's eyes flashed defiantly. "I will never betray the people of Middleworld."

Filth regarded her with interest. "Your selflessness is nauseating, but it gives me an idea. Let me rephrase my offer. You have until the new moon to return the White Jaguar, or it's Matchstick Boy's heart we'll take."

"Leave Hoop out of this. He isn't Maya. This is not his fight."

"Ever heard of globalism, Ix Sak Lol?"

"Stay away from him!"

A smile spread across Filth's rotting face. "I knew it! You might sacrifice your own life, but you would never sacrifice his!" He whooped in triumph like a sick hyena.

"You're insane," said Lola.

"I am inspired," replied Filth gleefully. "I can't wait to tell the guys about my idea."

"The guys? You mean the other Death Lords? You can tell them from me that your idea won't work."

"You'd let the Murphy brat die?"

"Of course," bluffed Lola, "if it would save the rest of humankind."

"You are lying, Ix Sak Lol. You do not have the stomach for this fight."

17

"Try me."

"Oh, we will try you. Return the White Jaguar, or you will have your little boyfriend's blood on your hands. . . ."

"He's not my boyf—," began Lola, but Filth had vanished.

All this time, the dream had taken place in what Lola had assumed was some dark and musty cavern in the underworld. Now flaming torches blazed into life, and she saw that it was a room built out of stone, its walls painted blood-red with toxic cinnabar. In the center, surrounded by jade carvings, quetzal feathers, painted pots, jaguar pelts, cocoa beans and spiny oyster shells, was a carved stone sarcophagus worthy of an ancient Maya king.

And then she understood that her dream was set in a royal tomb.

But why?

Was it to be *her* tomb?

She tried to wake herself. But like being stuck in quicksand, the more she struggled, the deeper the dream sucked her in.

There was a noise behind her, and she turned to see a stone slab descending to block the doorway. She wanted to roll out under it, but her feet seemed to be glued to the floor. With seconds to spare before the slab reached the ground, something— some*one!*—shot underneath and tumbled into the tomb.

"Hello, Monkey Girl," he said, getting to his feet.

"Very funny," said Lola. "I see you've remembered to tuck in your intestines this time."

"I'm sorry? Is that some kind of password?"

"Stand still and let me look at you."

Lola inspected her visitor from head to toe.

Max shuffled uncomfortably. "What are you doing?"

"I'm looking for a clue."

"What kind of—?"

"Got it!"

It was a trace of black hair dye, a few dark patches left over from Max's stint as a rock star in Spain. But it was enough to convince Lola that this was the boy from Boston and not a Death Lord in disguise.

"Hoop? Is it really you? What are you doing here?"

"You tell me. This is your dream. What happens next?"

Lola considered the question.

And suddenly, she knew exactly what happened next. She wanted to warn him, to tell him to run from her, and never stop running. But she couldn't speak.

Meanwhile, Max looked innocently around. "This place looks familiar. Have we been inside this temple before?"

His smile faded as she pulled a knife out of thin air and hurled it at him.

"Have you gone crazy?" he yelled.

She tried to hold down her own arm, to fight the force that was making her attack him. She focused her mind and tried to wrestle back control, but it was no use. The Death Lords were directing her dream as if it were a movie, and she was nothing but a puppet in their evil show.

All she could do was hope that Max saw the sorrow in her eyes as she aimed another blade at the boy she considered her best friend.

Whoosh! Whoosh! Whoosh! As soon as one knife left her hand, another one took its place.

Max jumped and dodged and ducked, like a character in one of his video games.

But no matter how agile Hoop was, Lola knew there could be no escape.

19

This royal tomb would also be Max Murphy's last resting place.

With a bloodcurdling scream, she shut her eyes and let loose the final volley that would chop him into little pieces.

Mission accomplished.

As the mutant corpse-eating tomb slugs slithered out to begin their feast, she turned away. *It's only a dream*, she told herself.

But when she woke, her face was wet with tears.

Now she knew that the Death Lords meant business: if she didn't return the White Jaguar, they would wreak their vengeance on Max—and it would be her fault, just as surely as if she'd killed him herself.

The new moon would be in two weeks' time.

Two weeks.

She had to warn him . . . before it was too late.

Chapter One

ROGUE OCTOPUS

"I like your purple hair," said Max. "It was black last time I saw you."

Nasty Smith-Jones combed her spiky bangs with her fingers. "Yours was black, too, in Spain, remember?" She peered at Max's thick reddish hair. "There are still some bits that haven't quite washed out."

"That was my rock-star look. I'm thinking of dying it again."

"No! If my parents realize you're the same boy they met in Spain, they'll ban me from ever seeing you again!"

Max looked offended.

"You can't blame them," Nasty pointed out. "You promised to take them to a high-society wedding, not a grudge match between an ancient Maya god and a talking howler monkey!"

"I guess they have a point." Max laughed. "So what did they make of it all? I thought they'd have dragged you back to Boston on the first plane out."

"I convinced them it was performance art and that we'd been lucky to see it. Once they'd calmed down, they decided to carry on with their grand tour of Europe."

"And now here you are in Venice."

Nasty smiled at him. "Here you are, too."

It was a golden afternoon. As their gondola floated down the Grand Canal, the sun bounced off domes and church bells and glass-fronted galleries, and transformed the water into shimmering emeralds as green and bright as the Monkey River in the jungles of San Xavier.

Nasty stuck out her tongue at some children on a bridge as the gondola glided underneath. "Bummer that you've just arrived and I'm flying home tonight. It would have been fun to hang out."

"I'll be back in Boston soon, too," Max assured her.

"You're not going back to the jungle?"

"Nope. All that Maya stuff is over now. The Death Lords can't get me anymore."

"So that gross guy in the eyeball headdress won't be back?"

"Ah Pukuh? No chance. According to the Maya calendar, he's next in line to rule the cosmos. But he'd need all five Jaguar Stones to do any real damage."

"How many has he got?"

"Four."

"Four!" Underneath her punky black eyeliner, Nasty's blue eyes were wide with alarm. "You mean he only needs one more?"

"Yes, but he can't get it. It's impossible. Trust me."

"Promise?"

"Promise."

"Good to know!" Nasty grinned at Max. "So call me when you get back and I'll give you the inside tour of Beacon Hill. Iggy Pop once stayed at a house on our street."

"Cool," said Max, trying to sound nonchalant, but inside his heart was pogoing for joy. Did Nasty Smith-Jones, the coolest girl in Boston, just ask him out?

He exchanged a knowing smile with Fabio, their stripy-shirted, straw-hatted gondolier, and sank back into the cushions.

Life was good.

His quest was over and he was finally free of the Maya and the Jaguar Stones and the twelve Lords of Death. Nobody was threatening him, nobody was chasing him, nobody was trying to kill him. He was an ordinary kid again, just one more American tourist in Venice, with nothing more pressing to worry about than what kind of pizza to try next. He closed his eyes and let the baking Italian sun burn away all memory of Xibalba, the cold and watery Maya underworld.

"*Attenzione!*" called Fabio.

Max held on tightly as the gondola lurched from side to side, rocking and spinning, as if it were caught in a whirlpool. The gondolier fought to keep control, but when his oar was snatched out of his hand by the raging water, he gave up and cowered in the back of the boat, every bit as scared as his passengers.

Max, Nasty, and Fabio screamed as the gondola was pitched upward.

Aware that what goes up must come down, Max braced himself for a splash landing. But the boat just hung in midair. It felt like the moment when a roller coaster pauses at the top of the first hill.

Peering cautiously over the side, Max saw that the whole Grand Canal was watching them.

All the boats below them had stopped in midstream, their crews and passengers frozen in surprise and horror. They seemed to be transfixed by something underneath the gondola, but Max didn't dare lean out farther to see what it was.

"What's happening?" he called back to Fabio.

"*Non lo so,*" cried the terrified boatman—"I don't know." Fabio had lost his straw hat and his jaunty little necktie, and his face was as white as mozzarella cheese. But even as he answered, their descent had begun and they plummeted back into the canal. As they hit the water, a small tidal wave washed over the gondola.

"Start bailing!" yelled Max, using his Red Sox cap to scoop out the water. "We're sinking!"

Nasty and Fabio didn't move.

"Help me!" he ordered them.

Still they didn't move. They were just staring ahead, wide-eyed.

Max turned and followed their gaze.

And looked straight into an unblinking black eye as big as a laptop screen, surrounded by a hood of rubbery pinky-orange freckled skin.

"Octo—" was all he could say, before a massive tentacle snaked up behind him and gripped him by the throat, wrapping itself around his neck and mouth.

His nose was filled by a briny, musty smell that made him want to vomit. Clammy blubber blocked his airways. He was suffocating in cephalopod. It was the biggest octopus he'd ever seen, bigger than he even knew existed. And it appeared to have singled him out for dinner.

He tried to pull it off, but as soon as he detached one tentacle, another would take its place. It seemed that there were tentacles everywhere—encircling his arms and legs, squeezing his flesh, freezing his blood—the icy-cold suckers locking tight to his skin.

He couldn't move, couldn't fight back, as the monstrous mollusk dragged him overboard, tipping the gondola and plunging Nasty and Fabio into the water.

Through a narrow gap between coils of slimy tentacle, Max caught a glimpse of them swimming toward the life preservers tossed from other boats.

But for him there was no rescue.

The giant octopus dragged him down, down, under the water, no longer shimmering but murky and cold, where hairy mussel shells clung to old boat ropes, and ugly, sharp-toothed fish stopped to stare at the colossal sea creature with its human captive.

Down, down, ever deeper, where Maya carvings were now visible in the stone walls of the canal.

Down, down, deeper even than the wooden pilings that supported the waterlogged city.

Down, down, past rocks and caves, until Max knew they were diving to the place where all waters met, the place of fear, the great icy pool of the Maya underworld.

His lungs were filling with water.

His eyes were closing.

He was losing consciousness.

Then he saw her, swimming toward him out of the darkness.

It was Lola, come to save him.

There was flash of metal, a knife blade, and suddenly the octopus was losing its grip. Max could move his legs, then his arms; then the tentacles around his face fell away.

Lola pointed upward, and his last sight as he kicked to the surface was of the octopus, its skin bright red with anger, its eyes sunk inward, its beak flapping, its inky blue blood leaking into the water.

"Max! Max!"

"Lola? What are you doing here?"

"Are you okay? That was horrible."

He was lying on hard ground.

Everyone was shouting in Italian.

The world was a blur.

He shut his eyes.

That was a close one.

But Lola had saved him.

She always saved him.

He reached for her hand. "How did you find me?" he asked.

"We were on the gondola. Don't you remember?"

He opened his eyes.

"Nasty? Where's Lola?"

"Lola? She's in San Xavier, isn't she?"

"No, she was in the canal. . . ." His voice trailed off as he watched a gang of fishermen haul up the octopus. It didn't look nearly as big as he remembered it.

"I don't think so," said Nasty gently.

"But she saved me. . . ."

Nasty's hair dripped on his face. Her black eyeliner was all smeared, making her eyes look even bluer. "Fabio saved you. I saw it all. He dived in and cut you free. The canal's not deep. It was over in a flash."

"But I saw . . ."

Nasty squeezed his hand. "People see all sorts of things when they're drowning. Some people see their whole life in action replay."

"But what about . . . ?" his voice tailed off.

"What?" she asked. "What else did you see? Tell me."

How could he tell her that he was going mad? That five seconds had felt like five minutes. That he'd seen Maya glyphs on the walls of a Venetian canal, and imagined that the warm tide from the summer lagoon had washed over him as cold and deep as the bottomless waters of Xibalba?

He hadn't realized how badly the whole crazy Jaguar Stones thing had messed up his head.

Nasty passed him a towel and wrapped another one around herself.

"Are you okay?" she asked. "How do you feel?"

How *did* he feel?

He felt wet, and he felt cold. But most of all, he felt like he wanted to see Lola.

He hugged the towel around him like a blanket.

After a while, as his heart rate returned to normal, he started to feel pretty foolish. He was fairly sure that one of the uncoolest things a guy could do in front of a girl was to get sucked off a gondola in a freak octopus attack.

And it wasn't like he could pretend it had never happened.

He groaned to think of all the tourist photos and videos that were being uploaded to social networks at that very moment.

He would never live it down.

He buried his head in the towel.

A cheer went up from the canal.

He peeked out.

"It's the fishermen," explained Nasty. "They're celebrating. Fabio said that the whole of Venice will be feasting on your octopus tonight!"

Max grimaced. "Where is Fabio? I should thank him for saving me."

28

"He's back in the water, trying to salvage his gondola. He told me to tell you that he's never lost a tourist yet."

"There's always a first time," said Max, rubbing his hair with the towel. "You must think I'm an idiot."

Nasty gaped at him. "What? No! I think you're really brave. It was totally cool the way you grappled with those tentacles."

"It was?" Max felt a little glow of pride.

And just like that, he put out of his mind what he'd known all along. That ancient Maya Death Lords were not the kind to forgive and forget. That Ah Pukuh, god of violent and unnatural death, still had a bone to pick with him. And that, as surely as a shark had carried him down to Xibalba on the Spanish Coast of Death, this giant octopus was an infernal messenger sent to drag him to the depths of hell.

"We should call your parents," said Nasty. "You might have a concussion."

"I'm fine," insisted Max. "Let's just sit in the sun and dry out."

Nasty looked around for a good spot.

"Over there?" She pointed at a café on the canal side.

As Max got to his feet, a ferry revved its engines at a floating dock and sent a wave splashing onto the paving stones. The water lapping at his toes reminded him of foamy fingers pulling him back to Xibalba. "Let's find somewhere more inland."

"Easier said than done," Nasty pointed out. "Venice is built on water."

Chapter Two

PIZZA GELATO

"Tonight, the chef recommends pan-fried octopus, fresh today from the Grand Canal. *Molto bene!*"

"My son helped to catch it," Max's father told the waiter proudly.

"We must order it!" chimed in his mother. "How fun!"

"Please don't!" Max begged her. "I don't want to see it."

His parents and the waiter looked at him with surprise.

"Why ever not?" asked his mother.

Still feeling slightly foolish about the whole episode, Max hadn't told his parents how close he'd actually come to drowning, nor about the strange Maya visions that had flooded his oxygen-starved brain. "It looked old and tough and rubbery. It won't taste good," was all he said.

"If *signor* prefers something smaller, we also have squid in its own ink," suggested the waiter.

Carla Murphy looked hopefully at her son.

"Nothing with tentacles," said Max firmly. "I'll have pizza Margherita."

While his parents meekly studied their menus, Max studied the hotel restaurant.

It was an old-fashioned kind of place with crystal chandeliers, wood-paneled walls, thick white tablecloths, upholstered chairs, and red velvet curtains. The waiters, too, were the epitome of elegance, in crisply ironed white shirts, black bow ties, and smart black pants. But their formal attire was somewhat undermined by the addition of thigh-high rubber waders that squelched and squeaked as they walked.

"What's with the fisherman's boots?" he asked his mother as they waited for their food. "Is it an Italian fashion thing?"

"They are expecting a high tide."

"What? Inside the restaurant?"

She nodded sadly. "Venice is sinking, *bambino*. At high tide, the water sometimes rises up through the floor."

Max scanned the marble underfoot for signs of leakage. "How could a whole city sink?"

"A better question might be: Why would anyone build a city on marshland?" Max's father warmed to his topic. "Many people think it's a wonder that La Serenissima—the Most Serene Republic of Venice—exists at all. It's really a collection of man-made islands, resting on wooden poles jammed into the mud."

Max looked alarmed. "Could it sink tonight?"

His father laughed. "It's lasted fifteen hundred years against the odds. I think we have time for dinner."

"It would take more than a high tide to close this restaurant," observed Max's mother. "We Italians love to eat."

Venice was Max's mother's hometown, and every time she returned, *we Italians* became her new favorite phrase.

"*Grazie*," she said, as a plate of stewed tripe was placed in front of her.

"*Prego*," said the waiter.

"*Grazie*," said Max's father, as he received a grilled lobster.

"*Prego*," said the waiter.

Max said nothing as his pizza was set down.

Aware that the waiter was hovering, he set about assessing it like a judge on a cooking show.

First, he tapped the crust with his knife.

Good. The center had a nice spring to it, while the edge was charred and flaky.

Next, the melted cheese.

He sniffed. It smelled divine. Best of all, it was still bubbling.

"*Grazie*," said Max, nodding.

"*Prego*," said the waiter. "*Buon appetito.*" He looked like his heart would burst with happiness as he headed back to the kitchen.

"I don't get it," said Max's father. "It's just pizza."

"This is Italy, Dad. The birthplace of pizza. They recognize an expert when they see one."

Max's father rolled his eyes.

"Let's eat!" said Max's mother. "*Mangia!*" She waved her hand expansively, knocking over the pepper mill.

"Steady on, Mom," said Max.

"Sorry, *bambino*, I can't help it. We Italians are famous for our flamboyant gestures."

We Italians. There it was again.

Max went to rip off a slice of pizza, but his mother stayed his hand.

Seriously? Max sighed. In exaggerated deference to the European gods of etiquette, he picked up his knife and fork and cut off a dainty triangle of pizza.

Frank and Carla Murphy smirked smugly to watch their offspring's mastery of silverware.

Not for the first time, Max reflected on the warped values of the adult mind. How was it, after everything his family had been through, that his parents could still care about table manners? Then again, there was something reassuringly normal about it.

And normal was something that had been missing in Max's life lately.

He decided to give his parents a treat.

Slowly and carefully, he unfolded his napkin and dabbed at his mouth.

His mother almost trembled with joy.

Yeah, thought Max, if he ignored the water that was now bubbling through the floor and lapping around his ankles, everything was normal again.

Was it possible that only a few weeks ago he'd been a tourist in Xibalba, the Maya underworld? He'd delivered the Yellow Jaguar to the Death Lords and they'd almost tricked him into staying. It was only thanks to the quick thinking of Princess Inez, the dead wife of one of Max's ancestors (a conquistador named Rodrigo), that he'd survived to tell the tale. Inez had taken his place on the Death Lords' ship and sailed away with them on a river of phosphorescent scorpions.

His mother's voice cut through his thoughts. "How is the pizza?"

"It's good, really good." Max took another chewy, cheesy, melty mouthful.

"But save room for dessert, *bambino*. I have something special planned."

"Aha," said Max's father. "Is that why you disappeared all afternoon, Carla? I knew you were up to something."

Max's mother smiled. "No more questions. I want it to be a surprise. I thought we deserved a treat after all that"—she searched for the right word—"*drama* we had recently."

"Drama" was a bit of an understatement, thought Max. She was referring to the time when their ordinary little Boston family had got sucked into an ancient Maya nightmare. It all started when Ah Pukuh, god of violent and unnatural death, decided to reassert himself with a little help from the Jaguar Stones, the five sacred stones of the Maya kings. He'd tasked his henchmen, the twelve Lords of Death, to find the stones—and they, in turn, had forced Max and his Maya friend Lola to do their dirty work.

With all five Jaguar Stones sitting in Xibalba, it would have been game, set, and match to the forces of darkness. But—and Max smiled to himself every time he thought about it—in a glorious, last-minute twist of fate, the good guys had managed to smuggle the White Jaguar out of Xibalba right under the Death Lords' noses.

And that, as far as Max was concerned, was the end of the story.

"I'm just glad all that 'drama' "—he made quote marks with his fingers—"is over."

His father nodded. "Well, you're safe enough here. The Death Lords won't be coming to Venice anytime soon." He chuckled to himself. "Can you imagine them sailing down the Grand Canal in a gondola?"

Max looked at him in horror. After his encounter with the octopus, he could imagine it all too easily.

"Enough about the Death Lords!" Max's mother quickly

changed the subject. "Did you have a nice afternoon with your friend from Boston?"

"I guess. Apart from the octopus."

"You should have invited your friend to join us for dinner, *bambino*."

"She's flying back to Boston tonight."

"She? It's a she?" Max's mother's eyes lit up. "Who is she?"

"No one you know."

Max concentrated on wolfing down his pizza.

"That boy can clean a plate faster than a column of army ants," muttered his father.

Max looked up. "How fast are army ants?"

"I've heard they can dissolve a wild pig, snout to tail, in a couple of hours."

"What do you mean, *dissolve?*"

"They liquidize their food before—"

"Frank! That is not dinner conversation," complained Max's mother. "No more jungle talk. We're on vacation."

Silence fell on the table.

His mother cast around for another subject. "This hotel is nice, isn't it?"

His father grunted. "So it should be, for what it charges. I don't know why we couldn't stay with your parents as usual, Carla."

"Their place is so small. I wanted us to have family time, just the three of us."

Max's thoughts drifted to his grandparents' dark little house in a Venetian backstreet. Every inch of it was filled with ornaments and knickknacks. It reminded him of the ramshackle hut of Chan Kan, the village wise man he'd met in San Xavier.

"Besides," his mother was saying, "we deserve a little luxury. The last few weeks have been very stressful."

"And the house needs time to recover," added his father. "It's still damp from having a rainforest growing inside it."

"I was thinking," said Max's mother, "that we should sell it."

Max and his father stopped chewing and stared at her.

"Why would we want to do that?" asked his father cautiously.

"So we can make a new start!" She reached across the table and patted Max's hand. "I have learned my lesson, *bambino*. I have not been the best mother but I am going to make it up to you. From now on, I am going to devote myself to looking after you. I want to stay home and cook all day."

Max sighed heavily. "Have you been reading that parenting book again, Mom?"

"This is my own idea. Home cooking binds families together. It is how Italian mothers express their love."

Max stared at her in disbelief. His mother's cooking did not express love so much as a desire to kill people by poisoning them. This was the worst plan he'd ever heard.

"But what about your job, Mom? You're the world's leading expert on Maya glyphs. You can't give up. So many archaeologists depend on you. And what about all your students at Harvard? No one else can teach that stuff like you can."

She hesitated for a second, then strengthened her resolve. "There is more to life than archaeology, *bambino*. We need to count our blessings. Look at Lola—"

"Where?" Max spun around in his chair, half expecting to see Lola walking through the restaurant as he had seen her in his drowning moments, still wet from the canal, with seaweed in her hair.

"Don't be silly, *bambino*, she is not here. I meant, look at Lola and how she has never known her parents. Poor thing. We should not take family for granted."

"Maybe we could just take more vacations together?" suggested Max.

But his mother had not finished talking about Lola. "I was wondering," she said, "have you heard from her lately?"

"No."

His parents exchanged a glance.

"You'll meet someone else, *bambino*."

"I don't want to meet anyone," mumbled Max.

"No point in moping." His father cracked a lobster claw. "How about this girl from Boston? Is she a Red Sox fan? As I remember, Lola wasn't interested in baseball."

Max could feel his cheeks burning. "Stop! Please! It's not like that. Me and Lola, we're just friends."

A passing waiter nodded in sympathy. "*Amore è gioia e dolori*," he muttered.

"What did he say?" asked Max suspiciously.

"Love—*amore*—is a joy and a sorrow," translated his mother. "We Italians are very romantic."

"It's not *amore*," snapped Max. He threw his napkin onto the table to signify how finished he was with both the meal and the conversation. "Can we go now?"

He half rose from his chair, but his mother pushed him firmly back down. "No, *bambino*. Not without dessert!"

"But Mom . . ."

"Humor her, Son," whispered his father.

His mother looked excited. "*Un momento*; I will be right back," she said as she sloshed through ankle-deep water, in the direction of the kitchen.

37

"We have to stop her," muttered Max.

"You don't want dessert, Son? I'll eat yours."

"No, Dad, I mean we have to stop her giving up her job. She'll poison us with her cooking."

"Come on, it's not that bad."

"Two words, Dad: salami soup."

He saw the fear in his father's eyes.

"I think she's made up her mind, Max."

"But you know she loves the Maya more than cooking. Can't you pull some strings, find a new research project, something she can't resist?"

"I'll do my best, but funding is in short supply right now. Besides, I'm sure she'll get bored of cooking in a year or two."

"A year or two?" Max repeated in horror. "How many dinners is that?"

A burst of opera rang out from his father's phone.

"I'm sorry, Max, it's a call from Harvard. Must be something urgent. If you'll excuse me for a moment, I'll take it in the lobby."

Max gazed out of the restaurant window. Duckboards had been set up to raise pedestrians above the flooded streets, and a never-ending line of tourists in yellow rain ponchos shuffled along in single file.

Somewhere in the darkness, a dog snarled.

Max stiffened.

It sounded like the savage, acid-dripping bark of a hellhound, one of the monstrous dogs sent by Ah Pukuh to pursue him all around Spain.

He shrank back in his chair, half expecting the vicious beast to burst through the plate glass window. "Calm down," he told himself. "The Death Lords can't get you here. They can't get you anywhere. You completed the mission. It's over."

As if to prove his point, the barking subsided into bad-tempered yaps, and a soggy poodle stared mournfully in at him as its owner stopped to read the restaurant menu.

Max smiled to himself.

He had to stop thinking that every barking dog was a hellhound.

He had to lose that hunted feeling.

A hand on his shoulder made him jump out of his skin.

He turned to see his mother holding out a little glass bowl.

"Try it, *bambino*."

Max looked in the bowl. Red sludge, flecked with green bits.

"What is it?"

"It's my new invention! Pizza Gelato!"

"Pizza Gelato?" repeated Max incredulously. "Ice cream and pizza? Mixed together? That's"—he was going to say "disgusting," but seeing his mother's excited expression, he stopped himself just in time—"unusual."

"I know, right? *Molto perfetto!* A stroke of genius! I feel like Leonardo da Vinci!"

She put down the bowl and took Max's hands. Her eyes were shining with excitement. "My vision is for a range of main-course gelati. You can be my chief taster! Pizza, spaghetti, clams . . . there is nothing we cannot make into gelato. We could even diversify into Pasta Popsicles. What do you think?"

Max disentangled his hands. His future was looking bleaker than ever. "Have you told Dad about this idea?"

"No, I wanted to surprise you both tonight. Where is he? Let's tell him together."

They found him slumped on a sofa in the lobby, staring at his phone. He looked shell-shocked.

"What is the matter? Did someone die?" cried Max's mother.

"No, but . . . sit down, Carla. We need to talk. Professor Delgado just called. She had some big news."

"Dolores Delgado? Our head of department? Was it good news or bad news?"

"I'm not sure."

"Frank, tell me. What did she say?"

"She said that an anonymous benefactor has offered her a grant to excavate the Black Pyramid of Ah Pukuh."

"But that is *good* news, Frank!"

"Well, it's just a cosmetic job at this stage. No tombs or interior rooms. They just want it all uncovered and smartened up a bit, so tourists can run up and down the steps."

"Doesn't she know that the Black Pyramid is a deathtrap?" interjected Max. "She should be telling the tourists to stay away. Lola was nearly sacrificed there and—"

"Now, now," said his father, "don't let your imagination run away with you. Things got a little crazy there for a moment with the Jaguar Stones but, these days, the Black Pyramid is just another overgrown ruin."

"What about—," Max tried to argue, but his parents were talking ten to the dozen.

"And it's in such a beautiful location," his mother was saying, "right by the sea. It would make a perfect stop for the cruise ships."

"That's exactly what this benefactor has in mind! They want to capitalize on the buzz about the so-called end of the Maya calendar and get started straightaway. So what do you think, Carla? Professor Delgado says the permits are in order and, with funding so scarce these days, she's keen to accept the offer."

"Absolutely," said Max's mother. "I would be happy to recommend some of my graduate students. They could make their names on a dig like this."

"Ah," said Max's father, "that's the bad news. It is a condition of the grant money that you and I undertake the job, Carla."

"Us? But that's impossible. We would have to relocate to San Xavier for months, maybe years. What about Max?"

"The benefactor has included a generous salary to compensate us for the inconvenience. Max could go to the best school in San Xavier, employ a private tutor, whatever he wants."

"Is anyone going to ask what I think?' asked Max.

His parents ignored him.

"Who is this benefactor?" asked his mother.

His father shrugged. "Some committee or other. I didn't catch the name. But as luck would have it, they're in Venice right now. They want to meet us at the Historical Society ball tomorrow night."

"A ball?" His mother brightened for a moment, then shook her head sadly. "We have to tell them no, Frank. It's out of the question."

"Won't you even consider it?"

"I promised Max I'd take a break from archaeology. We are going into business together."

"You and Max? What kind of business?"

She showed him the cup of rapidly melting herb-flecked red mush.

"What *is* that?" Max's father sounded appalled.

Max's mother looked hurt. "Savory gelato. It's our first flavor. Pizza Margherita."

"Is . . . is this really what you want, Max?" asked his father dubiously.

Before Max could answer, his mother answered for him: "Of course it's what he wants. It will be our family business."

"But we have a family business," his father reminded her. "It's archaeology."

They both turned to Max expectantly.

He looked miserably from one to the other.

Whichever parent he agreed with, he was doomed.

If his mother stayed home and cooked all day, he faced a lifetime of Pizza Gelato.

But if he chose his father's plan, he'd have to return to the Black Pyramid—where he'd already had two narrow escapes. (The first time he'd almost been tricked into signing away his soul; the second time, he'd narrowly avoided being hurled into the underworld for eternity.)

He sighed. "So let me get this straight. You promise that you wouldn't be working *inside* the Black Pyramid?"

"That's right. Our job is simply to make it look pretty so tourists can take photos and get back to the cruise ship."

"Maybe we could start up a gelato stand," mused his mother.

Max felt like a contestant on a game show.

He wished he could phone a friend.

Specifically, he wished he could phone Lola.

His father pressed him for a decision. "What's it to be, Max? What do you want?"

What did he want?

42

He thought about it.

What he really, really wanted was to see Lola.

Maybe his brain was addled from the octopus incident, but he'd been thinking about her nonstop ever since.

And Lola was in San Xavier.

Was it safe to go back?

Yeah, why not? He rationalized that all the bad stuff was caused by the portal-opening powers of the Black Jaguar. Since that stone—for better or worse—was now hidden away in Xibalba, there was no way anyone on Earth could reactivate the pyramid.

The question, he told himself, was not was it safe to go back to San Xavier, but was it safe to eat Pizza Gelato?

He took another look at the mush in the cup.

"Take the job," he said. "What's the worst that could happen?"

So that was how it started, the next round in the battle for planet Earth—not with a challenge or a war or a face-off, but with a cup of pizza-flavored dessert.

In the halls of Xibalba, a cheer went up.

"We did it!" crowed One Death, most senior of the Death Lords. "Now we will have our revenge."

"I can't believe they fell for it!" agreed the Demon of Pus. He took a handful of fried rat eyeballs from a gourd on the table and munched on them like popcorn. "That dame must be one bad cook."

Chapter Three
MASQUERADE

"**I**t will be a night you will always remember," Max's mother pointed out as she confiscated the video game controller. "Now stop playing games and start getting ready."

"But I don't want to go to the ball," wailed Max.

"Me neither," agreed his father. "But the benefactors will be there, and if we don't show up, we won't get the money."

"What's a ball anyway?" asked Max. "Is it all waltzes and footmen in wigs?"

"I hope not," said his father. "I'm planning to show off my new disco moves." He did an impression of a robotic rooster.

Max's mother looked from her husband to her son in despair. "What is the *matter* with you two? The Historical Society ball is a grand occasion. It is an honor to be invited."

Max shrugged. He was feeling jet-lagged and cranky. This was only their second night in Venice and now, thanks to last night's phone call from Harvard, his father had changed their tickets and they were flying back to Boston the next day. "Can't I just stay here and order room service?"

"Sorry, Son," said his father, "but the benefactors want to meet the whole family."

"Besides," added his mother, "you need to get out and see something of Venice. You've wasted the whole day in this room playing video games."

She had a point.

And, to tell the truth, he was getting a little bored.

Having girded himself in armor to fight lions in the Colosseum (*Gladiator Glory!*), donned doublet and hose to hunt down poisoners in medieval Florence (*Florentine Folly!*), and posed in a pin-striped suit to infiltrate gangsters in Sicily (*Mafia Meltdown!*), he'd come to realize that whoever had designed these Italian video games was more into fashion than special effects.

In any case, the real reason he'd stayed in the hotel all day was to wait for an e-mail from Lola.

As soon as he'd got back last night, he'd e-mailed her about his imminent return to San Xavier.

He'd expected an instant reply.

Maybe even a spontaneous outpouring of joy.

But nothing. Not a peep.

His mother, still talking about the ball, tried a new tack. "We can go for a big dinner afterward," she wheedled. "I heard of a place that makes pizzas the size of cart wheels."

Max sighed. He was helpless to resist the prospect of one last juicy, doughy, cheesy, real Italian pizza. "All right. Just promise that we won't stay long at this ball. And if you try to make me dance, I'm leaving."

"Deal." His mother smiled. "Let me show you your mask."

"Mask? What mask?"

"It's a masquerade ball. It's a Venetian tradition. Look, I'm a peacock"—she waved a greeny-bluey, feathery confection—"and your father is—"

"Wait, don't tell him!" Max's father ran into the other room.

"Okay now, Max," came his voice on the other side of the door, "imagine it's the Middle Ages. You're lying on your deathbed, covered in bubonic plague boils, waiting for the doctor and . . . knock, knock!"

A head popped round the door in a wide-brimmed black hat and a sinister white bird mask with wire spectacles and a long, thin, curving beak.

"Whoa! What are you? Doctor Death?"

His father stepped into the room, swishing his floor-length black coat. "Close. I'm a *medico della peste*, a plague doctor."

Max looked him up and down. "I don't get it."

"It was all designed to avoid contact with patients. Doctors stuffed the beak with herbs to ward off plague germs."

"Did it work?"

"I don't know. I'm more worried about how I'm going to eat anything while I'm wearing it."

Max brightened. "Will there be food?"

"Of course, *bambino*. We Italians would never throw a party without food."

Max's mother, who was now wearing a peacock-blue ball gown, handed him a black Zorro eye mask with a little gold braid at the edges. "Here, this is yours. It comes with a three-cornered hat and a cape, if you want to try the full effect."

Max put it all on and looked in the mirror. Much to his surprise, he looked pretty cool—like a mysterious and dashing highwayman.

"*Andiamo!*" said his mother, putting on her own mask. "Let's go."

It was getting dark, and a fog was rolling in from the lagoon. The wet streets bore evidence of an earlier high tide, but for now the canal water was staying within its bounds.

As Max's family crossed a little stepped bridge on their way to the water-taxi stop, a fat brown rat waddled across their path, its long tail dragging lazily behind it.

"And there's the culprit who brought the plague to Europe," said Max's father. "Or its fleas did, at any rate."

"Why isn't it scared of us?" asked Max.

"Why should it be? They say there are four rats in Venice for every human."

"There are three of us, so that makes twelve." Max looked nervously around for the brown rat's friends, then stamped his foot to scare it away.

The rat sat on its haunches, and looked straight at him.

It seemed to Max that they locked eyes.

What? Wait! Did that rat just wink at him?

As the rodent turned and plopped into the water, a bloodcurdling scream cut through the night air.

"What was that?" Max looked around nervously.

"Just a cat," said his mother.

"Or," said his father, his voice distorted by the plague-doctor mask, "was it the Blind Doge?"

"What's a doge?" asked Max, glad to drown out the spooky noises with conversation.

"Back in the days when Venice was a republic, the doge

was our elected ruler," replied his mother. "We do not have them anymore."

"No?" His father turned his sinister mask toward her. "And yet they say that the Blind Doge, Enrico Dandolo, still walks these streets at night, with burning coals for eyes. In life he was a ruthless warmonger. In death, to atone for the innocent blood he shed, he must carry a sword by its blade, constantly cutting his fingers on it and screaming in pain."

"Stop trying to frighten us, Frank. It was a cat," said Max's mother firmly.

"Are you sure?" teased his father. "Or was it that other famous Venetian, the Headless Doge? He was beheaded for treason and buried with his head between his legs. Now, with his hands still tied behind his back, his body wanders in search of his head, sobbing and crying out in shame."

"How can he cry out if he doesn't have a head?" asked Max.

"The point is," said his father, "that sometimes they pass on the street, the Blind Doge and the Headless Doge, but neither one can see the other."

Max's mother shuddered. "The streets of Venice are alive with ghosts." She pulled her shawl tighter around her, and her voice dropped to a whisper. "Tonight it reminds me of Xibalba . . . the chills and damp, the shapes in the mist, the smell of death and decay."

"And the rats," added his father.

It bothered Max that his parents could reminisce about their imprisonment in the Maya underworld as casually as other people's parents might discuss a weekend in Milwaukee.

Footsteps echoed in the alleyway behind them, and all three spun round to look, half expecting a phantom doge to emerge from the shadows. But the footsteps grew fainter again, and they were left standing alone by the landing stage.

Max willed the water taxi to arrive.

Venice had an ominous air tonight.

What was cool about attending a masquerade ball in a Venetian palazzo was arriving at the water gate, which was like a private dock in the basement.

What was not cool was a palazzo full of overexcited grown-ups in masks and costumes. You'd think they'd never been to a party before.

While his parents went in search of their benefactors, Max sought out the buffet table. It was unimpressive. Just platters of tiny toasts with fish eggs on them, like piles of frog spawn. He scraped the eggs off a piece of toast and tried to eat, but the fishy residue was overwhelming.

"*No mangia—danza!*" An old woman in a cat mask and a golden ball gown grabbed his arm. "No eat—dance!"

Max tried to escape, but Catlady dug in her painted fingernails.

He felt like a mouse in her clutches.

Soon he was caught in a hideous conga line of ancient merrymakers, all of them in grotesque animal masks and musty-smelling costumes, weaving unsteadily through the palace.

Max looked for his parents in every room.

He saw many men dressed as plague doctors, and many women in peacock masks, but none of them were Frank and Carla Murphy. (He also saw several Blind Doges and, intriguingly, a Headless one.)

He gave Catlady the slip and ran for the stairs, barreling straight into yet another plague doctor. This one looked nothing like his father. He wore a tricorn hat, a hooded cowl, and a voluminous waxed black cape to shroud every bit of his skin. His mask was old and yellowing, the eyeholes covered with circles of cloudy glass.

"Massimo?" he asked, his deep voice muffled by the mask.

Max nodded. "How do you know my name?"

"Your parents are looking for you."

"Where are they?"

"They had to go. There is a dinner in their honor."

"They left without me?"

"They could not find you."

"And I couldn't find them. These masks are a stupid idea!"

The plague doctor bowed. "The Venetian Tourist Board thanks you for your feedback."

"Who are you?"

"I am your guide. Your parents are waiting. You must follow me. Come."

Not knowing what else to do, Max followed the guide back down to the water gate, where a water taxi was moored. The guide took the wheel in the prow and gestured for Max to sit in the cabin.

Max hesitated.

Something felt wrong here.

But what else was he supposed to do?

And dinner, after all, was dinner.

Soon they were zooming down the Grand Canal, one

He wore a tricorn hat, a hooded cowl, and a voluminous waxed black
cape to shroud every bit of his skin.

more craft among all the other water taxis, ferries, gondolas, rowboats, police boats, motorboats, delivery barges, and garbage boats plying Venice's main waterway.

Crowds thronged the canal-side restaurants, and Max assumed that at any moment they would pull up at one of them. But the boat kept going and the canal broadened out, and soon Max could see the black spaces of the Venetian lagoon in front of them.

Where were they going? He tried to open the cabin door, but it was locked.

He knocked on the door and shouted, but the boatman did not turn round.

They passed the cemetery island of San Michele, the stucco decorations on its encircling walls gleaming white in the moonlight.

A light low in the water caught Max's eye.

Was it a fishing boat?

He started banging on the cabin windows and waving like crazy, not to be rescued exactly—he still was not sure that he needed it—but just so that another living creature would know of his whereabouts and could, if necessary, report the sighting.

Of course, as he later realized, his plan was doomed.

In his panic, he'd overlooked the fact that he was wearing a mask and a hat. His most distinctive feature, his hair (which he called brown but which he knew, in his heart of hearts, bordered perilously on ginger) was covered. If any hardworking fishermen had seen him, they would have rolled their eyes to see a high-spirited reveler, homeward bound in a wave-making, fish-disturbing water taxi.

But as it happened, all that was irrelevant.

Because as they drew nearer, Max saw that the light was not from a fishing boat but from a ring of candles burning on a floating wooden box.

Max's blood turned to ice.

The box was a coffin.

A coffin the size of a child.

And then the sea was full of them. Little coffins bobbing on the water, each one lit by candles that even the choppy waves could not snuff out.

Was it a macabre vision? Or was it an art installation?

You never knew in Venice.

As Max looked on in horror, his boat headed out to the open sea.

The coffins were gone. All around was blackness and swirling mist.

Max refused to admit that he was in trouble.

He pictured a map of the Venetian lagoon and told himself there were many islands in it. It was perfectly possible that his parents and their hosts were dining at some trendy trattoria on the farthest one. After all, he reasoned, in a city of living history, the Historical Society would be sure to choose somewhere off the beaten track.

He watched the tour guide as he steered, trying to anticipate their direction.

Just then a sea breeze carried off the guide's hat and blew back his cowl, revealing the back of his head. It was hard to see in the darkness, but he appeared to have rippled brown hair that rose in a little tuft on each side.

Max was studying this curious coiffure, when a land mass solidified out of the darkness. The guide cut the engine and allowed them to float in to the shore with the waves. Then

Little coffins bobbing on the water, each one lit by candles
that even the choppy waves could not snuff out.

he unlocked the cabin door and jumped over the side of the boat.

In a flash, Max had flung open the door and burst out, venting all his questions. "Where are we going? Why did you lock me in? What is this place?"

"Follow me, if you please," came the guide's voice from the shore.

Max jumped off the boat and splashed through the shallows to catch up.

In the misty moonlight, there was now no disguising the fact that the messenger's head was covered not in hair, but in . . .

. . . feathers.

"I know you," said Max.

"Then let us end the masquerade!" The messenger pulled off his costume and tossed it back into the boat. Underneath the beak of the plague doctor, just as Max had suspected, was hidden the beak of an owl.

He tried to stay calm.

"Why have you brought me here? Where are my parents?"

"How should I know?" said Lord Kuy, the owl-headed messenger of the Death Lords. "It is you they wanted to see."

"Who's *they*?"

"Who do you think?"

A wind blew off the sea and ruffled the owl-man's feathers.

"The Death Lords? You're lying. They can't leave Xibalba."

"Their touristic options are limited, I grant you. But La Serenissima is always open to them."

"That's ridiculous. What's the connection between ancient Maya Death Lords and Venice, Italy?"

"Of all the cities in Middleworld, Venice is the most liminal."

"Liminal? You mean criminal?"

"I mean liminal, on the threshold, between worlds."

"I don't get it."

"Venice is a city built on water like Xibalba—a place of swamps and marshes, mists and fog. Now if you would just follow me up this hill—"

"Where are we?"

"They call it *l'isola della peste*, the plague island. It was used to quarantine victims during a plague epidemic. You are lucky to be here. It is usually off-limits to tourists."

"*Help!*" screamed Max.

"No one will hear you. And if they did, no one would come. Venetians think this place is haunted. They never dream that the lights and movements they sometimes glimpse from the mainland are the Lords of Death on vacation."

Max looked around in desperation. There was nowhere to run.

"This way," said Lord Kuy, pushing him forward.

Crunch, crunch, crunch. The brittle earth broke up beneath his feet.

"What am I walking on?" asked Max. "Is it seashells?"

Lord Kuy snickered. "I was hoping you'd notice. It is bones, all bones."

"What, like fish bones?"

"Bones of plague victims. Thousands of them."

Max looked around in horror. As far as he could see, the ground shone calcium white.

"Is that you, Kuy?" boomed a voice from the top of the hill. "It is about time. The rest of the guys have gone to the casino. I was just about to join them. Did you find him?"

"He is here, Lord One Death."

And out of the darkness stepped the fearsome leader of the Death Lords.

"Bow down!" Lord Kuy instructed Max.

Max tipped his head slightly, still studying One Death. He looked different from the last time Max had seen him. On that occasion, he'd been riding on the scorpion boat in Xibalba, and had looked like a rotting cadaver in a black feather headdress. Tonight he was dressed up to the nines.

He wore a black top hat trimmed with black feathers, a tailored black leather suit, and a blood-red silk tie. His bulging yellow eyes were lined in black, and his thin black hair was slicked back into a ponytail. He sported skull rings on his fingers, studs through his nose, and a clutch of black feathers hanging from his ears. The overall effect was like an undertaker to a motorcycle gang, with a hint of psychotic rock star.

Despite his eccentric outfit—or possibly because of it—One Death exuded menace from every pore.

"*Buonasera*, Massimo Francis Sylvanus Murphy," he said. "Long time no see."

"Not long enough," said Max. "What do you want?"

"What do I want? What kind of a question is that? By the most serendipitous of coincidences, we are both in Venice at the same time. It would have been impolite of me not to engineer an encounter. So how have you been?"

Max said nothing.

"That costume suits you," continued One Death, looking Max up and down. "You look like one of us. I trust you are having a pleasant vacation?"

"What do you want?" asked Max again.

"How about a thank-you?"

"What for?"

"Don't tell me you didn't notice the honor guard I arranged for you? All those adorable little kiddies floating in the sea."

"The coffins? You did that?"

One Death took a bow. "Spectacular, wasn't it? It took a lot of effort to dig up every tot who'd ever drowned in these waters, but I think it was worth it. Call me a perfectionist, but I even drowned a few extra to make up the numbers."

"You mean those were real coffins? With bodies in them?"

"What else?"

Max stared at him in horror, at a loss for words.

One Death smiled. "You mortals are so sentimental. That is what inspired me to add the candles. They represent the tykes' families, and the people who loved them." He pretended to wipe away a tear. "Touching, isn't it? Can you imagine how much your mother would cry if she was to lose you?"

"What's your point?" asked Max.

"It's just a bit of fun to remind you of your own mortality."

"Look, I get it. You don't need to remind me. Ah Pukuh and all you Death Lords would like to wipe out humankind, starting with me. But dream on, because that is never going to happen. Lola and I beat you, fair and square. Now leave me alone!"

"Leave you alone? We will never leave you alone."

Max rolled his eyes. "You need to move on." He spoke slowly, as if he was explaining the situation to a small child. "You have no power over me anymore. I know the rules.

It's like a video game. And I won the last level. End of story."

"Rules? Games? Levels?" scoffed One Death. "Have you forgotten that I am a Death Lord? Rules mean nothing to me. I cheat at games. The only level that interests me is the level of pain I will inflict on you."

"That's not how it works. I completed my task. It's over."

"But another's task has just begun. And you are the prize."

"You can't do that! I'm not a goldfish in a bag!"

"No? Your hair is the same color. And your eyes are bugging out."

"Oh, very funny. At least I don't have worms crawling out of my nose!"

One Death grabbed the offending worms and ate them in one bite.

He looked furious. "Where is your respect? Where is your obedience? How dare you question me in any way? Your puny life has always been ours for the taking! The clue is in our name: we are Death Lords!" He stamped his foot. "We want what we want, and we want it now!"

Lord Kuy gave a raspy cough. "If I may be so bold, your lordship, the tantrum approach did not go down well with focus groups. Today's mortals respond better to chilling inscrutability. If the ancient Maya Death Lords as a brand are to have relevance to the modern consumer, we need to stay on message."

One Death took a deep breath. "And the message is . . . ? Remind me, Kuy."

"The message, your lordship, is one of ultimate evil."

"Did you hear that, Massimo Francis Sylvanus Murphy? I am the embodiment of ultimate evil. I will stop at nothing to destroy you." He leaned in so close that Max could smell the half-chewed worms.

"Why me? What have I done?"

"It's what you haven't done."

"Is this about the White Jaguar?"

"You think?" boomed One Death sarcastically, his voice echoing around the lagoon. The hill of bones seemed to scrunch together in fear and grow smaller. "Of course, this is about the White Jaguar. Why else would I go to all this trouble on my vacation? Come over to our side, Massimo Francis Sylvanus Murphy. And bring the White Jaguar with you."

Drawing courage from his mask and his highwayman cape, Max tried to stand up to the Death Lord, but his cracked and shaking voice betrayed his fear. "You're wasting your time," he bleated. "You'll never get it. Never."

"Oh, please. Just listen to yourself. The White Jaguar is as good as ours. It will be home in Xibalba before the new moon, you mark my words. And then your precious Middleworld will melt into oblivion and take you and your fellow mortals with it. Thus will the ancient Maya prophecy come true."

"You're not still pushing that end-of-the-world stuff?" Max gained courage. "No one believes it anymore, not even the History Channel. There *is* no ancient Maya prophecy. We humans are not as stupid as you think."

One Death smirked at Kuy. "We'll see about that."

Lord Kuy sank his head into his owlish shoulders. "Why waste your breath, your lordship? Let us join the other Death Lords at the casino. You have given the boy fair warning. He will find out soon enough what you have in store for him."

"And my revenge will be all the sweeter." One Death

turned to Max. "Tonight you have signed your own death warrant, mortal. Until we meet again, *arrivederci!*"

"Wait!" called Max. "What was that about me being a prize?"

But with a diabolical laugh and a beating of owl wings, One Death and Lord Kuy had vanished.

Max's façade of bravery vanished with them, and his knees buckled beneath him. His body shook violently as he tried to process what had just happened. He'd thought he was free of the Death Lords. He'd thought they had no power over him. He'd thought he would never see them again.

But now it sounded like they had a new plan and he was somehow mixed up in it.

This was a worrying development.

But right now, his biggest problem was getting back to the hotel.

What had he been thinking to follow Lord Kuy?

More crucially, what was he doing, in the middle of the night, wearing a Halloween costume and stranded on a hill of bones at the far reaches of the Venetian lagoon?

And then it occurred to him that his situation was so ridiculous, it had to be a dream or an effect of concussion. If he just stopped for a moment and closed his eyes and pinched himself, he would wake up in the hotel room. It would still be afternoon and he would have fallen asleep playing video games, and the whole masked ball would never have happened.

He closed his eyes and took some deep breaths.

His heart slowed down a little.

He pinched himself until it hurt.

Now everything swam into focus.

Frog spawn on toast?

A geriatric conga line?

Coffins in the sea?

It was all so obviously the stuff of nightmares.

Confidently, he opened his eyes.

On the far-distant horizon, the lights of Venice twinkled.

It was still the middle of the night. He was still wearing a Halloween costume. He was still stranded all alone on a hill of bones.

No, not alone. Somewhere close by, a child was weeping.

Chills ran up Max's spine. As he peered through the darkness, he was thinking of the little coffins in the sea. "Hello?" he called. "Is anybody there?"

Helloooooooo, his voice blew back at him, as the wind flicked his hair and rustled his cape.

Helloooooooo, boomed the waves as they broke on the shore below him.

He stood completely still and listened.

The weeping was all around him now. But it wasn't from a child. It was, Max realized, from the sound of the bones as they shifted and rolled with the wind. On this island of dead souls, in groans and shrieks and whispers, the wind carried the pain of the people who had died here.

And they wanted Max to join them.

In chilling breaths, the wind urged Max to accept his fate like the plague victims in the bone pile. Like him, they, too, had once had lives and loves and families; but in the end, it all came down to bones and ashes. . . .

Ashes and bones, sighed the wind.

Already, Max's toes were sinking down into the bones, where the fingers of heartsick mothers pulled at his feet and hungry maggots waited to feast off his flesh.

He stumbled down the hill, pulling out his feet with every step, flicking away maggots, pushing away bits of finger that tried to hold on to him.

On the shore—of course—the boat was gone.

Stay, stay, moaned the wind, pulling at him with invisible arms.

He paused to consider what to do next, but the bones still crunched as if invisible feet walked all around him.

He knew he was not alone.

But instead of being frightened, he remembered for some reason a chili farmer named Eusebio who had once explained to him about the web of life in the jungle and how everyone was connected.

He turned to face the hill.

"I'm sorry," he called, above the wind. "I'm sorry for how you were treated. I'm sorry for how you were dumped here and left to die of a horrible disease. I'm sorry for all the mothers and fathers of the children who died in the sea. But you know who isn't sorry? The Maya Lords of Death. You might not have heard of them because Europe probably didn't find out about them until after you were dead. But take my word for it, they laughed the day you died. And they're laughing at me now. They just don't get it, how we humans look after each other, even people we don't know. But if you keep me here, and grind down my bones, they will have won again. So please, I beg you, let me go. Please send me home to my parents."

There was a moment of stillness, like the calm before the storm, and then the wind screamed louder, and the waves crashed furiously onto the shore.

Great, thought Max. *I've made the island even angrier.*

But then he noticed a light coming toward him, across the churning sea.

It floated closer and closer until he saw that it was one of the coffin candles.

And it was sitting on the dashboard of a water taxi.

Expertly steered by the raging waves, the boat was swept up onto the shore in front of him. Max noticed Lord Kuy's discarded masquerade costume on the floor and knew it was the same boat that had brought him here. More importantly, he also noticed the key in the ignition.

"Thank you!" he said, saluting the island.

The ground underneath his feet was vibrating with little pulses, as if the chips of bone were impatiently urging him on. As soon as he climbed aboard, the shingle formed itself into a moving slipway, and launched him into the open sea.

Max turned the ignition key and pressed the starter button. The motor whined and wheezed, but the engine refused to catch. He tried again and again, but nothing—not even a splutter.

He sensed the disappointment of the bones, who'd evidently expected him to zoom away like the action hero he'd pretended to be.

Even the wind died down, and the island seemed to be holding its breath, watching him in disbelief.

Feeling decidedly unheroic, he looked under the seat, found a small oar, and began to paddle.

Venice was impossibly far away, and getting farther all the time as the current washed him farther out to sea.

Not a single other boat was visible in the vast expanse of moonlit water.

Now the water lapping the shore sounded like sighs of exasperation.

"Hey, I can do this," he called to the island. "This is nothing."

Max searched his memory for examples of his seamanship. "I've shot the rapids in an underground river. I've ridden a shark to Xibalba. I've . . . I've . . . I've escaped across the ocean in a Zodiac inflatable. . . ."

Yeah. That time when Uncle Ted had helped him flee from Landa's yacht. He hadn't been able to start the boat then either.

In his mind's eye, he saw Uncle Ted on the deck of the yacht, yelling instructions.

He saw Uncle Ted's lips moving.

But what was he saying?

Pull, moaned the wind.

Choke, crunched the bones.

That was it! Pull the choke!

Max found the choke, pulled it out, turned the key, and tried again to start the engine.

It roared into life.

It was a beautiful moment, a good guys' moment.

He felt the current reversing, the water buoying up his boat, and the wind stroking his back. He sat for a moment, bobbing on the water, listening to the melodious thrum of the engine. Then he pushed the throttle lever forward and sped toward the shimmering lights of Venice.

His mother had been right about one thing.

It had been a night he would always remember.

Chapter Four
THE BLACK PYRAMID

The wailing began, as it always did, in the deepest, darkest night. Max lay in his tent, wide awake, listening to the ghostly cacophony. From the booming roars and unearthly cackles, it sounded like the legions of hell were gathered outside his tent flap.

It's just the howler monkeys, he told himself. But their racket was so loud and so close, he knew that nothing on Earth would persuade him to venture outside his tent until morning.

His thoughts wandered to Lord 6-Dog and Lady Coco, the ancient Maya king and his mother who were currently subletting the bodies of two howler monkeys. Were they howling now in their cells at San Xavier airport? They'd been impounded on their way back from Spain with Zia, the Murphy family's housekeeper, and so far nothing, not even bribery (Uncle Ted's idea), had got them released.

Max hadn't even been allowed to visit them as he passed through the airport.

In fact, coming back to San Xavier had been disappointing all round.

Even Lola, supposedly his best friend, had not been there to welcome him back. Uncle Ted said she'd left in a hurry the day before Max arrived.

No note, no card, no explanation.

Half of him was pretty sure she was arranging some kind of surprise for him. The other half was pretty sure she'd forgotten all about him.

He tried to act as if he didn't care either way.

So with Lola gone and the monkeys languishing in quarantine, that left just Uncle Ted and his butler, Raul, to form Max's official welcome committee at the Villa Isabella.

They'd both been pleased to see him, but it was hardly the wild party he'd expected. Of the two prisoners Max had rescued from Xibalba, Hermanjilio was working at the university and Lucky Jim, Uncle Ted's former bodyguard and foreman of his banana business, was studying to become a teacher.

It seemed like everyone had moved on.

Disappointed by this lukewarm reception, Max had decided not to be there when Lola got back. After all, he wouldn't want her to think that he'd looked forward to seeing her every single moment of every single day since he'd got home from Venice, or anything like that.

"Will you have a chef on this dig?" he'd asked his parents.

"We will have a cook," replied his mother. "Why?"

"Because I think I'll come with you, just for a few days."

"To the Black Pyramid?" His father looked at him with surprise. "I didn't think you'd want to go near that place after what happened last time."

"I'll hang out on the beach. It's pretty nice from what I remember."

His mother was grinning from ear to ear. "It will be so much fun! We can sit by the campfire and tell stories—"

"Or," Max interrupted her, "I could pitch my tent on the beach."

"Absolutely not," said his father. "It's too dangerous. There could be jaguars and who knows what else roaming around."

"Jaguars on the beach?"

"Jaguars hunt on land, in water, in trees, and, most probably, on beaches, too. You're sleeping at the site with us."

Afterward, Max wondered if the Death Lords had controlled his brain in some way to make him agree to this arrangement. Because now here he was, zipped into a little tent in a clearing and way too close for comfort to the Black Pyramid.

Like a skunk gives off a stink cloud, the pyramid's malignant presence radiated evil. With the howler monkeys roaring outside, and his recent encounter with a Death Lord on his mind, Max realized that coming here might have been a big mistake.

In the morning he would see about getting out.

He just had to survive the night.

He imagined looking down on himself from the top of the pyramid. He saw his tent, so fragile and crushable, like a little brown moth.

He knew he wouldn't sleep.

He looked around for a book and saw only one of his mother's, a history of Maya glyphs. With a heavy heart, he reached for it and began to read.

It felt like only five minutes later when he awoke to sunshine and the reassuringly normal smell of frying bacon.

Following the call of breakfast, he walked groggily across the plaza to the mess tent. Straight in front of him was the Black Pyramid. He stole a glance and was relieved to see that, in the morning light, it didn't seem as menacing as it had the night before. In fact, now that he took in the dig set up around it—the thatched shelters, the rope markers, the wheelbarrows, the shovels, the buckets, the survey equipment—he saw it for what it was: an overgrown pile of old stones.

His fears from the night melted away. It was a beautiful day, and he was looking forward to lazing on the beach.

Breakfast was served on long tables under an open tarp. While not up to Raul's standards, the camp cook had laid on an appetizing spread of scrambled eggs, crispy bacon, black beans, freshly made tortillas, and slices of pineapple.

His parents were slumped at one of the tables. As Max piled up his plate and went to join them, he felt the eyes of the workers following his every move.

"Why are they staring at me?" he asked as he sat down.

"I think they might have heard about your encounter with Ah Pukuh on your last visit," replied his father. "Don't ask me how, but word gets around."

His mother yawned. She had dark shadows under her eyes.

"Did you hear the howlers last night?" Max asked, stuffing an egg-filled tortilla into his mouth.

Both his parents nodded wearily.

"It's a sound I never get used to," mused his father. "You'd think it was a herd of angry dinosaurs, not a few hairy primates. They're the loudest land animals, you know, on account of—"

Max tried to head off the lesson. "How's the dig going?" he asked his mother, spraying crumbs as he spoke.

She looked like she was going to object to his table manners, then evidently realized that she was too tired and they were in a jungle anyway and decided to let it pass. "It's going well," she said, standing up and brushing herself off. "In fact, I must drag myself to work right now. My glyphs won't read themselves. I will see you both at dinner. Have a good day, *bambino*—and don't forget your sunscreen!"

When she'd gone, his father told him more. "We've made excellent progress, Max. It's a fascinating site." He lowered his voice. "Between you and me, I've applied for the permits to go inside. I keep thinking about that army you told me about."

"The Undead Army?"

"That's the one. Generations of Maya warriors going back to the earliest times. I'd give anything to see it."

"Forget it, Dad. It's too dangerous."

"But the armor, the weaponry . . . it would tell us so much about Maya warfare. It would be the find of the century. It would make our fortune!"

"We wouldn't live to spend it, Dad. Why do you think they're called the Undead Army? They're zombies."

"Zombies?" His father laughed. "You've been playing too many video games."

"Exactly. Which means I know a zombie when I see one."

A wind blew through the plaza, making the corners of the roof tarp flap like giant wings.

"Looks like the locals might be right." His father peered anxiously at the sky. "They say there's a hurricane coming in the next few days."

Max looked around the mess tent. The eyes of every worker were still fixed on him. "What else do they say, Dad?"

"I don't know. It's all superstition. They're always spooked about something."

"Maybe you should listen to them." Max wrapped up a little picnic of crispy bacon, tortillas, and pineapple for his lunch.

"So what's on your agenda today, Max?"

"A snooze on the beach, followed by some lying around, and maybe a little light sunbathing. How about you?"

"I have a big survey project to finish."

"Well, have fun, Dad. Just promise me you'll stay away from the Undead Army. Remember, they're called that because they're not dead, they're only sleeping. And trust me, you really don't want to be the one who wakes them up."

Chapter Five
WAKING THE DEAD

It was windy on the beach and not quite as pleasant as Max had imagined, but he found a sheltered spot behind some rocks, slathered himself with sunscreen, sprayed himself with bug repellent, and lay down on his towel. Eventually he managed to tune out the wind-lashed rustling of the palm trees and the constant buzzing of mosquitoes enough to relax.

A smell of rotting fish assailed his nostrils.

At least the sun felt good.

"This is nice, isn't it, Hoop?" said Lola's voice.

Max leapt to his feet.

"Monkey Girl! What are you—"

"Gotcha!" said Ah Pukuh.

Well, that explained the bad smell.

The god of violent and unnatural death winked at Max from behind his sunglasses. He was sitting on top of the rocks, under a palm-leaf parasol. His belly bulged over his floral Bermuda shorts and, as he laughed, it quivered like blotchy milk pudding.

"What do *you* want?" asked Max, horrified.

"For starters, I want to borrow your sunscreen. I need to preserve my waxy pallor."

Max regarded Ah Pukuh's pockmarked skin with disgust. "Get your own."

"Charming. And after I have ventured into the noonday sun purely to welcome you back to the Black Pyramid, and introduce you to some friends of mine."

Max looked up and down the beach. It was empty. "You don't have any friends," he said.

"*Au contraire*." Ah Pukuh pointed out to sea.

Emerging from the waves was the Undead Army—or at least a spectral version of it. Max stared at the ranks of shimmering, translucent, weed-draped Maya warriors. "How did they get out of the crypt? Who woke them? It wasn't Dad, was it?"

"Even your father is not fool enough to wake the Undead Army. No, these are but shades, come to warn you. For the moment, all but one of them sleep on."

"All . . . but one?"

"His name is Eek' Kitam. I'll call him. You guys will get along like a house on fire." Ah Pukuh picked up a large conch shell and blew into it. The wind carried its mournful sound up to the Black Pyramid. "Or do I mean he'll set your house on fire?"

"This is stupid," said Max. "Don't you have anything better to do than follow me around, making idle threats? As I explained to One Death—"

"That's *Lord* One Death to you. And our threats are not idle."

"As I explained in Venice, I have fulfilled my mission. It's over. You have no power over me anymore."

Ah Pukuh took off his sunglasses and looked Max right in the eyes. "No? Then why are you here? Who lured your parents back to my pyramid?"

"*You* brought us here?"

"It was a masterly subterfuge, was it not?"

Max groaned. "I should have guessed. But why? What do you want with us?"

"I want the White Jaguar."

"I don't know where it is."

"But you know someone who does know. And you need to make her give it back."

"Do your own dirty work. It's got nothing to do with me."

"It has *everything* to do with you." He reached his fat fingers over to Max's bare chest and traced a line, like a surgeon planning an incision. "Your heart is the prize."

"What do you mean?"

"It's simple. Your girlfriend gives us the White Jaguar, and you keep your heart." His sharp nails scratched Max's skin. "But if she keeps the Jaguar Stone, we get your heart. So what do you think she'll do, eh, *Hoop*?"

Max swallowed hard. "She's not my girlfriend. And she will never give you the White Jaguar."

"I thought you might say that. That's why I've awoken Eek' Kitam. If you can't persuade her, he will persuade her for you."

Max followed Ah Pukuh's eyes to the cliffs that bounded the beach. A figure was descending the sheer cliff face as easily as a spider scuttling down a wall. "Is that him?" asked Max dully.

"It is indeed. In life, he was a merciless killing machine. In death, he is literally unstoppable."

As Max watched the figure's progress, he saw movement on the cliff top. It was his father, setting up survey equipment.

He waved, but his father was looking the other way.

He shouted, but the wind drowned out his cries.

Wasn't there some unwritten law that parents always sensed when their offspring were in danger? How could his father be oblivious to his perilous predicament?

It reminded Max of a day, long ago, on the school playground, when his father had come to collect him and got so wrapped up in chatting with another parent, he'd missed the fact that his little son was getting roughed up by the class bully, almost in front of his eyes. "Your mother's not going to be happy about this," he'd said to Max when he saw his ripped shirt and muddied schoolbooks. "What on earth have you been doing?"

But the figure that now swaggered across the sand was more intimidating than any school bully.

Evidently a recent recruit to the Undead Army, he still had some flesh on his bones and patches of crispy brown skin. His headdress was the skull of a snarling peccary—a kind of wild boar—with sharpened tusks, trimmed with feathers. His other adornments were a tattered and ancient jaguar-skin cape, and a deerskin loincloth. A flint battle-ax hung from his belt, a bow and a quiver of arrows were strapped across his back, and he pointed a wooden spear ahead of him as he crossed the beach.

"Massimo Francis Sylvanus Murphy, meet Lord Eek' Kitam," boomed Ah Pukuh, when the warrior stood in front of them. "In Mayan, Eek' Kitam means Black Peccary. But for you, he means bad news."

At a nod from Ah Pukuh, Eek' Kitam stuck his spear in

A recent recruit to the Undead Army, he still had some flesh
on his bones and patches of crispy brown skin.

the sand, took his ax, and, with jerky movements, swiped it lightly across Max's cheek.

"Ow!" Max's fingers touched blood.

"Sharp, isn't it?" crowed Ah Pukuh. "We Maya may not have had metal, but our obsidian blades were sharper than your steel scalpels. Now watch this."

Ah Pukuh took the ax and plunged it deep into the warrior's chest.

Eek' Kitam didn't flinch. He didn't blink. He didn't bleed.

He just calmly pulled the ax out of his wound and stood to attention.

"Ta-da!" The god of violent and unnatural death turned to Max. "So you see, you cannot win. If the girl does not return the stone, I will send Eek' Kitam to get it. And he will take both your hearts."

Eek' Kitam smiled and nodded. He made a noise like a death rattle.

"No! You can't do this! You keep changing the rules! It's not fair!"

"It's good to be working with you again, Max Murphy. I've missed your constant bellyaching. Remember how we rode the tour bus across Spain with the band? Those were the days, weren't they? I think I could have made it in the music business." Ah Pukuh's ponytail bounced wildly as he rocked out to some air guitar.

Eek' Kitam tried to copy him, using his ax as a guitar.

"Nice ax!" quipped Ah Pukuh. He nudged the zombie. "Get it?"

Eek' Kitam remained expressionless.

"That's the trouble with the living dead. No sense of

humor." Ah Pukuh turned back to Max and affected a rock-star drawl. "Still playin' rock 'n' roll, Maxie? Wanna get together and jam some time? Play some licks?"

"I'm a drummer. I don't play licks."

"No? Pity." Ah Pukuh stuck out his fat tongue and wiggled it. "Licks sound like something I'd be good at."

Max looked away, disgusted. "Why don't you just get out of my life?"

"No can do, Maxie boy. And here's something else I should make very clear. If you mention a word about this to your doting parents, I will drag them back to Xibalba faster than you can empty a room with one of your drum solos."

"You can't do that."

"You keep telling me what I can and can't do. But the fact is, you're on my turf now, and I can do anything I like."

As Max took in the bad news that once again his life was in the hands of this bloated bully and his deathly cohorts, gray rain clouds gathered and blocked the sun.

"There's a storm coming," said Ah Pukuh. "You might want to take cover."

He nodded toward the sea, and the phantom army marched out of the water and lined up on the beach. The first rank somehow hoisted Ah Pukuh's massive weight onto their insubstantial shoulders and bore him away, sitting cross-legged and holding up his palm-leaf umbrella like an Indian raja, with Eek' Kitam leading the charge.

Max leaned against the rock, his legs buckling beneath him. The smell of Ah Pukuh, the ferocity of Eek' Kitam, the impossibility of what had just happened, made him feel nauseous. As the first raindrops began to fall, he put his towel over his head and trudged back up the path to the site.

The first person he met at the top was his father.

"Perfect timing, Max! Come and help me get this equipment out of the rain."

"Didn't you see me down there, Dad? I was waving at you."

"Were you? I'm sorry. Must have had my reading glasses on." His father took a closer look at him. "Are you all right, Max? You look like you've seen a ghost." He noticed the blood on his son's cheek. "Your mother's not going to be happy about this," he said. "What on earth have you been doing?"

Chapter Six
MIDNIGHT MEETING

"Tell me again how this happened, *bambino*," said Max's mother that evening as she cleaned the cut on his cheek. "It looks like a knife wound."

Max winced at the sting of the antiseptic. "There are some sharp rocks on the beach, Mom," he explained lamely.

"Stop fussing over the boy, Carla," snapped his father. "The big question is, what about the looting in the pyramid?"

"What looting?" asked Max.

"One of the workers spotted signs of activity on the top platform. It looks like someone has forced their way in."

Or out, thought Max.

"What I don't understand," said his mother, "is how this could happen in broad daylight?"

"We'll leave that to the police to work out." Max's father put his head in his hands. "This is such bad news. It will mean weeks of paperwork. I hope it won't derail the dig. The workers are spooked enough as it is, without this kind of trouble."

"Calm down, Frank. There may be a simple explanation."

Max wished he could tell them that the culprit was almost certainly a dead Maya warrior called Eek' Kitam. But Ah Pukuh had sworn him to secrecy, and the last thing he needed right now was to send his parents back to Xibalba. It had been hard enough to rescue them the first time.

Besides, Max reasoned, by reporting a looting at the Black Pyramid, his parents might save themselves from Ah Pukuh's clutches. The police would move in and the dig would be canceled and the Murphy family could escape to safety.

But where was safety?

It was a problem that Max was still mulling over, long after his parents had gone to bed. As he methodically snapped dry branches and fed them into the fire, the same questions went round and round in his brain:

Did Ah Pukuh and the Death Lords really have the power to follow through on their gruesome threats?

And if they did, should he try to find Lola and persuade her to give them the White Jaguar?

Or should he be braver than any fourteen-year-old had ever been in the history of the world, and sacrifice his own life to make a stand?

That last option made him feel sick to his stomach.

Far across the plaza, the hulk of the Black Pyramid squatted like an evil toad, and even the shimmering moonlight couldn't lighten its air of brooding menace.

Max wondered if Ah Pukuh and Eek' Kitam were in there now, high-fiving each other to celebrate a job well done. He could imagine Ah Pukuh's many chins wobbling with mirth as he recalled how much they'd frightened the kid from Boston.

He listened for a moment, half expecting to hear their cackles of laughter on the night breeze.

But all he could hear was his father's snores, the buzzing of insects, the snuffling of small animals, and the cries of night birds hunting. Way in the distance, the ocean crashed on the rocks of the headland.

But what was that?

Somewhere in the forest, twigs snapped and leaves rustled.

Surely Eek' Kitam was not on the prowl again?

With a noise like a squealing of brakes, an animal burst into the clearing. It looked like a small hippopotamus with a bendy nose like an anteater.

Max leapt up in fear, but the strange creature didn't even notice him as it charged across the plaza and back into the undergrowth.

Heart pounding, he sat back down at the fire.

And then he heard the laughter.

His blood ran cold.

Someone was behind him.

Very slowly, he turned around, braced to see Ah Pukuh, come to torment him some more.

But standing there, hands on hips, long dark hair shining in the moonlight, backpack on her shoulders, huge smile on her face, was Lola. "Sorry if the tapir scared you, Hoop! He panicked when he saw me, and stampeded."

"Oh," said Max, "it's you." He didn't smile.

82

"What's wrong, Hoop? I thought you'd be glad to see me."

"How do I know it's even you? You could be a Death Lord for all I know. Tell me something only Lola would know."

"Like a memory, you mean?" She thought for a moment. "Like how you were jealous of Santino?"

Max pretended to look puzzled. "Santino who? The name doesn't ring a bell."

Lola raised an eyebrow. "Santino García. We met him in Spain."

"Oh, him. The law eh-student. Why would I be jealous of that pretentious mommy's boy?"

"He e-mailed me the other day. He sent his greetings to the *pelirrojo*. That's what they call people with your color hair, remember?"

"He's got a nerve. At least I don't use a jar of hair gel every day."

And just like that, Max and Lola fell back into companionable bickering, like old times.

"At least I know it's you," said Max. "No one else would stick up for Santino."

Lola ignored this gibe. "Now it's your turn. Tell me something only Hoop would know."

"I can tell you that I've had a really, really bad day. Ah Pukuh sneaked up on me on the beach, and he showed me the whole Undead Army standing in the sea, and then this one guy, who's an unstoppable killer zombie, cut me with his ax and—"

"It *is* you!" said Lola, clapping her hands. "Only Hoop whines like that."

"Oh, ha-ha. It's actually not funny. And you're in big trouble, too."

"I know." She groaned. "It's all starting up again, the whole thing with the Jaguar Stones. I'm so sorry you've been dragged back into it."

"So why weren't you at the villa when I got back?"

She avoided Max's eyes. "I needed to think things through. The Death Lords have been pressuring me."

"Look, it's okay. I know the deal. They told you that if you don't give up the White Jaguar, I can say good-bye to my heart."

She nodded. "Pretty much."

"So, did you think things through? What did you decide?"

Lola didn't hesitate. "They can have it."

"My heart?"

"No, of course not. The White Jaguar."

Max stared at her. "You'd do that for me?"

She blushed. "It's for me as well. I'm sick of it, Hoop."

Max breathed a sigh of relief. "Me, too," he agreed. "Besides, if you don't hand it over, Ah Pukuh will stop at nothing to get his hands on it. So we really have no choice."

They sat in silence, staring at the fire.

Max tried to process what it felt like to stop fighting, to surrender, to take his chances with the rest of planet Earth. It didn't feel nearly as good as he'd hoped. "But it's the right thing to do," he reassured himself, thinking aloud. "We never could have won."

Lola nodded. "I feel that way, too."

Max looked at her curiously. "You do?"

"When we first got involved with the Jaguar Stones, I thought we could outwit Ah Pukuh and the Death Lords. But the more I think about it, the more I realize it's hopeless.

We're just two kids. What do *we* know? The world will have to save itself."

"Wow, you *have* changed. What's the matter, Monkey Girl? Where's your fighting spirit? You sound so down."

"It's the Death Lords, Hoop. They've got to me. They appear every night in my dreams and they taunt me about having no family. They tell me I'm worthless."

"But—"

Lola cut him off. "And you know what? They're right. I'm nothing. I'm no one. I don't even know my real name. Who am I to stand up to them?"

"What? That's crazy talk. What's happened to you?"

"You wouldn't understand. It's a Maya thing. Ever since the first kings claimed to be descended from the gods, bloodline is everything to us. And I haven't got one."

"It's an *ancient* Maya thing."

"Things change slowly around here, Hoop."

"Anyway, you do have family. You have your adopted family in Utsal. You told me yourself that Chan Kan is like a grandfather to you."

"But he's not my blood."

"Why is it always about blood with you guys?"

"Whatever." Lola sighed. "I just want it to stop."

"So what does Hermanjilio say? He's the one who risked everything to steal the White Jaguar back."

Lola shrugged. "I haven't asked him. He's been out of town."

"What? When's he coming back? We only have until the next new moon to—"

"I'm waaaaay ahead of you." Lola opened her backpack and extracted a football-sized object wrapped in deerskin. She pulled back a corner to reveal a glimpse of alabaster stone, as creamy white as the moon itself.

"You stole it from him?"

"Hermanjilio isn't the one getting threatened. Besides, he's really busy at the university. He has a lot to catch up on. He won't even notice it's gone."

"He will when Ah Pukuh activates all five Jaguar Stones and all hell breaks loose."

"Then he shouldn't have left me in charge of it."

"Can I . . . can I touch it?" Max asked.

She passed him the deerskin bundle. Gently, as if there was a real cat inside, he unwrapped it and stroked the carved jaguar head of cold white stone. "This is it," he said. "This is the stone that started everything. This is the stone that my parents activated at the White Pyramid, and kicked off this whole mess. Then they disappeared and I came to San Xavier looking for them, and then I met you." He smiled at her. "Funny to think we would never have met if it wasn't for the White Jaguar."

"My people believe that everything was meant to happen," said Lola. "If we met, we met for a reason. If we say good-bye, we will meet again."

Max studied her in the firelight. She had shadows under her eyes and hollows in her cheeks. She looked thinner. She looked small and sad and flat and cold and empty.

By contrast, the White Jaguar in his hands was feeling warmer and heavier. It seemed to settle in his arms and rest its weight on him.

Afterward, he thought it must have been the Jaguar Stone that gave him courage.

Because what he said next was so out of character he knew that, if he lived past the next new moon, he would spend his whole life reliving this moment. All he knew was that the old Max Murphy of Boston, Massachusetts, would have done everything he could to avoid another confrontation with the ghouls of the Maya underworld. And, last time he checked, the new Max Murphy was of the same pacifist opinion.

But looking at Lola's huddled form, something inside him disagreed and he found himself clenching his fists in anger. Up to this point, it was usually Lola who was the brave one, the fighter, and Max (often reluctantly) followed her lead. But now he understood very clearly that she needed his help. If he could not convince her to stand up to the bad guys, the battle was already lost. Lola was the strongest person he knew. If the Death Lords could break her spirit, they could break every man, woman and child on the planet.

He cleared his throat. "Were you planning to give the White Jaguar back tonight? Is that why you came here?"

"I came here to talk to you. And then . . . yeah . . . I guess . . . I thought . . . maybe . . . we could give it back together."

"Is that really what you thought? Or were you hoping I'd change your mind?"

"What? No! Why would you even—?"

"Here's the thing. The Death Lords are wrong. And you know it. You're not worthless. You're the opposite of worthless. It's not about who your family is, or how rich they are. You, Lady White Flower, are the coolest person I have ever met. You're"—he searched for the word—"invincible!"

Max did not like where this was going. He wanted to stop himself talking. But somehow the White Jaguar was egging him on.

And Lola was listening. "Are you saying we should fight?" she whispered.

Max felt himself nodding.

Even as she said, "No, Hoop, it's over, we can't do this," he could see the spark coming back to her eyes.

"Sure we can do this," he heard himself saying. "Think about what we've done already. We changed the weather. We floated in time and space. I played in a rock band, and you almost became Queen of Spain or whatever your title would have been. And let's not forget that we took on the Maya underworld—not once, but twice—and we won! We did amazing things, and it didn't have anything to do with our blood or our genes or our families. We did them because we worked together and we trusted each other, and when one of us lost heart, the other one was brave enough for both of us. I couldn't have done any of this stuff without you. If I'd been on my own, Ah Pukuh would've rolled me up in a tortilla and eaten me on day one. After everything we've been through, I just don't think we're meant to give up."

Lola sighed. "This isn't your fight, Hoop. You're not Maya—"

"It doesn't matter. We're a team. Like those trees Eusebio showed me, the ones that always grow together. . . ."

"Poisonwood and gumbo-limbo?"

"Yeah, one hurts and one heals."

"Which one am I?"

"My point is that we don't have to be the same to work together. Being different is sometimes better."

Lola laughed. "That sounds like something I'd say."

"I've been paying attention, Monkey Girl. You've taught me a lot."

Lola raised one eyebrow. "Like what?"

"Like when you told me that if the Maya had stood together

against the Spanish, they would have been invincible." Well, it seems to me that Ah Pukuh is trying to do to Middleworld what the conquistadors did to the Maya. He's trying to split us up and play us off against each other. He's a bully and he needs to know that humankind is not going to take it anymore." Max gulped. He knew this speech had only one ending. "It starts with us, Monkey Girl. Right here, right now."

"You really think we can do this?" Lola looked half scared, half thrilled.

Max shrugged. "We have a pretty good track record against those morons!"

"They may be morons, but they're powerful morons."

"We have power, too. We're smarter than them."

"This is not one of your video games, Hoop. It's deadly serious. You could get hurt . . . or worse."

"I know that. And if there was an easy way out, I'd take it. But I know something about bullies. And I'm pretty sure that if we hand over the White Jaguar, they'll ask us for something else. And they'll beat us up anyway. Honestly, I think we're safer keeping hold of the White Jaguar and calling their bluff."

Lola stared at him. "I hate to admit it, but you're right."

An owl screeched nearby. They saw it swoop out of the trees and fly toward the Black Pyramid.

"That's probably Kuy or one of his minions," said Lola. "I bet he was eavesdropping on us."

Max passed the White Jaguar to her, then stood up and cupped his hands around his mouth. "You can tell them that the Hero Twins are back in business!" he shouted after the owl.

As soon as the words left his lips, a conch-shell trumpet boomed out from the Black Pyramid.

Lola trained her hunter's eyes on the top platform. "There's someone up there!"

"Don't tell me," said Max. "He's wearing a headdress with tusks."

She nodded.

"It's Eek' Kitam," he told her, "the zombie from the beach."

"Eek' Kitam? Black Peccary? Catchy name." Lola threw earth onto the fire to extinguish it. "But we also call peccaries skunk pigs. I think that suits him better."

Max was staring at the pyramid. "I see him! He's coming down!"

Lola took a deep breath. In an instant—as if a fairy godmother had waved a wand and erased the Death Lords' taunting—she snapped back to her old self. She quickly packed away the White Jaguar, and swung her backpack onto her shoulders.

"Ready, Hoop? It's time to put our master plan into action."

"And what was our master plan exactly?"

"*Run, Hoop, Run!*"

Chapter Seven
CLAUSTROPHOBIA

Max was concentrating too hard on not tripping over tree roots or impaling himself on low branches to think too much about what was happening. The good thing about running through rainforest was that not much grew on the sunlight-starved forest floor—so the going was relatively easy. The bad thing was that the tree canopy also blocked moonlight, making it very hard to see.

Lola paused. "Listen!"

Max was no jungle hunter, but even he could hear Eek' Kitam following their trail.

Evidently, this zombie was not your usual silent tracker type.

Where Max and Lola picked their way carefully, the zombie crashed along. Where Max and Lola stepped gingerly over tangled tree roots and skirted leaf litter for fear of snakes, the zombie stomped on everything in its path.

Lola looked back. "He's gaining on us."

She was running at full speed, and Max had to push himself to keep up.

Where was she headed? Where could they hide?

Whumph! Max tripped over a root and fell face-first onto the forest floor. Lola grabbed his hand and dragged him along the ground. "Get up! Get up!" she yelled at him.

"Ow! Ow! Ow!" Even as he struggled to regain his footing, he saw the flash of an arrow. It landed—*thunk!*—in the tree behind Lola.

"Get up!" she shouted again, but Max's shaking legs wouldn't bear his weight, and his feet couldn't get a grip on the damp roots beneath them. He felt sharp pain, like his arm being pulled out of its socket, heard Lola scream, then nothing, just a strange silence, a sense of weightlessness, as the world collapsed around him.

The next thing he knew he was being dragged through water in a lifeguard armlock. For a moment, he thought he was back in Venice and kicked out at an imaginary octopus.

"Don't fight me!" yelled Lola. "We're almost to the bank."

She pushed Max onto a rock. "That was lucky," she spluttered, pulling herself up next to him.

"Lucky?" Max was sick and dizzy and his lungs were full of water. "How do you work that out?"

"The ground gave way beneath us! We fell through the roof of an underground cave!"

"You call that lucky? We must have fallen twenty feet."

"But we landed in water! We're alive!"

"That's quite a low bar for defining lucky."

"Hey, city boy, you're back in the jungle. It's all about survival, remember?"

Morning was breaking, and a shaft of weak sunlight shone down through the opening and illuminated the cave. It was a narrow, oval-shaped cavern about the length of a basketball

DIAGRAM OF CAVE-IN

Open to surface
Rocks & debris
Water
Water Flow

Top View

Side View

Scale = 8 ft

court with a shallow creek running through the middle into a deep pool of water at one end.

"And now we're trapped," said Max, "and no one knows we're here."

"At least we lost Skunk Pig," Lola pointed out.

Even as she spoke, a shower of rocks and debris splashed into the water. Eek' Kitam's head appeared in the opening, close enough for Max to register the jade beads implanted in his teeth.

"Or not," she whispered. "We need to move. With him stomping around up there, the rest of the roof could come down at any moment." She looked around the cavern. "Let's try upstream. These caves usually lead somewhere."

As they splashed their way up the creek and into the gloom, an arrow whizzed by.

"Keep down, Hoop!"

It was unnecessary advice, as the ground was sloping upward and the cave roof was getting lower.

"Where are we going?" he asked.

"I don't know. We're following the stream."

The problem with that plan became apparent when the water disappeared into a crack and left them facing a wall of solid rock.

"What now?" Max ducked as another arrow missed its target and bounced off the rock.

"We'll have to fight."

"He's a zombie. We don't stand a chance."

"But we're smarter than him."

"Are you suggesting a pop quiz? Because I don't think he'll play along."

"It's not funny, Hoop! How do they kill zombies in movies?"

Max flinched as an arrow missed his head by inches.

"You can't kill them. That's the thing about zombies. They're already dead. You have to destroy their brains."

"So we'll need ammunition." Lola tucked her backpack behind a large rock and began to gather stones. "Guava size is perfect! As many as you can find!"

"How big is a g—?" Over Lola's shoulder, Max saw the end of a rope made of thickly plaited vines drop down through the hole. *"He's coming!"*

"This size," replied Lola calmly, showing him a baseball-sized stone. "Ignore him and keep collecting the ammo."

By the time the feet of their enemy came in sight, they'd amassed a good cache of stones and stacked them up like cannonballs.

They hid behind the rock and watched as Eek' Kitam lowered himself down the vine rope until he hung just above the surface of the water. He looked around the cavern. Evidently the lack of eyeballs in his empty eye sockets did nothing to impair his vision.

He swung on his vine in their direction and landed at the edge of the pool. Pointing the obsidian blade of his spear ahead of him, he walked straight toward Max and Lola.

"Ready?" whispered Lola. "Aim at his head."

Max swallowed hard and lifted a stone.

"Fire!"

Disappointingly, even when their stones found their mark, they didn't have much effect. Max hit Eek' Kitam square in the face and cracked his jaw, but the zombie didn't notice a thing. Lola hit the back of his skull dead on, but the stone bounced off as if his cranium were armor-plated.

He was on them like a whirlwind, spinning his spear in a blurry arc above his head like a kung fu master.

First he dealt a hard swipe with the spear shaft to Max's neck, then, whirling around, brought a sweeping blow to the back of his legs, knocking him off his feet.

With Max laid low, Eek' Kitam turned on Lola. The spear shaft felled her just as quickly. When Max looked up, the zombie had one foot on her back and was pulling her head up by the hair to expose her neck. With his other skeletal hand, he took his battle-ax and raised it to deliver the killing blow.

"*Stop!*" yelled Max, between gasps for breath.

Eek' Kitam paused and slowly turned his head. A slight tilt of his chin told Max he was interested in making a deal.

"The White Jaguar's in here." Max crawled forward with Lola's backpack. "Take it!" he said, tossing it at the zombie. "This is what you're programmed to find! Just take it and leave her alone!"

Eek' Kitam made his death rattle noise, which Max mistakenly assumed was an expression of agreement. (In retrospect, he would realize it was a zombie approximation of a villainous laugh.)

Eek' Kitam let go of Lola's hair and replaced his battle-ax in his belt. Keeping his spear pointed at Lola's throat, he picked up the backpack. Then he reversed away, toward the pool.

"Thanks for saving me, Hoop," whispered Lola. She sighed. "I guess Skunk Pig won that round."

"At this point, I don't care. I just want him to go away."

Spear in hand, Eek' Kitam waded into the pool, and tied the backpack onto the end of the vine. Then he turned slowly to face them. His empty eye sockets seemed to stare straight at them.

"What's he doing?" said Max. "Why doesn't he climb up the vine?"

Eek' Kitam made the death rattle noise again.

Then, thrusting the spear point in front of him, he marched straight toward Max and Lola.

"He's coming back!" cried Max.

"Quick!" yelled Lola. "He's downhill from us. Help me move this big boulder." Together they pushed and shoved and kicked until the great stone came free. Then, with a mighty heave, they launched the boulder at the zombie, screaming all the while like madmen.

Eek' Kitam stepped nonchalently out of the way, and the boulder hit the rock wall behind him with a deep thud. The impact sent a tremor through the cave, the sound echoing around them like rolling thunder.

There was a groan from the cave ceiling, as if the earth above them—all the teeming leaf litter and tangled roots and rain-weakened limestone—was apologizing for the destruction to come.

Then a loud crack.

"Take cover!" yelled Lola.

Instinctively, Max crouched against the back wall with his hands over his head. Lola huddled next to him. They barely had time to exchange a look of terror before the rest of the cave roof imploded. The noise was deafening, as an avalanche of stones, trees, and earth crashed down in front of them, settling in layer upon layer of rubble and building a wall between themselves and the zombie.

When all was still, Max opened his eyes. It was pitch-black. He couldn't see his hand in front of his face.

"I'm blind!" he screamed.

"You're not blind, Hoop, it's just dark. The rockfall has blocked us in."

"My eyes are stinging!"

"It's just dust. Please, stop shouting. You're not helping."

"We're trapped!" yelled Max.

"Come on, Hoop, jungle one-oh-one. In a situation like this, what do we do?"

"Scream for help? Like this: *Help! Help!*"

"Wrong answer. What we do is we stay calm and we find the matches that we always keep in a waterproof bag in the pocket of our cargo pants."

"I don't have any matches! I'm not wearing cargo pants!"

"Really, Hoop? I thought you said you'd learned a lot from me?"

"I wasn't expecting to go hiking when I went to bed last night."

"Well, lucky for you, one of us came prepared."

Max heard several failed strikes of a match before—yay!—a tiny burst of flame appeared a few paces away. They were in a space the size of a small closet—a small closet with a creek trickling through it.

The zombie was somewhere on the other side of the wall.

"He must have been crushed," said Lola. "Even Skunk Pig couldn't survive that rockslide. See, Hoop? I told you we're lucky."

She dropped the match before it burned her fingers.

"Yeah," Max agreed. "I feel very lucky to be barricaded inside this tiny, dark, airless space. So, Monkey Girl, how do we get out?"

By the light of a few more matches, she confirmed Max's worst fear. There was no way out. The rockfall was immovable. To his almost equal horror, he also saw that they were not alone. Scuttling around busily trying to find new homes were giant centipedes as long as rulers, pill bugs like toy tanks, and a scary-looking tailless scorpion with eight legs.

"What is that thing?" asked Max in horror.

"It's a cave spider."

"It's got pincers."

"That's how it grabs its prey."

"It won't grab me, will it?"

"Of course not," said Lola, but she didn't sound too sure.

"Light another match. I think one crawled into my shirt."

"We need to conserve matches, Hoop."

"Where's your flashlight?"

"It's in my backpack. On the end of Skunk Pig's vine."

They sat in darkness and a silence so deep that Max could hear the insects crawling and burrowing.

"I wonder," said Lola after a while, "if your parents will notice you're gone?"

"Of course, they will," snapped Max. "Do you think they're so wrapped up in their work that they wouldn't notice that their own son is missing? That's so insulting."

"I'm sorry, Hoop. I like your parents. And I'm

obviously no expert on parental behavior. But it's just that it always seems to be you rescuing them, not the other way round."

She had a point.

A few pebbles tumbled from the wall of stone, dislodged by a moving creature.

Max screamed.

"It's okay, Hoop. It was just a cave spider or a centipede. It won't hurt you. Calm down."

"It's got me! It's got me!"

"Stop shouting. Whatever it is, it's harmless. Just swat it off."

Max croaked out one word: "Zombie."

"What? What are you talking about?"

"Zombie!"

Lola lit another match.

A skeletal hand was clawing at Max's neck, digging into his flesh with its bony fingers.

It took two of them to detach it and pry off its fingers one by one.

The zombie hand fought like a demon, but eventually they wrestled it to the ground. While Max held up the match, Lola smashed the bones with a rock. When the fingers tried to escape individually, both Max and Lola pounded them until the last wriggling bone had been pulverized.

"I thought you said zombies were controlled by their brains," complained Lola as they sat back, exhausted. "So how could its hand have drilled through the wall on its own?

"Remote control?" guessed Max. He shrugged. "I never said I was an expert on Maya zombies."

"Let's hope the rest of it is buried under some big

boulders," said Lola. "Or we'll have to destroy it bit by bit. And we're running out of matches."

They sat very still and listened for rampaging zombie body parts.

"I think I should warn you," said Max, "that I'm getting claustrophobic. And I'm starving. I feel like I might suddenly start screaming and turn cannibal and eat you."

"Get a grip, Hoop. We've only been in here an hour or so."

"How much air do we have?"

Lola ignored the question. "Let's try some positive thinking. Send a message into the universe. See in your mind what you want to happen next. But not the cannibal stuff, okay?"

"Okay."

Max closed his eyes and imagined his parents finding him gone and radioing for help. He visualized the rescue helicopters hovering over the surface. He saw teams of burly rescuers descending into the cave to clear the rocks. It all looked so real and felt so likely that he started to relax.

"Hoop? Are your feet wet?"

Lola lit another match. Its course blocked by the rockfall, the little stream that had flowed through the cave had found its way into their hidey-hole. The ground was slick and wet. In the time it took for one match to flare and die, the water rose several inches.

So this was it.

After the best efforts of the Death Lords to devise a suitably innovative and gory end to Max Murphy's life story, it was to be death by drowning, pure and simple.

What the octopus had started, this cave was going to finish.

"We can't just sit here and wait to go under," he said.

Lola was silent.

"Talk to me!" he begged her.

"What about?"

"Anything. Tell me what you're thinking. Please, just keep talking."

"I just . . . I was thinking about my parents, Hoop. Why did they abandon me?"

"Chan Kan loves you."

"Chan Kan wants me to be someone I'm not. He hates it that I want to go to college and travel round the world. He wants me to stay in the village."

"It's your life. What does it matter what Chan Kan wants?"

"Ever since that freak show in Spain when Landa pretended I was a Maya princess, I've felt kind of unbalanced. I'm sick of other people projecting their stuff onto me. I need my own stuff. My own history."

The water had risen to waist level.

"Can't Chan Kan tell you anything?"

"He just repeats the same old story about how Hermanjilio found me in the forest and brought me to Utsal. But there must be more to it than that. Someone must know something. I wasn't a newborn, so where had I been living? It's impossible to keep secrets in these little Maya villages."

"No one ever reported a missing baby?"

"Weird, isn't it?"

The water was up to their necks.

"Hey, Hoop, I can feel a little ledge. Come and sit on it. It will raise you up a bit. You might find a pocket of air."

"What about you?"

"I'm taller than you, remember?"

"Just so you know, I would have grown this year. My father

is six foot two, so I probably would have been way taller than you in the end. If we'd lived."

Lola felt for his hand and squeezed it. "I've heard drowning isn't so bad. It's like going to sleep."

"I almost drowned in Venice. A giant octopus dragged me under. But you saved me. . . ."

"Me? I wasn't in Venice. . . ."

"Yes, you were. In my head anyway. Although it was Fabio who—" The water reached his mouth and he couldn't talk anymore.

Lola let go of his hand.

The water was nearly up to his nose when he saw her slip under the water.

Max knew he had to follow her.

Of all the stupid things he'd done in his fourteen-year existence, thinking that he could stand up to Ah Pukuh and his killer zombie had to be the most stupid of all. But, to his surprise, he realized that it wasn't the thing he regretted the most.

As he counted down the last moments of his life, his thoughts turned to a little Maya boy called Och. A boy who'd adored him and copied him and been the little brother he'd never had—until Max had done something idiotic—actually several idiotic things—and turned Och's adulation into contempt. As he held his breath and waited to die, he could see Och's face so clearly. The little boy seemed to be reaching out to him.

A bright light shone into Max's eyes.

He heard a voice talking in Mayan.

Lola was right. Drowning wasn't so bad.

But was this the Maya heaven or the Maya underworld?

103

Chapter Eight
A NEW PLAN

ch's face was so close that Max could smell beans and tortillas on his breath.

Max stared at him. "Are you an angel?"

The little boy didn't answer him, but turned and whispered in Lola's ear.

"Monkey Girl! What's going on? Are we dead?" Max asked her.

"No, we're fine—thanks to this guy!" Lola ruffled Och's hair. "He's brought some workers from the site. They've let the water out and they're taking down the wall. Och squeezed through the first little hole they made."

"Thank you, Och," said Max. "You saved our lives."

Och bit his lip and stared at the ground.

"What's the matter with him? He speaks English. Why isn't he talking to me?"

"I don't know. He won't tell me what's wrong."

"He's not still mad that I ate his porridge?"

Lola rolled her eyes. "No, Hoop, I'm sure it's not the porridge."

"He looks so sad."

"Maybe it's about Chan Kan. He's like a grandfather to all the kids in the village. Och says he's dying and he wants to say good-bye to me. That's why Och came looking for me, to take me back to Utsal."

Max tried to look sympathetic, but the truth was that the old man gave him the creeps. "Did you know Chan Kan was sick?"

"I know he's old."

"What is he, like, a hundred?"

"Or more. But he's pulled this trick before, just to make me visit."

"You don't think he's dying?"

"I don't know. I'll find out when I get to Utsal."

"When you see him, you should interrogate him again. Try and get some answers."

"Interrogate him? You make him sound like a criminal. But maybe I'll ask him again about the day I was found, see if there were any details he forgot to tell me. They say that when people get old, they start to remember the past more clearly."

Max could hear the singing of Maya workers as they removed more and more rocks from the wall. "How did Och find us, anyway?"

"He saw the big hole where the ground had caved in and climbed down to investigate. Apparently my backpack is still hanging on the vine, so he guessed I was here. And he ran to the site to get help."

"So there's no sign of Stink Pig?"

"Skunk Pig. Och thinks he might have seen a few toes scuttling around."

"Ugh. That's enough to give me nightmares."

As the next rock was lifted out of place, a face filled the void. "I see them," said his mother's voice.

"Thank goodness," said his father's voice. "But this place could collapse at any moment. We all need to get out fast!"

As soon as the opening was big enough, Max, Lola, and Och wriggled into the main cave—where the first thing they saw, dangling like a prize at a fair, was Lola's backpack still tied to the vine.

She waded over and untied it.

Even before she gave him the thumbs-up, Max could tell from the weight that the White Jaguar was safe inside.

"I can't believe it survived," she said.

Max extricated himself from his mother's arms. "I can't believe *we* survived."

"Hero Twins, one; Death Lords, none," announced Lola, as the workers helped them back up to the forest.

Max's stomach did a victory roll. Somehow, crazily, they had foiled the felons of the underworld yet again. But he knew Ah Pukuh would come back stronger.

The battle for the White Jaguar had only just begun.

Back at the camp, Max's mother fussed around as if they were royal guests. She handed out towels, made hot tea, and broke into her emergency supply of Italian licorice candies (which nobody wanted). "I will get you both dry clothes," she said, "then I will make some food."

"Don't eat it," whispered Max to Lola. "If Ah Pukuh can't kill you, my mom's cooking will."

Oblivious, his mother continued her ministrations. "We have a spare tent, Lola; you are welcome to stay here."

"Thank you, Professor Murphy," said Lola, "but Och and I have to get back to Utsal."

"Can I go with them, Mom?" asked Max, keen to put as much distance as he could between himself and the vengeful remains of Eek' Kitam. "There's nothing for me to do here."

"Absolutely not," said his mother. "No offense to you, Lola, but you two are a bad influence on each other. You are always getting into some kind of trouble."

"But Mom—"

His protestations were drowned out by engine noise.

Och pointed to the sky. A light aircraft was heading straight toward them over the Black Pyramid.

For a moment, Max thought the Undead Army was launching an aerial attack.

"What the . . . ?" began his father. "Duck! Duck! Everyone get down!"

They threw themselves to the ground as the small plane buzzed over and then turned, in a wide arc, to come back.

"Its wheels are down—I think it's trying to land," said Lola.

"It's not going to make it," said Max's father. "There's not enough space."

The closest thing to a landing strip was the patch of cleared earth between the pyramid and the camp. They watched between their fingers as the small plane came down lower, lower, lower . . . but just before landing, the pilot seemed to lose his nerve, and the plane gained altitude again. Then, with a decisive throttling-back of the engines, it suddenly swooped down and the wheels thumped onto grass. The pilot threw the engine into reverse and, with a squealing of brakes (not unlike the sound of the tapir), the plane bumped and skidded across the plaza until it came to a stop in the middle of the camp.

As the propellers made their last, slow spins, the cockpit door flew open.

Max shrank back, half expecting Ah Pukuh to step out in a flying helmet and goggles.

But this was a thin man, in a cream linen suit and panama hat.

He gave them a wave. "Hello, all!" he called, before jumping down to terra firma.

"Ted? What are you doing here? That was quite an entrance." Max's father strode over to greet his brother.

"I just thought I'd pop in and see how the dig was going," said Uncle Ted, taking off his hat and mopping his brow with his pocket handkerchief.

"What a nice surprise." Max's mother kissed her handsome, if slightly haggard, brother-in-law on both cheeks. "I did not know you had a plane, Ted."

"It belongs to a friend of mine, the chief of police. He lets me borrow it from time to time."

He turned to Lola. "I was worried about you, but I had a hunch you might be here." He grinned at Max. "It's good to see you, too, Nephew."

"I'm so sorry," said Lola. "I'm . . . I'm not used to people worrying about me. I didn't mean to drag you all this way."

"You're safe, and that's all that matters. Between the two of us, I was looking for a reason to get away." Suddenly he looked back at the plane, as if he'd forgotten something. "Excuse me for a moment, but I have to check on my passenger."

"You have a passenger?" asked Max. "Who is it?"

"Someone you know very well," Uncle Ted called as he ran back. "I thought he'd followed me out."

A light aircraft was heading straight toward them
over the Black Pyramid.

A large black howler monkey appeared at the cockpit door. He was massaging his temples with his hairy fingers. "Confound it, Lord Ted, I have decided that neither howlers nor Maya kings were meant to fly. Thou hast befuddled my brain and bruised my body. I am only glad that of all the great inventions of the mighty Maya, flying machines were not amongst them."

"Lord 6-Dog!" cried Lola happily. "You're free!"

The monkey-king jumped nimbly to the ground. "We have Lady Zia to thank for that. She stormed our quarters with a sheaf of papers and demanded our release. The quarantine officers were reluctant to comply, but in the end she wore them down."

Uncle Ted rolled his eyes. "I know the feeling. She's at the Villa Isabella now. That's partly why I had to get away. That woman is intense."

"Is Lady Coco there, too, Mr. Murphy?" asked Lola eagerly.

"She's renewing her acquaintance with Raul. The two of them have been cooking up a storm. Which reminds me, if you'd like to join me for refreshments, Raul and Lady Coco have sent something for you all."

He unloaded a large wicker hamper from the plane.

Max looked anxiously between the Black Pyramid and the picnic hamper. With no movement on the pyramid, he decided to risk checking out the hamper. There were mango scones and buttery corn cakes and cocoa-nib cookies. The fresh-baked smell was heavenly.

He waited impatiently as his mother arranged a little cloth on a camping table and decorated it with a jar of tropical flowers, snipped from a nearby bush. He was interested to see that she'd brought her flowery apron with her, and had instantly reverted to domestic goddess.

"Isn't this nice?" she said, as she set out fresh limeade and a large bowl of just-picked cashew nuts. "Would you care for a nut, Your Majesty?" she asked Lord 6-Dog.

"In all honesty, dear lady, I would prefer thy flowers."

Without a second thought, she plucked the bouquet out of the jar and passed him the dripping stems. "Let me get you a napkin for those," she said, with all the aplomb of a hostess passing round hors d'oeuvres.

How strange, Max thought, that his mother in a housewife apron in the middle of the jungle serving a bunch of flowers to an ancient Maya king in the body of a howler monkey was the most reassuringly normal thing to have happened all day.

"Could Och and I take ours to go?" asked Lola. "We need to be on our way. It's three days' walk to Utsal, and Chan Kan is waiting for me."

"But I only just got here," objected Uncle Ted. "Can't you stay a little longer?"

"Och says Chan Kan is dying." She hesitated. "Again."

"Chan Kan? The guy who raised you? I'm so sorry to hear that," said Uncle Ted, as Max's parents murmured in sympathy. "Of course, you must go. In fact, let me fly you there! You'll get to Utsal in no time!"

"Really? You'd do that?"

"It would be my pleasure. I'd love to see where you grew up, Lola—as long as you'll be my navigator."

"It's easy," Lola assured him. "Just follow the Monkey River!"

"I'm surprised you've never been there, Uncle Ted," said Max.

Uncle Ted smiled ruefully. "Back in my smuggling days, I was not exactly welcome in traditional villages like Utsal. Word got around the Maya that I was selling off their heritage."

"Which you were," Lola pointed out sternly.

"Well, I'm a reformed character now. And I've donated my ill-gotten gains to the Maya Foundation in San Xavier City, so I think I can walk into Utsal with my head held high."

"Please let me go with them, Mom," begged Max. "We won't get into trouble, I promise. And Uncle Ted will be there to keep an eye on us."

"Fine by me," said his uncle. "The more, the merrier!"

"Are you sure you know how to fly that thing?" Max's father asked him.

Uncle Ted looked offended. "I have a pilot's license, you know, Frank."

"But it does not look safe," put in Max's mother.

"Don't be fooled by all the dents and scratches, Carla— that's just the reality of bush planes."

"Besides, we'll be flying low and we'll have the tree canopy beneath us, like a safety mattress!" added Lola. She saw the appalled expression on Carla Murphy's face. "I'm joking, of course!" She nudged Och. "You want to ride in the plane, don't you?"

He looked unsure.

"We'll get there faster," Lola encouraged him.

Och nodded straightaway.

Max turned to his parents. "Please let me go with them. It's important. Last time I was in Utsal, I was kind of a jerk. This is my chance to say sorry and show them I've changed. You're always worried about my manners, Mom. I'm trying to do the right thing here."

"I don't know, *bambino.* . . ."

"Come to think of it, Carla," said Max's father, "it's not such a bad idea. It sounds like it would be a character-building experience. And, like it or not, you and I have to go to San Xavier City to report the looting. Ted could look after Max while we're away."

"I promise," said Uncle Ted, "to make sure he cleans his teeth."

Max's mother sighed. "*Allora* . . . all right. I hope I do not regret this."

"But no more caves," added his father.

Max nodded.

And, just like that, he was free.

Free to board a clunker of a plane that looked like it was held together with Band-Aids and chewing gum. Free to revisit the village that had mocked and humiliated him. Free to pay his last respects to the ancient shaman who'd scared him out of his wits. But free also to put as much distance as he could between himself and the Black Pyramid.

"All aboard!" said Uncle Ted.

"I will meet thee at Utsal," said Lord 6-Dog, heading for the trees. "Nothing would persuade me to reboard that rust bucket."

"That's the first sensible thing old 6-Dog's said since he put on the monkey suit," sneered Xibalba's president of marketing.

A titter ran around the room.

"I am not paying you to make jokes," thundered Ah Pukuh, at the head of the table. He clapped his hands, and a pack of slavering, razor-toothed hellhounds ran in. They took down the president of marketing and dragged him screaming out the door. "We are running out of time," continued the god of violent and unnatural death, without missing a beat. "I need the White Jaguar and I need it now."

The Demon of Jaundice yawned so hard that his teeth fell out. It had been a long meeting and it showed no signs of ending anytime soon.

The meeting was taking place in the deepest, darkest level of the Maya underworld, where Ah Pukuh had brought together his Death Lords and other close advisers to discuss the progress of what the Marketing Department had dubbed (making quote marks with their fingers) "the Jaguar Stones campaign."

That title was neatly printed in glyphs on all the files and binders and boards and charts that Ah Pukuh was now sweeping angrily off the table.

"Eek' Kitam has failed!" he yelled. "So much for your so-called hearts-and-minds initiative. If a charmer like Eek' Kitam cannot win their hearts and minds, we need to bring on the big blowguns. So let's have no more talk about brand values, or hypertasking, or reality sandwiches. From now on, we do it my way!"

The vice president of marketing cleared his throat. "Lord Ah Pukuh, without going down the blamestorming route, I do think we should whiteboard a few—"

Ah Pukuh clapped his hands.

The hounds ran in.

The vice president was removed from the meeting.

Ah Pukuh nodded in satisfaction. "It's time to show those brats who's boss! We will release the entire Undead Army and tear them from limb to limb!"

The Death Lords broke into applause. "Crush them! Crush them!" they chanted.

A corpse so disintegrated that it was impossible to tell its gender put up its hand.

"Who are you?" snapped Ah Pukuh, sitting back down at the head of the table.

"I'm . . . I'm the new intern in social media," stammered the corpse nervously.

Ah Pukuh narrowed his eyes. "Meaning?"

"It's m-my job to exploit web-b-based technologies to b-build an interactive dialogue with your consumer b-base."

Ah Pukuh moved to clap his hands and summon the hounds.

"Wait!" The intern swallowed nervously. "It's just that . . . I was thinking . . . you could get a lot more bang for your buck if this thing went viral." He had one eye on the hellhounds, which were straining to attack him. "You want all of Middleworld to quake at the sound of your name, right? So what you need is a promo that rams home your message."

Ah Pukuh stayed the dogs. "Go on . . ."

"The Hero Twins are headed to Utsal. And you know what's just upriver from there . . ."

"I do know." Ah Pukuh smiled. "So tell me your idea."

And when he'd heard it, he had to agree that it was a very fine idea indeed.

"Now, this is what I call a hearts-and-minds campaign," he announced to the room. "I win the hearts of those two brats on a platter, and I terrify everyone in Middleworld out of their minds! Someone bring snacks! I have some serious evil to plan."

Chapter Nine
CRASH LANDING

At first the plane swooped through the tropical sky like an eagle riding on the breeze. But as they turned inland, threatening gray clouds loomed in front of them and made it hard for Lola, as navigator, to find her way.

Max swallowed nervously.

He was sitting in the backseat with Och. It was noisy in the plane and he'd long ago given up trying to talk; the boy seemed lost in a world of his own. So Max stared gloomily out at the storm clouds and hoped Uncle Ted would find somewhere to land before the thunder came.

He gave a yelp of terror as they hit a pocket of turbulence.

"Look down!" Lola called from the front seat. "Skunk pigs!"

Max looked where she pointed, and saw a herd of grayish black peccaries grazing in a clearing. At the sound of the plane, they stampeded into the undergrowth.

As the plane soared over the treetops, Max remembered the first time he'd seen the rainforest. He'd stood on the balcony of his room at his uncle's house in Puerto Muerto, trying to spot some wildlife in all the greenery and thinking how much the tight-packed tree canopy looked like broccoli, his most hated vegetable.

It was a bad beginning.

Now he understood better how things worked down there.

As it turned out, the rainforest was a lot like school. So many different species all crammed together, all competing for a spot in the sunlight. Some bullied, some cheated, some formed alliances. Some were poisonous, some were extroverts, others hid in the trees.

But they all did whatever it took to survive.

Only the jaguar stalked the forest without fear.

So what was he? A jock? A prom king? A—

"*Monkey River!*" shouted Uncle Ted from the front seat.

And there it was, snaking below them, the mighty river that flowed right across San Xavier from the mountains in the west to the Caribbean in the east. Perhaps because the sky was gray and drizzly, the river didn't look as sparkly green as Max remembered it. In fact, it looked dark and sluggish.

"If you head upstream," shouted Lola, "we'll soon be at Utsal."

Max peered down. He knew exactly what he was looking for: a bustling little village of thatched huts around a clearing beside the river. There would be smoke from the cooking fires, men working in the cornfields, women washing clothes, children jumping in the water, dugout canoes pulled up on the banks.

As they approached a long, wide bend in the river, Och looked animated for the first time and pointed down at a settlement.

"That's not Utsal," said Max.

The place that had attracted Och's interest was more

like a construction site than a village. It had a few traditional thatched huts, but everywhere new buildings of gray cinder blocks were taking shape. The new houses had patchwork tin roofs that glinted in the sun; many of them had satellite dishes. There were no people, no cooking fires, no dugout canoes; just piles of smoldering garbage and a few skinny dogs poking around on the riverbank.

"That *is* Utsal," yelled Lola over the engine noise. "Looks like things have changed."

"Get ready for landing!" warned Uncle Ted.

They flew over Utsal again, coming in lower and lower.

Max could see what his uncle was aiming for: a patch of scrubland parallel to the river, where the foliage had been cleared. The drizzle turned into a downpour, and rain lashed the windshield like a volley of rocks.

Lola looked back at Max and grimaced. She was holding her backpack on her knees and now she clutched it so tight, her knuckles shone bone-white through her skin.

Max glimpsed water below them, very close below them.

Then everything turned to chaos.

Uncle Ted was shouting and Lola was batting things, white things, away from his face, while he tried to land the plane. Max guessed it must be some kind of insect infestation, like stinging larvae or biting maggots. Then one of the white things came flying over the seat and scratched his face, and he realized it was a piece of bone. Zombie bone! He tried to capture it, but it ran down the seat and disappeared.

Och drew his legs up under him and covered his face.

"Hold on for your lives! Brace yourselves!" yelled Uncle Ted in all the chaos.

With Uncle Ted pulling back on the throttle and Lola

helping to steer, they hit the ground hard, the impact sending a shock wave through the plane.

It shuddered and groaned like it was breaking apart.

They bounced high, leaning crazily to one side, before falling back down for another hard impact. Max was thrown against the window and then thrown against Och and then thrown against the window again.

He looked to the front and saw his uncle pulling wildly at the controls.

Boom, boom, boom! Then another hard bump.

They were sliding now, barreling toward the tree line way too fast.

The plane resounded with the constant thwack of trees and bushes. A stream of chopped leaves and branches sprayed the windows as the propellers diced their way through the brush like runaway wood chippers.

With a final thud and a nauseating splitting sound, the plane spun wildly and came to a stop. There was an eerie silence as everyone looked around in wonder, hardly believing they were still alive.

Once he was sure that his passengers were unharmed, Uncle Ted let out a sigh of relief. "Sorry for the rough landing, kids, but something . . . did you see them?. . .those *things* . . . attacked me. They poked me in the eyes. I couldn't see. Did anyone get a look at them? What were they? It seemed like they jumped out of your bag, Lola."

She nodded ruefully. "It was Skunk Pig. Some of his bones must have sneaked into my backpack after the rockfall. We have to find them all and destroy them, or they'll keep coming after us."

"Skunk Pig?" Uncle Ted sounded dazed.

"He's a zombie warrior," explained Max. "From the Black Pyramid."

Uncle Ted groaned. "Please don't tell me that you kids are up to your old tricks. What have you got yourselves involved in this time?"

"Hey, we didn't start it," protested Max. And he quickly explained about the chase and the cave and the rockfall.

"It creeps me out to know that Skunk Pig is on this plane somewhere." Lola shuddered.

"Check your stuff," Max advised her. "Make sure there's no more bits of him lurking in there."

"You do it," she said, passing her backpack over the seat, "while your uncle and I check the cockpit."

Realizing that she didn't want Uncle Ted to see the White Jaguar (a former smuggler would easily recognize a Jaguar Stone, even in its deerskin wrapping), Max carefully placed the stone on his knee, emptied the backpack, and turned it inside out. "All clear. So how do we destroy the bones on the loose?"

"First of all," said Uncle Ted, "we need to get ourselves off this plane." He tried his door. It was jammed shut. "Does anyone's door still open?"

"Mine does," volunteered Lola.

Uncle Ted's craggy face was beaded with sweat. A small cut over his eyebrow gave him the air of an action hero. "Okay, so we exit on Lola's side, watching carefully to make sure that none of our surprise guests escape. Everybody out!"

One by one they leapt down from the plane, wedged the door shut again, and stood in the drizzle, surveying their surroundings.

They were on dry land, but only just. The plane had crashed

through a grove of bamboo and come to rest at a crazy angle on the bank of the river. Even if it hadn't lost one of its wings, it was so smashed up, it looked unlikely to ever fly again.

"Welcome to Utsal," said Uncle Ted.

"Just one problem," observed Lola. "Utsal is miles away, on the other bank."

"First things first," said Uncle Ted. He took a first aid kit out of the cargo hatch, and handed it to her. "You three take this and go shelter under that fan palm."

"But none of us are injured," Max pointed out.

"It's got medical tape and trash bags inside. I need you to make some rain gear before the storm gets any worse," Uncle Ted explained. "We have a long walk ahead of us."

"What are *you* going to do?" asked Max.

"I'm going to make absolutely sure that the journey ends here for our stowaways."

"We'll help you," offered Lola.

Uncle Ted shook his head. "If you want to be helpful, just make the ponchos. And don't forget hoods. This hat is brand new—I don't want it getting ruined."

As Max and Lola stood arguing about the best way to turn a trash bag into a rain cape and Och peered anxiously across the river, an explosion rocked their bit of rainforest.

"He's set fire to the plane!" said Lola.

A rather singed and smoky Uncle Ted joined them under the palm tree. "I don't think Skunk Pig will bother us again."

"What about the plane?" asked Max.

"I'll tell my friend that it developed a dangerous malfunction and promise not to sue him. It was ready for the scrap heap anyway." He clapped his hands together. "So, how are those ponchos coming along?"

"I don't see why we need them," said Lola. "It rains in the rainforest every day."

"Not like this it doesn't."

There was a crack of thunder and the downpour began in earnest: sheets and sheets of water, so loud that they could hardly hear each other speak.

Lola hastily donned her hooded trash bag. "Let's walk downriver until we're opposite Utsal," she shouted. "Someone is sure to see us and come to help."

Och was delighted with this plan and led the way for a mile or so along the bank until the tin roofs of Utsal came in sight. The village looked deserted.

Och stood on tiptoe to whisper in Lola's ear.

"He wants us to swim for it," she explained. "He's in a hurry to get home." She regarded the fast-flowing water dubiously. "I guess it's not that far. And we couldn't get any wetter than we already are."

"What about the crocodiles?" asked Max.

"And the water snakes?" added Uncle Ted.

Lola bent down and conferred with Och. There was a lot of head shaking on Lola's part until they seemed to come up with a new plan. Standing side by side, they put their fingers between their lips and whistled as loudly as they could. Against the noise of the rain, they sounded like drowned birds.

An old woman emerged from one of the huts.

She put up an umbrella, and stared across at them.

Lola shouted to her in Mayan.

The old woman shouted a hoarse reply and went back into her hut.

"Do you know her? What did she say? Is she sending someone?" asked Max.

"I've never seen her before. She said to wait for the worker boat."

"What's a worker boat?"

"How do I know? I can't believe that she didn't offer to help."

They stood there for a good while longer, whistling and shouting and hoping to attract the attention of someone a little more neighborly.

But no one came.

Eventually, the worker-boat mystery was solved by the appearance of a wooden motorboat that cruised around the bend of the river, belching smoke. It was packed with passengers, Maya villagers, who looked at the trash bag–clad castaways without interest.

Max, Lola, and Uncle Ted waved their arms and yelled for help.

The boatman, who was shrouded in a yellow rain slicker, glanced across at them. He made a money sign with his fingers.

"He's saying it will cost us," said Max.

"What?" Lola was outraged. "No one around here would ask for money to help a stranger."

"Why not? He's entitled to make a living." Uncle Ted waved back to accept the deal. "It will only be pennies. No big deal. I just want to get out of the rain."

Ignoring the protests of his passengers—his very wet passengers—who evidently did not approve of this extra stop, the boatman set a course toward them.

When he was level, he cut the engine.

"Hello!" Uncle Ted called over. "Can you take us to Utsal?"

"One hundred dollars, mister."

"A hundred dollars? Just for taking us across the river?"

"One hundred dollars. Each person."

"Four hundred dollars? Are you mad? It's a hundred yards."

"Take it or leave it," snarled the boatman. He started up the engine.

"Surely you're not going to leave us stranded?" protested Uncle Ted. "We've been in a plane crash. There are children here."

Och pushed his way to the front and put down his hood so the boatman could see him properly.

"Eusebio!" called Och.

Lola looked from the little boy to the boatman. "Eusebio? It can't be!"

The boatman took some sunglasses from his pocket and quickly put them on, as if trying to disguise himself.

"It is Eusebio!" cried Max. "I gave him those shades!"

Max and Lola gaped at the boatman in disbelief. Could it really be their old friend Eusebio, the kindly chili farmer who'd once given them a lift from Utsal to Itzamna, and stopped along the way to teach Max a lesson about the importance of working together and helping other people?

What could have happened to turn this gentle, jolly man into a grasping profiteer?

Embarrassed by their accusing stares, Eusebio relented.

"You can owe me," he said, throwing a mooring rope to Uncle Ted.

As they made the short journey across the river, Lola surveyed the other passengers mournfully. "What's the matter with everyone? They all look so miserable. Not a single person has smiled at me."

"It's raining," Max pointed out.

"We're in the rainforest, Hoop. It always rains here. But Utsal used to be the happiest place in the world."

"You make it sound like Disneyland."

"In a way, it was. We were like one big family. Now everyone feels separate. Even Och has hardly said a word to me."

"Chill. Everyone's wet and tired and they want to go home."

"What about Eusebio? You can't tell me he hasn't changed."

Max thought about it. He remembered Eusebio's booming laugh and his generous nature. Now the boatman was only interested in lining his own pockets. Max shrugged. "Maybe he's gone to the dark side."

125

"Don't even joke about it."

When the boat docked, the passengers tramped sullenly off. Some of them even sneered at the castaways as they passed.

"Did you see that?" asked Lola, indignantly.

Och pushed his way through and jumped off the boat.

"Aren't you going to say good-bye?" Lola called after him. He gave a halfhearted wave, without turning round, and ran off through the village. She watched sadly as the boy made his way home. "I wonder what's wrong with him?"

"At least it's not my fault this time," said Max.

"Excuse me, Lola." Uncle Ted was extracting banknotes from his wallet. "Please give this to our miserly mariner, while I try to get a signal on my cell phone."

The rain had stopped as suddenly as it had started.

Eusebio was unloading cargo on the dock.

"Let's go help him, Hoop," suggested Lola.

"Help him? He tried to fleece us."

But Max followed her over.

"It's good to see you, Eusebio," she said, passing him the money. "How are you?"

The boatman counted the banknotes, with a sour look on his face. "Out of pocket, that's how I am."

"Why are you talking like this? It was only a few weeks ago that you gave us a lecture on the evils of the consumer society. You said that helping each other was the most important thing—like the ants and the trumpet tree, remember?"

"I was wrong."

"So what's changed?"

"Helping people does not put tortillas on the table."

"Neither does neglecting the cornfields. I saw them from the plane; they're overgrown."

Eusebio waved a hand dismissively. "Who has time to grow corn and grind it and pound it into dough for tortillas? Anyway, the young people prefer french fries. It's called progress."

Max nodded in agreement.

Lola pursed her lips. "What does Chan Kan think about all this?"

"Have you seen him lately?" asked Eusebio warily.

"That's why we've come."

"You will find him changed."

"It seems like everyone's changed. Everyone and everything."

"We are moving with the times, Ix Sak Lol."

"I liked it better before."

"Before the tourists? Me, too." For a moment, Eusebio's face softened and he looked like his old self. "But there is no going back. Tourism is our future."

"Where did all these tourists come from, all of a sudden?" asked Max.

"You haven't heard? A big hotel has opened upstream in Limón. We all work for them now. They pay good money, so we can afford tin roofs, electricity, satellite TV. . . . They gave me this boat. It is better than my old dugout, no?"

Lola stroked the boat admiringly. "It carries more people, that's for sure. But those passengers today, who were they? Why didn't I recognize any of them?"

"A lot of new people have moved into the village, to be near their work at the hotel."

"Why do they all look so miserable?"

"We have to smile all day for the tourists. So when we finish work, it's a relief to rest our face muscles. Most of us prefer not to talk at night. We just want time to ourselves. We

like to put our feet up, and watch TV or surf the Internet."
He nudged Max. "It's like your New York City around here
these days."

Max smiled inwardly at the comparison. Then he
considered the trash and the blaring TVs and the blank faces
of the commuters, and he realized that Eusebio had a point.

Lola put on a bright voice. "So how's the chili business?"

Eusebio frowned. "Not good. I have nowhere to sell them.
The market at Limón is all popcorn and hot dogs now. They
say the tourists don't like spicy food." He nudged Max. "Hey,
remember that pepper-soup trick we used to play on them?"

Max nodded. "How could I forget?"

Eusebio chuckled, then remembered himself and tried to
look penitent. "It is not allowed anymore."

"Who says?" asked Lola.

"The hotel. The hotel controls everything now."

"What's the name of this hotel anyway?" asked Lola.

"The Grand Hotel Xibalba."

"Did you hear that?" fumed Lola as they walked through the
village to Chan Kan's house. "The Grand Hotel Xibalba? The
Death Lords are behind this, I know it!"

"It could be a coincidence," said Max.

"Oh really? So Utsal has been the same close-knit little
village for hundreds of years and then the minute this hotel
opens up, it turns all mercenary and modern—and you think
that's a coincidence?"

"But why shouldn't the people who live here have fast
food and laptops? Everyone else does."

"Let's see what Chan Kan has to say about it."

The shaman lived in one of the last remaining thatched huts.

"*Ko'oten!* Come in!" came his impatient voice, almost before they arrived.

Max followed Lola into the hut. "Grandfather! I've come back to see you! And I've brought Max Murphy with me, so please talk in English."

Chan Kan was lying in a hammock. This time around, he looked a little less like Gandalf and a little more like a vagrant. His long hair was dull and matted. His impossibly old face was even more wrinkled than Max remembered it, especially when it contorted with rage at the sight of him.

"Is this your husband?" he demanded of Lola. "I told you that I will not meet him. How dare you bring him here?"

"I am not married," said Lola gently. "It's me, Ix Sak Lol."

The old man peered at her through dim eyes. Then he peered at Max. "Who is he then? He is not one of us."

"He's my friend. His name is Max. You met him once."

"You told me to trust the howler monkeys," Max reminded him.

Chan Kan stared at him, then started laughing. The creases in his face were now so deep that his eyes vanished completely. "I remember you! You're the one who ate the soup! Do you still bury your head in the sand like a burrowing snake? Or have you learned to soar with the hawks?"

"As a matter of fact," said Max, "I flew here today."

"We came to see you, Grandfather," added Lola.

Chan Kan slapped his knee. "So, the Hero Twins have returned at last! Are you ready to play ball?"

Chapter Ten
CHANGES

"How are you, Grandfather?" asked Lola.

"I am preparing to enter the water."

Max had hung around with Lola long enough to know that *entering the water* was an archaic Maya way of referring to death. It was a lesson he'd learned the hard way, when he'd literally entered the water in Spain to follow a ship of dead souls on his journey to the Maya underworld. Now death and water were forever linked in his mind, like a flotilla of little coffins bobbing on a moonlit lagoon.

He looked around Chan Kan's hut and remembered how alien it had seemed the first time he'd come here: the sickly smell of incense and beeswax candles; the shelves stacked with sinister-looking objects in jars; every surface piled with leaves, twigs and berries waiting to be made into potions; all the skulls and bones, furs and feathers that decorated the walls. It didn't look like any doctor's office Max had ever been in, but now he understood that Chan Kan's rainforest remedies were often as effective as medicine from the drugstore, sometimes even contained the same ingredients.

It was Chan Kan's soothsaying act that freaked him out. On his previous visit, the old man had compared Max and Lola to the Hero Twins of Maya myth, and announced that the fate of the world was in their hands. Max shuddered at the memory. He hoped the old man would keep his crazy ramblings to himself this time.

Lola put her hand on Chan Kan's shoulder. "Och said that you . . . that you wanted to talk to me, Grandfather."

He ran his wrinkled old fingers over her hand, as if he was reading Braille. "I have missed you. Where have you been?"

"We went across the ocean to Spain. The south was hot and dry like a clay oven. But you'd like it in the north. It's wild and green, and the people believe in magic."

Max noticed that she left out any mention of ghosts and weddings and fires and Jaguar Stones.

"Do *you* believe in magic?" Chan Kan asked her. Then, without waiting for her answer, he went on: "If only I had a magic spell to undo what I have done. But I can no more change the past than I can stop fallen fruit from rotting."

"Grandfather, you are a great shaman. Your wisdom has helped many people in this village."

"And yet I cannot help myself. I cannot remember the old ways, the rituals, the prayers. The words have flown from my mind like startled parakeets. I am nothing but a corn husk, dried out in the sun. Utsal does not need me anymore."

"I need you," said Lola.

"You?" A look of pain crossed Chan Kan's face. "How can you say that—you of all people—after everything that has happened?"

"You mean the way Utsal has changed? That's not your

131

fault. In fact"—she lowered her voice—"I think Ah Pukuh is behind it."

"Ah Pukuh?" Chan Kan looked confused. "What does he have to do with anything?"

"Think about it. It would be so much easier for him to take over Middleworld if all the people were distracted by money and TV and fast food!" Lola's eyes widened. "That's it! Maybe he's putting chemicals in the food!"

"Um, the food companies already do that," Max pointed out.

Chan Kan looked at Max as if he'd never seen him before. "Who is that?" he asked Lola.

"He's my friend," said Lola patiently. "But we were talking about the new hotel. Have you heard about it, Grandfather?"

Chan Kan nodded. "It is a source of great trouble. But I hear the pizza is good."

Max's ears pricked up. "Deep-dish, or thin and crusty?"

"Is he your husband?" Chan Kan asked Lola once again.

Max rolled his eyes at her, amused by the old man's goldfish memory.

"Why don't you wait for me outside?" she said, coldly.

So Max went outside and sat on the ground and watched another boatload of weary workers wend their way home. He was hoping to see Och and his younger brother, Little Och, but no children played in the streets. Max could hear cartoons blaring from the houses and guessed they were all watching TV. He wondered if anyone would mind if he just entered a random house and sat down to watch it with them.

But he didn't dare give it a try.

So instead he watched the ants marching, millions upon millions of ants, in platoons, brigades, regiments, a mass of black stripes converging on some shared mission, and he wondered, uneasily, if the Undead Army still slept in peace in the Black Pyramid.

When Lola came out, she was carrying a little deerskin pouch.

Loud snoring noises issued from inside the hut.

"Boy, he's really losing it," said Max. "The way he kept forgetting things and repeating himself. I hope I don't end up like that."

"You will. We all will." Lola sighed. "He's an old man. You should show some compassion."

Max had never liked Chan Kan and felt absolutely no pity toward him. He looked for a change of subject. "What's in the bag?"

"He gave me his crystals, his most treasured possession. He said they will connect me with my future."

"Like fortune-telling? Can you do that stuff?"

"No, it gives me the creeps. I would never want to be a shaman."

"Well, at least you have something to remember him by."

"It was odd, though. I think he has me mixed up with someone else. He talked about how I played with the crystals when I was little. But I remember distinctly that I was never allowed to even *touch* them. Maybe I should give them back."

"Nah. He's just confused. So did you manage to interrogate him?"

"About the day I was found? No, it's too late. His memory's gone. I think that maybe"—her voice trembled—"maybe this really will be the last time I'll ever see him."

"We can come back in the morning. His memory might be better after a good night's sleep. You can ask him some more questions and give back the crystals, if you still think they're meant for someone else."

Lola weighed the bag of crystals in her hand. "I think they're meant for another time and another place. I feel like there's a whole world in this little bag, a world that's almost gone."

As they walked back through the village, Max couldn't help but notice how different it was from the last time they'd been here. On that occasion, the women had fussed over Lola, and the children had crowded around Max, and there had even been a feast in their honor. Today, only one scrawny dog looked even remotely pleased to see them.

The villagers looked down as they walked, lost in their own thoughts or isolated by headphones, all hurrying home from the ferry. Max noticed that most of them carried a bag of takeout food, and good smells of fried chicken wafted by.

"Can we get dinner?" he asked. "I'm starving."

Lola thought for a moment. "Let's visit Och. If we're lucky, his mother will be making tortillas on the fire. She makes the best tortillas in town."

"Why are you Maya so obsessed with tortillas?" pondered Max as they set off for Och's house. "You make fun of me and pizza, but I don't eat it every day."

"You would if you could," Lola pointed out.

"But the Maya have tortillas with every single meal. Don't you ever get sick of them?"

"They're more than just food; they're who we are."

"That's how I feel about thin-crust pepperoni."

"And were your ancestors were made out of pizza dough?"

"What? No! I'm half Italian, but I wouldn't go that far."

"Well, that's the difference. Our creation story tells us that after laying down the cosmic hearthstones, what you call the three stars in Orion's belt, the creator gods formed the first humans from corn dough. So every morning, when I see women crouched over their hearthstones shaping dough for tortillas, it gives me goosebumps. It's like we get born again every day." She sneaked a glance at him. "Does that sound silly to you?"

"No, I like it. I like most stories with food in them."

Lola laughed. "Let's hope Och's mother is making tortillas."

He recognized Och's house straightaway, and the porch where he'd slept in a hammock for the first time in his life. He hadn't exactly been the perfect guest on that occasion, and he was looking forward to making amends—so he was disappointed to find it all dark and quiet.

"Looks like there's no one home," he said.

"Hello?" called Lola. "*Baax kaw aalik?* How are you?"

"*Ko'oten,*" came a woman's voice. She sounded sad and tired.

They went inside.

The first thing Max noticed was no cooking fire. The three hearthstones sat cold and unused. So much for homemade tortillas.

A single candle burned on the table, where Och's mother sat in the gloom.

Lola bowed to her politely and went to Och, who was standing in the corner of the room, swinging his little brother in a hammock.

"Chan Och?" said Lola, delighted. "Little Och?"

Max remembered with a start that Och's younger brother was also nicknamed Och (meaning "possum"), as were most of the children in the village; a cunning ruse to fool the spirits of the rainforest, who liked to steal away human babies.

Och put a finger to his lips to show that his brother was sleeping.

Now that they were closer, Max and Lola saw that the boy in the hammock was wrapped in bandages.

"What happened to him?" whispered Lola.

"*K'aak'*—fire," replied Och.

Lola clapped a hand to her mouth. "Och, why didn't you tell me?"

Och shrugged. "*Baaxten?* Why? We are not blood. It's not your problem."

Lola threw her arms around him. "How can you say that? We don't need the same blood to be family! I would do anything to help you."

"Can you make my brother well again?" asked Och.

"No, but—"

Och turned his back on her and continued rocking the hammock, singing what Max assumed was a Maya lullaby.

Visibly upset, Lola went to sit at the table, and Max followed. Och's mother emptied a small bag of tortilla chips into a bowl and offered them to her guests. Lola declined, kicked Max under the table to do the same, and passed the bowl to Och. He took one and carried the bowl back to his mother, encouraging her to eat.

Max guessed that there would be no more food in this house tonight. He sat at the table, smiling awkwardly and trying not to eat the last of the chips, while Lola chatted in Mayan with the boys' mother.

After a while, she got up. "Say good-bye, Hoop; it's time we were going."

"So now we know why Och was so preoccupied," said Max, back in the street. "What happened to his brother?"

"His mother was doing a tortilla-making demonstration for the tourists. They all crowded round and Little Och got pushed, and he fell into the cooking fire."

"Will he be all right?"

"They don't know. Chan Kan has given his mother herbs to help the healing, but he needs an operation or he'll be scarred for life." Lola's eyes filled with tears.

Max leapt over a wide column of ants. "Why don't they take him to the hospital?"

"The nearest burn unit is in San Xavier City, but it might as well be on Mars. Even if Och's parents could somehow afford the treatment, it would be impossible for them to get him there."

Max clicked his tongue. "I bet Uncle Ted could pull some strings."

"Hoop, you're a genius!"

A cheer went up behind them and they turned, smiles at the ready, expecting to see old friends. But it was only the shrieking of a game-show audience from somebody's TV.

"Come on," said Lola, running down the street, "let's find your uncle."

They found him sitting on the dock, waiting for them.

"Just in time," he said. "The pizza will arrive any minute!"

Max's stomach growled at the thought. "That's not funny! Don't torture me!"

"I would never joke about such a serious matter, Max. Apparently a pizza shop has just opened upriver, so I took the liberty of ordering—pepperoni with extra cheese, isn't it?"

To Max's astonishment, a delivery boy pulled up in a small motorboat and handed up several large, flat boxes.

"I must say," said Uncle Ted, as he paid, "Utsal is not what I expected. From everything you told me, Lola, I pictured one of those traditional Maya villages that keeps to the old ways. I thought we'd be eating homemade tortillas tonight, not pizza."

"Me too," agreed Lola. "But that's what I need to talk to you about. Those old cooking fires are dangerous. Och's little brother fell in and got burned and—"

"Poor kid! Is he okay?"

"He needs to go to the hospital in San Xavier City but—"

"I take it his family is not rich? How will they get him there?"

"That's the problem. You have so many connections, I was hoping you might know someone who could help."

Uncle Ted took out his cell phone and started jabbing in numbers. "If I can't persuade the air ambulance service to take him, I'll charter a plane and fly him there myself."

Lola did a happy dance, right there on the dock.

"Aren't you going to have pizza?" Max asked her. "It's good."

"Let me take one to Och's family and tell them the good news!"

"First," said Uncle Ted, "let's agree on a plan. I'm happy to stay behind and sort out matters for the little boy, but I'd like to get you two out of here. After seeing those critters on the plane, I'd feel happier knowing that you're safely tucked up in the Villa Isabella. But we need to move quickly. There's a hurricane blowing in and, from the way the ants are marching, it looks like it will be a big one. We need to get you on your way before everything grinds to a halt around here."

"Suits me," said Max. "But how?"

"I know!" answered Lola. "There's a new tourist bus between Puerto Muerto and Limón. Och's mother mentioned it."

"Splendid!" said Uncle Ted. "So you'll take the first worker boat in the morning, catch your bus in Limón, and be back at Puerto Muerto before nightfall." He waved his cell phone. "What's your number, Max, so I can keep tabs on you?"

"I left my phone with Dad. It doesn't work since it got wet in the cave."

"Never mind. They're more trouble than they're worth in San Xavier. You've got my number if you need it." He waved his phone above his head, trying to get satellite reception. "I'll try and get a call through to Raul to tell him to expect you."

"Will you ask him to make a big dinner for us?" Max's mouth was already watering at the thought of the feast that would await them the next evening.

"Of course I will! I just wish I could call your parents and tell them of the change of plan, but there's no signal at the Black Pyramid. I'll ask Raul to keep trying."

"We'll be fine," said Max, who was keen to leave Utsal as soon as possible, especially on a comfortable tourist bus.

"It'll be fun!" added Lola.

Uncle Ted looked at them thoughtfully. "I hope I won't regret this."

"It's one boat ride and one bus ride," Lola assured him. "What could possibly go wrong?"

"Do you really want me to answer that? You two have a bit of a track record."

"Stop worrying, Uncle Ted," said Max. "We're not children. We'll be fine."

Uncle Ted sighed. "I hadn't realized how stressful it is to be a parent. Look, whatever happens, just promise that you'll stay together and look after each other?"

They nodded earnestly.

"That's settled then! Lola, grab a pizza, and let's you and me go talk to Och's family. Max, you find Eusebio and ask him how much he wants to take you two upriver in the morning. If he says a hundred dollars each, tell him to forget it. And you're only going one way, so don't let him charge you for a round trip."

In the event, Eusebio—evidently ashamed of his earlier rapaciousness—agreed to take them to Limón for nothing. He even offered them all a hammock for the night.

"This is very kind of you," said Lola, stretching out.

"I just want to be sure you wake up early," said Eusebio gruffly. "My passengers will be angry if we don't leave on time—they get their pay docked if they're even one minute late for work."

"Sounds like the hotel has strict management," replied Lola. "*Death Lords*," she mouthed to Max.

Max rolled his eyes at her and turned over in his hammock. There was no way that Filth, Pus, and their cronies

140

had enslaved the people of Utsal just to run a tourist hotel. That was ridiculous.

Wasn't it?

But hotel or no hotel, the fact remained that unless he and Lola could think of a way to stop it, the whole human race would soon be enslaved by the ancient Maya Lords of Death.

He fell asleep imagining a monochrome world where blank-faced humans, their spirits broken, trudged to their joyless work like robots.

And that was exactly the scene that greeted him on the dock next morning.

Chapter Eleven
HURRICANE HOTEL

It was still dark when the passengers filed aboard, most of them looking half asleep. No one said a word as the boat filled up and Eusebio started the engine.

As they roared upriver in a cloud of evil-smelling smoke, the sky turned slowly from grayish black to grayish pink.

Max chewed on leftover pizza and watched the forest go by. "I keep looking for Lord 6-Dog in the trees. I thought he'd be here by now."

Lola smiled. "There's an old mango orchard between here and the Black Pyramid. He probably got distracted."

"Just as well," said Max. "There's nothing for him to eat here." He pointed to a grove of black, leafless trees. "It's as bare as fall in Boston."

"I'd like to see your famous fall. Rainforest trees don't do that synchronized leaf-dropping thing." She squinted at the trees. "That looks like a blight to me."

"And where are all the animals? Last time we came up

this river, there were monkeys, iguanas, turtles, crocodiles . . . remember?"

"Hey, Hoop, for a city kid, you're beginning to sound like a nature lover."

"I am? Yeah, I guess I am. It's just kind of sad, seeing the jungle all empty like this." He clapped his hands to catch a mosquito and missed. "Still lots of bugs though."

"Even more than usual," agreed Lola, waving away a cloud of blackflies. "It must be all the trash."

He followed her eyes and saw, bobbing like ducks on the oil slick in the boat's wake, a flock of fast-food containers, plastic bags, and soda bottles. The wind was getting up, and for a while Max and Lola watched a candy wrapper dancing on the breeze, before it, too, was sucked into the oil slick.

The closer they got to Limón, the more trash floated in the water.

By the time they reached the landing stage, the magnificent Monkey River, main highway of San Xavier, had been reduced to a liquid garbage can.

"I wonder," said Lola, "if the river will ever get so clogged that one day it will just stop flowing."

Limón itself was equally trashy.

Neon lights flashed through the early-morning haze.

Everywhere billboards promised gastronomic excess: BELLYBUSTERS BURRITO BUFFET! TRIPLE-STUFFED TACOS! NACHOS-A-GOGO! Normally that kind of thinking would have got Max's juices flowing, but when he saw the HOME OF THE TEN-FOOT TAMALE, he knew that even he was beaten.

They waited for the workers in front of them to disembark.

"Look at that old guy with the big bag. He looks like Chan Kan, but even nuttier." Max was pointing at a hunched figure

143

in a long white tunic, with an elaborate shawl arrangement on his head and a large woven tote bag across his chest. The bag weighed him down and, combined with a cane that seemed to indicate impaired vision, made it difficult for him to step off the boat. The passengers behind him grumbled impatiently, but no one offered a hand. Eventually someone pushed him from behind and he launched himself onto the quayside, grabbing blindly at a wooden post to stop himself from falling. A squawk of protest erupted from his bag.

"What . . . who . . . ?" murmured Lola distractedly, still mesmerized by the neon signs.

"He's gone now." Max watched as the old man disappeared, tip-tapping with his cane, into the crowd of workers, hawkers, and beggars who thronged the quayside. "So did you get to say good-bye to Chan Kan this morning?"

"I went to his hut, but it was empty. He was probably out looking for dewdrops or spiderwebs or something. Shamans are always collecting weird ingredients."

"Well, he can't be on his deathbed if he's still getting up at dawn and doing that kind of stuff."

Lola nodded happily. "I hope you're right."

By the time Max and Lola finally stepped ashore, Eusebio, too, had vanished.

"So which way to the bus station?" asked Max.

"I'm not sure," replied Lola, looking anxiously around. "Everything's so new. I don't recognize this town anymore."

A man wearing an old-fashioned box camera around his neck approached them. With one hand he made sure that his straw hat didn't blow off in the wind; in the other he cradled a long, shaggy green animal that looked like a creature from a Doctor Seuss book.

"Picture?" asked the man, trying to pass the hairy beast over to Max.

Max jumped back in alarm. "What *is* that thing?"

Lola waved her finger and shook her head at the man before muttering to Max: "It's a sloth."

The sloth looked at him with sleepy eyes.

Max eyed it back suspiciously. "Why's it green?"

"That's algae. It grows in the sloth's fur."

"Gross."

Lola rolled her eyes. "It's not gross, it's symbiosis. They're helping each other out. The algae gets a place to live, and the sloth gets some excellent camouflage. Plus, if the sloth gets hungry, it can lick the algae for a snack."

Max looked at the sloth with new respect. "Wow! That's genius! It's like I carried popcorn in my hair."

"Except that would make you *more* visible to predators."

"I'm top of the food chain. I don't have any predators."

Lola raised an eyebrow. "You can't think of anyone who wants to kill you?"

"Oh," he said. "You mean Ah Pukuh."

"And . . . ?"

"The Death Lords?"

"And . . . ?"

"Stink Pig?"

"Correct. And I'm sorry to break this to you, but covering yourself in popcorn is not going to save you from any of them. Come on, let's find the bus station."

They walked along the riverfront, still closely followed by the sloth man. A man with a snake wrapped round his neck stepped in line and was soon joined by a man with a parrot on his head. Every time Max and Lola paused, the three men would crowd around, jostling each other and urging them to pose for photographs.

"No photo!" Max exclaimed. "Where is the bus station?"

The men pointed down a side road, and Max and Lola set off again, followed by the little menagerie.

They came to a large, trash-strewn square, lined on three sides with banks, fast-food restaurants, and souvenir stores—every one padlocked and shuttered. In the middle of the square were parked three tourist buses, all silent and empty. On the fourth side sat a small yellow adobe structure shaped like a Maya pyramid. The sign over the door read:

GRAND HOTEL XIBALBA
★★★★★

"That's it?" said Max. "That's your big, scary hotel run by the Death Lords? It's tiny! It looks like it's run by two little old ladies and a pet parrot."

"Looks," announced Lola mysteriously, "can be deceiving. But I wonder why everything's closed around here? It's like a ghost town."

"The hotel's open," Max pointed out. "We could check it out."

"No! We're not going anywhere near that place. Let's go and find our bus."

An electronic billboard behind the hotel spewed out a loop of red neon ticker-tape letters:

```
LUXURY HOTEL, CASINO AND CONVENTION CENTER
...JUNGLE-THEMED POOL AND BEACH...SALON
...WORLD'S BIGGEST PIZZA BUFFET...
HOMEMADE ICE CREAM...LIVE ANIMAL SHOW
...BIG-NAME ENTERTAINMENT TONITE...!
```

"Aren't you the slightest bit curious about it?" asked Max. "It doesn't look big enough to have all that stuff inside."

Lola looked at him in mock surprise. "You're not suggesting that the Death Lords would tell lies, are you?"

"But you still haven't explained why you think they'd want to own a hotel. I'm sure they have enough to do, plotting the end of the world, without trying to run the world's biggest pizza buffet." Max licked his lips. "That does sound good, though. I wonder if it's thin crust."

The ticker-tape letters began to flash:

```
THIN-CRUST PIZZA OUR SPECIALITY...
INFINITE CHOICE OF TOPPINGS!
```

"*Infinite?* Oh, come on!" exclaimed Max. "We *have* to try it!"

"Really, Hoop? You had pizza for dinner last night, and cold pizza for breakfast this morning, and now you want more pizza? Boy, the Death Lords really know how to reel you in."

"Have you ever been to Las Vegas, Monkey Girl?"

"No."

"Well, there are tons of places like this in Vegas, and I promise you that not one of them is owned by the Death Lords."

147

"How do you know?"

The wind blew a small piece of paper over Max's eyes, blinding him for a second. He peeled it off and looked at it. "It's a flyer for the buffet! 'Scratch here to release the irresistible fresh-baked aroma of our award-winning gourmet pizzas!'" He scratched and sniffed, almost burying his face in the paper. "Oh, that is good. Here, try it."

Lola grabbed the flyer off him, scrunched it up, and threw it in the nearest trash can. "Let's find the bus to Puerto Muerto and get out of here."

She set off toward the parked buses. "You'll be hungry later," Max called after her, before giving in and following.

Trash blew like tumbleweeds across the deserted square.

The three would-be animal photographers gave up pursuit and hunkered down with their creatures against a wall in front of the hotel. They sat there, watching.

Lola headed for the large double-sided blackboard that listed the day's bus trips but, before she reached it, it blew over with a crash. As she struggled against the wind to pick it up, a little boy ran out to help her.

When the board was upright, she stood back to read the options:

SAN XAVIER CITY:
MUSEUMS AND MALLS!

IXCHEL: TEMPLE OF
THE MOON GODDESS!

PUERTO MUERTO:
PIRATE PLUNDER!

"What time is the bus to Puerto Muerto?" Max asked the boy.

He shook his head.

Lola asked him in Mayan.

He shook his head again.

Before they could press him further, he took a rag from his pocket and wiped the blackboard clean. Then he produced a bit of paper and a piece of chalk, and began to copy down what was written on the paper. Max and Lola watched in horror as the words took shape: NO BUS TODAY.

Lola exchanged a few words in Mayan with the boy before he ran off again. "He said they've canceled all the buses. The hurricane's hitting land sooner than expected. That's why the stores are shuttered. He said the hurricane warning will be sounding any minute."

"It is getting very windy." Max caught his Red Sox cap as it was about to fly off his head. "What should we do?"

"We'll get a boat back to Utsal and try again tomorrow. Unless you have a better idea?"

Max kicked the wheel of the nearest bus. "Rats!"

"There's no point getting mad about it."

"No, two big rats! They were under the bus. They ran out when I kicked the wheel."

Lola wrinkled her nose in distaste. "Let's go back to the dock."

"Can we get something to eat first? I'm starving."

"No."

"Why are you being so bossy?"

"We need to get out of here. For one thing, there's a hurricane coming. And for another thing . . . don't laugh at me, but the Death Lords are near. I can sense it."

149

"Oh come on. Just one quick slice of pizza."

"It's too risky."

"But we'd be safer inside the hotel when the hurricane hits than out here in the storm."

"So you'd take that chance? You'd walk into enemy territory?"

"Think of it as reconnaissance. As Lord 6-Dog would say: *Know thine enemy*."

"I don't like this, Hoop. It feels like a trap."

Around the square, sirens rang out to alert the populace to the incoming hurricane.

"You're overthinking it. We need to take shelter."

"Let's find somewhere else then."

"There is nowhere else. Look, we'll just go into the hotel, grab something to eat, and find out what's happening. I mean, I assume you don't think the Death Lords are working in the lobby?"

"No, but—"

"So they must have a tourist-information desk. We'll ask how long the hurricane will last and when the buses will start running again. We could even phone Uncle Ted."

Lola looked torn. "Okay, you win. I guess we'll be all right if we act like ordinary tourists and don't call attention to ourselves."

"Deal! Let's go! That pizza smelled so good. . . ."

As they approached the hotel, the three photographers jumped up and posed their creatures appealingly. The sloth's green fur rippled in the wind.

"Picture! Picture! Picture!" they cried.

"Let's do it!" said Max. "We're supposed to be acting like tourists!"

It was impossible to choose one photographer over the rest, so Max gave a little money to each of them. Then, after some minor bickering about who took what, Lola held the sloth, the parrot perched on Max's finger, and the snake looped over both their shoulders, with Max being careful to make sure that Lola got the end with the head.

The sloth man handed Max a piece of paper. "Collect your photograph at the concierge desk," he said.

"You work for the hotel?" said Max, surprised.

"Everyone works for the hotel," said the sloth man. As he spoke, thunder rumbled in the distance and a light rain began to fall. "You should go inside. There's a hurricane coming."

As the automatic glass doors parted for them, Max and Lola were hit by a blast of icy air that made them gasp.

As they went in, a group of tourists came out—a mother chivvying her reluctant family, all kitted out in yellow rain ponchos. "Hoods up!" she piped with false jollity. "It's only a shower. A drop of rain never hurt anyone!" She proceeded to force her offspring to pose for a photo with the animals. "Smile, everyone; say cheese!"

The children remained sullenly tight-lipped and refused to touch any of the animals, so that the resulting pose showed the inanely grinning woman just visible under a sloth, a snake, and a parrot, while her family scowled all around her.

Laughing, Max pointed out the scene to Lola. "What is it with parents on vacation? Did yours ever force you to . . . ?" His voice tailed off as he remembered that Lola had never been on vacation with her parents, had never even met her parents.

Idiot! he said to himself.

"Fatso!" said a woman's voice.

He turned to see the owner of the voice, a small woman

with frizzy bleached blond hair. Incongruously in this jungle setting, she wore a tight business suit, high heels, and shiny red lipstick. "Fatso?" she repeated, pen poised over her clipboard.

"Fatso yourself," said Max, offended.

The woman forced a smile, showing a smudge of lipstick on her teeth. "No, it's F-A-T-S-O," she said, spelling out the letters. "It's short for Forest Asset and Tree Stripping Operations. Clever, isn't it? We're the new strip-mining and logging consortium that's going to put this place on the map. We're having our annual conference here today. But if you haven't heard of us, I assume you're not attending?"

Lola put her hands on her hips. "So it's F.A.T.S.O. who've been cutting down all the trees around here?"

The woman nodded. "We've done a great job, haven't we? Leave nothing behind, that's our motto. Here, have a button."

Lola grabbed the button and threw it back at her.

"Sorry! She has a button phobia!" Max called over his shoulder to the woman as he hurried after Lola and pulled her to one side. "What was that about? We're supposed to be not calling attention to ourselves, remember?"

"So you expect me to smile sweetly while that woman and her stupid buttons destroy the rainforest?"

"She's just doing her job."

"You could say that about the loggers, too. It's no excuse."

"Well, you better calm down, or you'll get us thrown out of here."

"Good. I hate this place."

It was cold and dark in the lobby, lit only by flickering candles. Black-clad figures moved like wraiths behind the reception desk. Sheets of water trickled artistically down the sloping black walls, to be reflected in the polished black tile floor. There was a sitting area with wooden stools and low stone tables; on each table stood a vase containing one bare twig.

"It reminds me of a Japanese restaurant," said Max. "All they need is a sushi bar and a—" He was going to say "fish pond," but his musings on interior design were interrupted by a blast on a conch shell.

A hand gripped his shoulder.

"Congratulations!" squeaked a voice in his ear. "You are our octillionth visitors!"

Max turned around to face a thin, rat-faced man in a shiny black suit. In place of a shirt and tie, he wore a black hotel T-shirt, emblazoned with the words I LEFT MY HEART AT THE GRAND HOTEL XIBALBA.

"What's an octillion?" asked Max.

"It's a one followed by twenty-seven zeros," replied Lola instantly.

Max looked puzzled. "That can't be right."

"It's true," insisted Lola. "Some people think the ancient Maya computed time across seventy-two octillion years."

"No, I mean we can't be the octillionth visitors. This hotel looks brand-new."

The man narrowed his eyes. "Forgive my English. What did I mean to say?"

"Thousandth?" suggested Max.

"That's the one. Congratulations! You are our thousandth visitors! Your prize is a one-night stay at the luxurious Grand Hotel Xibalba!"

The conch-shell trumpet sounded again, and a uniformed bellboy marched across the lobby, carrying a thick vellum envelope on a jaguar-skin pillow. He stopped in front of Max and looked at him expectantly.

Max took the envelope and opened it. "Vouchers!" he exclaimed, flicking through the contents. "Luxury Suite," he read, "Ice Cream Parlor, VIP Backstage Tour, Pizza Buffet, Casino, Beauty Salon, Entertainment, everything! And it's all free! That's fantastic!"

"Give them back," said Lola.

"No," said Max. "I've never won anything before."

"It's a trick," said Lola.

"Don't be so paranoid," replied Max, still rifling through the vouchers. He pulled one out and waved it at her. "You should go for a free massage and chill out."

She glared at him.

"I'll use it then." Max stuffed the voucher back into the envelope.

"Allow me to introduce myself," said the rat-faced man. "I am Concierge and Head of Guest Services here at the Grand Hotel Xibalba. Would you care for a VIP tour?"

"VIP?" Max could feel himself smirking.

"It stands for Very Idiotic Person," said Lola.

"What's the matter with you?" he muttered.

"What's the matter with you?" she replied.

The concierge pretended not to be listening.

"Just give him back the vouchers and let's get out of here," hissed Lola.

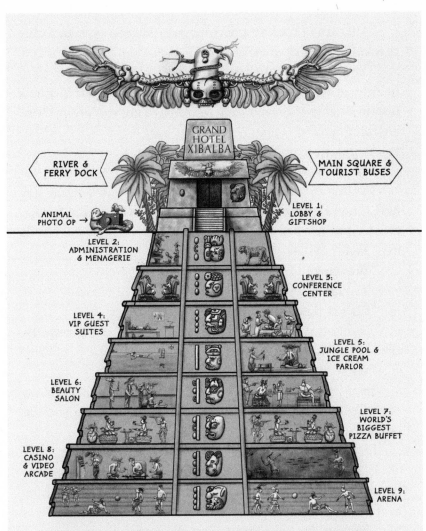

RIVER &
FERRY DOCK

MAIN SQUARE &
TOURIST BUSES

ANIMAL
PHOTO OP →

LEVEL 1:
LOBBY &
GIFTSHOP

LEVEL 2:
ADMINISTRATION
& MENAGERIE

LEVEL 3:
CONFERENCE
CENTER

LEVEL 4:
VIP GUEST
SUITES

LEVEL 5:
JUNGLE POOL &
ICE CREAM
PARLOR

LEVEL 6:
BEAUTY
SALON

LEVEL 7:
WORLD'S
BIGGEST
PIZZA BUFFET

LEVEL 8:
CASINO
& VIDEO
ARCADE

LEVEL 9:
ARENA

SOUVENIR HOTEL MAP

LOSE YOUR HEART (BUT NOT YOUR WAY!)
AT THE GRAND HOTEL XIBALBA

★★★★★

Max turned back to the concierge. "Could we take a rain check? Come back another time?"

The concierge touched his hand to his chest as if what he was about to say gave him great pain. "Your prize is nonnegotiable and valid only for today. I am sorry, but those are the rules."

He reached out to take back the vouchers.

Max held on to them.

"Think about it," he whispered to Lola. "We could stay here tonight and get the bus to Puerto Muerto in the morning. No need to go back to Utsal. It's perfect."

"No."

"Why not."

"You know why not."

"Let's at least take a quick look around."

"Perhaps you'd like to see your suite?" suggested the concierge. "You have the best rooms in the hotel."

"We're not staying," said Lola.

"No? I am sorry to hear that." The concierge made a show of wringing his hands in dismay. "May I ask where you are going?"

Lola glared at him. "It's none of your business."

The concierge glanced over to the door, where the poncho family was trooping back in, soaked to the skin and squelching as they walked. This time the mother looked as miserable as her children. "I ask only because the hurricane has arrived. There will be no transport out of Limón today."

"What about the worker boat?" Lola challenged him. "We'll go back to Utsal."

The concierge shook his head. "Nothing moves until the storm blows over. There is no going back."

"You mean we're trapped here?" From the look Lola gave him, Max knew she blamed him for this development.

"Not trapped." The concierge smiled. "Cocooned in luxury."

Lola looked like she might blow a fuse. "If you think for one minute that I don't know—"

"—how lucky we are," cut in Max quickly. "We're so lucky. Lucky us. We're lucky, lucky tourists. Shall we have a look at our rooms?"

Lola narrowed her eyes at him, but said nothing more. In fact, she was possibly not speaking to him.

"Your suite is on the fourth floor," said the concierge. He set off across the lobby. "This way to the elevator."

"Cheer up," Max muttered to Lola as they followed him. "It could be worse. We could be out there in the storm."

She looked at him with a face like thunder.

"Going down!" announced the uniformed elevator operator, who didn't look more than ten years old.

"Going *up*, you mean," Max corrected him. "Our rooms are on four."

"In the Grand Hotel Xibalba, sir, everything is down. It is the world's first subterranean hotel." The elevator boy smiled proudly. "Safest place to be in a hurricane."

Chapter Twelve
IN THE DARK

"I don't care how Resplendent they are! Are those Quetzal birds paying rent?" yelled the red-faced businessman into his cell phone. "I thought not. Then they can find someone else to mooch off—I need that cloud forest cleared *yesterday!*"

He'd barged into the elevator just as the doors were closing—using his briefcase to prize them open again—then he'd pushed his way into the center, forcing the rest of the passengers to squash against the sides. "Third!" he'd barked to the elevator boy, before continuing to shout self-importantly into his phone.

The elevator bumped to a stop.

"Third floor," announced the little operator. "Convention center."

The doors opened on a large sign, pointing the way to the conference. It bore the F.A.T.S.O. company logo of a buzzing chainsaw.

"He's one of the enemy," muttered Lola. "I should have tripped him when I had the chance."

"Or," whispered Max, "you could stick to the plan of acting like a tourist."

"Excuse me, " Lola said to the elevator boy, "but I see there are nine floors in this hotel, like the nine levels of Xibalba, the Maya underworld."

The eyes of the elevator boy darted nervously to the concierge.

"Bravo," said the concierge to Lola. "I see you've done your homework."

"So," Lola pressed on, "why would you design a hotel around a place we Maya call the Well of Fear?"

The concierge smiled, showing his teeth. "It's called a concept. All the best places have them these days."

"Like Disneyland," suggested Max.

"Yeah, Xibalba is just like Disneyland," hissed Lola through her teeth, "if Mickey was a bloated corpse covered in plague boils and Minnie was a decaying mouse skeleton!"

The elevator boy tried to stifle his giggles.

Max sensed that Lola was going to be difficult company for the next few hours.

The elevator doors opened onto a stone corridor lit by electric-powered torches. It reminded Max of the Yellow Pyramid back in Spain—except there, of course, the flaming torches had been real.

"Fourth floor—VIP suites!" announced the elevator boy.

"This way," said the concierge, leading them to a set of double doors at the end of the corridor. "The Ak'bal Suite."

He threw open the doors to reveal a palatial—if cold and gloomy—sitting room. Jaguar-patterned curtains were draped along one wall to give the illusion of windows, and jaguar-patterned rugs were scattered on the baked-tile floor. The walls were painted in Maya-style murals. The one closest to Max depicted a gruesome sacrifice scene.

"How do you like it?" asked the concierge.

"It's kind of"—Max searched for a polite word—"dark."

"Dark?" echoed the concierge. He flicked on a plastic wall torch over the desk. "Is that better?"

Max winced as the light shone its beam directly onto the agonized face of the sacrifice victim.

"He meant dark in the sense of forbidding," explained Lola. "It's oppressive in here, like a Maya temple."

The concierge looked pleased. "I knew you'd like it. You each have your own room"—like a flight attendant pointing out emergency exits, he gestured to two doors facing each other on opposite sides of the sitting room—"so please make yourselves at home. I'll leave you to settle in now. If you need me, I will be in the lobby."

As soon as he'd gone, they each opened the bedroom door closest to them.

Max whistled in approval. "I'll take this one!"

"Fine by me," called Lola, from the depths of her room.

In Max's room, there was a small bed covered in jaguar-print bedding. The rest of the room was taken up with a state-of-the-art home theater system, including a huge flat-screen TV and a game console. The electronics contrasted strangely with the rough-hewn walls and plastic torches, but Max wasn't judging the decor. He saw only the library of video games. Without a second thought, he kicked off his shoes, stretched out on the bed, and reached for the array of remote controls.

A moment later, Lola stuck her head round the door. "Don't get too comfortable, Hoop. We need to keep our wits about us." She looked about in amazement. "Wow, look at all that gear! This room is perfect for you!"

"I know, right? It's better than my room at home."

"Mine's completely different," continued Lola. "It's got books, music, paints, a loom—like it was designed for me."

"So now aren't you glad we came?"

"No. I don't like it at all. It's almost as if they were expecting us. . . . I smell a rat."

Max sniffed the air. "Could it be Mickey's bloated corpse, by any chance? Or Minnie's decaying mouse skeleton?"

Lola laughed in spite of herself. "Okay, so I lost it a bit in the elevator. But I'm telling you, I still think this is a trap."

"A mousetrap?"

"It's not funny. We need to get out of here while we still can."

"Please, Monkey Girl, relax. We're in the VIP suite. One room is for playing video games and one's for chilling and being creative. You're making a big deal about nothing."

"Am I?"

"*Yes.* You've been acting weird ever since we walked into this place. One minute you tell me to stay quiet and act like a tourist; the next minute you're freaking out over some woman with a button, or cross-examining the elevator guy."

"I'm sorry; you're right. But everything about this place makes me jumpy."

"I can't believe that we've won an all-expenses-paid stay in a luxury hotel, and you can't just relax and enjoy it. It's not like we have anywhere else to go until the hurricane's over."

"How do we know that the Death Lords didn't send the hurricane?"

"Okay, now you're being paranoid. Just let me check out this game system, then we'll go and explore the rest of the hotel, and I'll try and convince you that everything's normal."

"Good luck with that," commented Lola, as she peered at another lurid sacrifice scene on the wall over Max's bed.

"Why don't you call Uncle Ted," suggested Max, "and tell him what's happened? I bet he'll say to stay in the hotel until the buses are running again."

Lola picked up the phone. "It's dead," she said.

"Okay. Just give me a few minutes and we'll go down to the lobby and phone him from there."

"I don't trust him," said Lola as she left the room.

"Who? Uncle Ted?" Max was still looking for the game controller.

Lola's head reappeared round the door. "The concierge."

"Why not?"

"He looks like a rat."

If Max hadn't been so distracted by the game console, Lola's words might have put him on his guard. They might have reminded him of a night in Spain, when a leather-clad rock band had reverted to a pack of scurrying sewer rats, right in front of his eyes. And he might have remembered that Death Lords and rats tended to hang out in the same places.

But Max wasn't interested. He'd found the controller and he was focused on playing his games. "What's with your rodent obsession today? The concierge can't help how he looks."

Lola massaged her temples. "You're right. This place is getting to me. I've got such a headache. Maybe I'll lie down for a moment."

"Better close the door. It could get noisy in here."

"Have fun."

The door clicked loudly as she pulled it shut.

Max sank back into the pillows. This was the life. He

understood that Lola didn't like anything about this hotel, but she needed to get real. Just because a place had soft beds and state-of-the-art electronics didn't make it the work of that devil Ah Pukuh.

He pointed the controller at the screen, and the room was plunged into darkness.

What?

He heard a noise, a scuttling noise.

Something ran over his face. An insect? He knocked it off.

He was jabbing at the controller furiously now, trying to undo whatever he'd just done to make the lights go out.

But the lights stayed out.

He jumped off the bed to go find a light switch on the wall.

Something crunched under his feet.

He wished he'd worn socks.

"Lola!" he called, but there was no answer.

Something was running up his leg, under his jeans.

Slapping at his leg with one hand, he found the door with the other, and grabbed at the wooden doorknob. He pulled it, turned it, pushed it. It refused to move.

"Lola! Where are you? Help me!" he shouted.

"What have you done?" she yelled from the other side of the door. "The power's gone out! I think you've blown a fuse with your games."

"It wasn't my fault; I hadn't even started playing. Can you call someone to fix it?"

"The phone's out, remember? I'll go down to the lobby."

"No! Wait! My door's jammed. Help me get out of here first."

He heard the handle jiggling on the other side.

"It's stuck," called Lola.

"That's what I just said!"

"Let me grab my flashlight."

Max waited.

Sweat ran down his face. Every so often, a bug ran over his bare feet.

Then Lola's voice again. "Hoop? I'm back! Are you there?"

"Of course I'm here. And there are *things* in here!"

"What things?"

"I don't know—bugs! Big bugs! They crunch when I step on them!"

"Stand back! Here goes. . . ."

She thumped and kicked the door, but it was no use.

Next a series of blows and sounds of wood splintering suggested she was using a piece of furniture as a battering ram.

Still the door held firm.

As far as Max could tell, all she'd succeeded in doing was scaring the bugs. He could hear them skittering around the floor in panic. Every time he moved, he trod on one; but if he didn't keep moving, they crawled over his feet—which was worse.

He started doing jumping jacks to keep them from running up his legs.

"Hurry!" he called. "Get me out of—"

Something big with a hard shell fell into his mouth.

Max gagged and spit it out in disgust and kept spitting and retching until his eyes watered and he felt dizzy. His mouth tasted foul, like dried blood and clogged drains.

"Lola!" he whimpered, steadying himself against the door.

"I've found a corkscrew. I'm working on the lock," she called back.

A lot of scratching and banging and gouging was followed by several very hopeful-sounding clicks.

At last, the heavy wooden doorknob fell off the door and straight down onto Max's foot. He'd have a bruise for weeks to come, but the pain didn't even register . . . because just as the mahogany globe was making its brutal descent, the connecting door swung open and he realized what had been in his mouth.

In the beam from Lola's flashlight, the floor was a writhing carpet of cockroaches.

"Gross!" She shone the light around the room, and the roaches scurried for darkness, scuttling under the bed, disappearing into cracks, vanishing into the walls.

"I think I'm going to puke," said Max.

"Don't," said Lola. "Let's just grab our things and get out of here."

Out in the corridor, they checked their belongings thoroughly for stowaway roaches.

"You have to admire them," said Lola, "they're the ultimate survivors. Did you know that a cockroach can live for a week with no head?"

Max shuddered. "One fell in my mouth."

"What did it taste like? I've heard they taste like apples when they're grilled."

"Who grills cockroaches? I can't believe we're having this conversation. But no, for your information, the massive black cockroach that fell into my mouth did not taste like an apple. It tasted like essence of rusty sewer pipe."

"So maybe now you'll reconsider my theory that the Death Lords are behind all this?"

"No. It's a stupid theory. Why would the Death Lords open a hotel?"

"I've been thinking about that. Maybe they wanted to begin their reign of destruction by destroying the rainforest. Or maybe they were feeling out of touch in Xibalba and wanted a base of operations in Middleworld. Or maybe they just wanted to lure us here with the White Jaguar."

"You're crazy," said Max.

But, at that very moment in the bowels of the Maya universe, a cluster of malevolent faces were listening to Lola's words and nodding in agreement. In fact, some heads nodded so furiously that they snapped off their rotting spinal cords and rolled clean away.

"She's a smart cookie, that one," said the Demon of Pus.

"But the boy hasn't got a clue," added the Demon of Jaundice.

Back in the gloomy hotel corridor, Max (who—it has to be said—really did *not* have a clue) was still in denial. "If this is all about getting the White Jaguar, building a nine-story subterranean hotel doesn't seem like the easiest way to go about it."

"Have you ever read Maya mythology, Hoop? The Death Lords don't think easy; they think big."

"Are there any hotels in Maya mythology?"

"No, but did you notice the name of our room? It was called the Ak'bal Suite. *Ak'bal* is Mayan for 'darkness.' When the Hero Twins went down to Xibalba, the Death Lords set a series of tests for them—and their first test was in the Dark House."

"That's all you've got? You can't blame the Death Lords for a power cut. The power goes out all the time in this country. And it's hurricane season. And this is a new building. Doors jam. Fuses blow. It happens."

"But it only happened in our—"

Max put his hands over his ears. "I'm not listening. I don't want to hear any more about the Hero Twins or the Death Lords or the ancient Maya. It's the first time I've ever won anything and I just want to enjoy my prize."

"But you can't ignore—"

"Yes, I can. I can ignore anything I want to. Especially the fact that I nearly ate a cockroach. So can we please change the subject?"

"Okay. But keep your wits about you. I'm telling you, this place is not what it seems."

"You sound like Lord 6-Dog."

"I wish he was here. He'd agree with me, for sure."

"Yeah, and then you could both watch the Conspiracy Channel on TV."

"Is there one?"

"No, I'm being sarcastic."

They went back up to the lobby, where they found the concierge playing dice with the bellboy. He looked surprised to see them, but quickly jumped to his feet. "Is everything to your satisfaction?"

"No," said Max, "it isn't. My door got jammed, the power

went out, the phone doesn't work, and the room is crawling with cockroaches."

"How unfortunate." The concierge's eyes narrowed. "And yet here you are."

"I broke down the door," explained Lola.

The concierge pursed his thin little lips. "On behalf of the management, let me express our most sincere apologies."

Lola pounced on his words. "Who is the management? Who's in charge here? Who owns this hotel?"

The concierge ignored her questions. "I deeply regret that you have not enjoyed an optimal guest experience. I will send Maintenance to your room immediately. Meanwhile, may I offer you some refreshments? An ice cream, perhaps?"

"We're not children!" snapped Lola. "You can't make everything better with ice cream."

"Ah," said the concierge, "but you've never had ice cream like this. It's all homemade, here on the premises. And we're famous for our unusual range of flavors."

"I'd like an ice cream," said Max.

Lola rolled her eyes. "There's a surprise."

"It might take away the taste of cockroach."

"All right. I suppose you've earned it."

The concierge clasped his hands together unctuously. "If you'll follow me to the elevator, our ice cream parlor is on the fifth floor."

"It better be good," muttered Lola.

"Good?" The concierge smiled, showing his sharp little teeth. "I think you'll find it's to die for."

Chapter Thirteen
TERMITE TAMALE

"Fifth floor," announced the elevator boy.

Max and Lola stepped out of the elevator into what looked like a cave.

"What is this place?" asked Max. "It looks like a cave."

"It's our jungle-themed pool and beach," replied the concierge. "We modeled it on one of San Xavier's famous cenotes. Most tourists are too scared to venture into the real thing, so we provide an authentic cenote experience."

Max and Lola looked around in disbelief. It was the least welcoming swimming pool that either of them had ever seen. The walls were faced with slimy green stones, and the water was green with algae. The so-called beach was a thin strip of black volcanic grit around the rocky edge of the pool. There were no sun loungers or deck chairs, just a line of boulders, each one topped with a small brown plastic crocodile.

Max thought back to the day he'd first met Lola. They were being pursued by Antonio de Landa and they'd escaped down an underground river. They'd ended up in the cenote underneath the Pyramid of Chahk, the rain god. That had been a beautiful place, with clear blue water sparkling in a shaft of sunlight—nothing like this grim and airless cavern filled with stagnant sludge.

A very large, very sunburned, very bald man waddled up to the water's edge. His belly hung over the top of his floral swim shorts as he dipped a toe into the murky pool. "It's freezing!" he exclaimed.

"We call it refreshing," the concierge corrected him.

"This is supposed to be a luxury hotel," complained the man. "I expected a heated swimming pool."

"Expect the unexpected, that's our motto," said the concierge as he pushed him off the side.

The man hit the water and disappeared from view.

Max gaped at the concierge in disbelief. "What did you do that for?"

"I did him a favor. He needed help taking the plunge."

The man's bald head popped up like a beach ball. "I can't swim!" he screamed, flailing around wildly, then suddenly realized that the water was shallow enough to stand up in. "What are you waiting for?" he said to Max nastily. "Give me a hand."

Max couldn't quite reach, so he grabbed a toy crocodile to extend his grasp. He held it by the tail, intending to use it as a pole, but the creature swung its head around and tried to bite him.

"It's alive!" he yelled in surprise, dropping it into the pool.

For one serene moment, the bald man and the crocodile faced each other.

Then the man redoubled his panic, while the crocodile—no doubt planning its attack—floated like a log nearby.

Quickly, and with a great deal of splashing, during which they both got soaked, Max and Lola pulled the man out of the water.

Lola handed him a towel. "Are you all right?"

"Of course I'm not all right! What kind of place is this?" He jabbed a finger at Max. "You threw a crocodile at me!"

"I didn't throw it. I dropped it."

The man spit out a mouthful of pondweed. "I could have been eaten alive! I'm suing you for everything you've got!"

The concierge, who'd been busying himself with setting out towels, was entirely unconcerned for his guest's plight. He pointed to a sign on the wall: "All patrons swim at their own risk. You signed the waiver when you checked in. And if I could draw your attention to the small print, veterinary fees will be added to your bill should any of our creatures be traumatized by contact with you." He sniffed. "I'm no expert, but that crocodile does not look happy."

"Do you work in this madhouse?" the bald man asked Lola.

She looked horrified. "No! We're visitors like you."

"Well, take my advice and leave while you still can!"

"Have a nice day," called the concierge as the man stormed off. He turned to Max and Lola. "He'll treasure the memory when he gets home. Now, who's ready for ice cream? Follow me."

"This has to be the worst hotel in the world," whispered Lola as the concierge led them around the pool toward the back of the cave.

"It makes Doña Carmela's seem like the Ritz," agreed Max, thinking about the shabby little place where they'd stayed in Spain.

There was a buzzing in the darkness at the far end of the cave, and a red neon sign reading ICE CREAM flickered to life.

"Come in, come in," called the concierge. "We're a little early, so you'll have to serve yourselves."

Max could have punched the air with joy. Ever since he was little and he'd read a book about Curious George being left in sole charge of an ice-cream parlor, he'd dreamed that the same thing might one day happen to him.

And now that glorious day had arrived.

He entered the store with a proprietary air. As the concierge buzzed about, opening cupboards and pulling out drawers to find bowls and spoons and jars of cherries, Max strutted around his domain of dairy desserts. He was relieved to note that it looked clean and free of cockroaches, all scrubbed white tiles and gleaming stainless steel.

But it was missing one important detail.

"Where's the ice cream?" he asked.

"They keep it in the main freezer overnight." The concierge pointed to an enormous white door at the back. "It's the largest refrigeration unit in San Xavier. I suggest you have a look inside and help yourselves, while I go and soothe my crocodiles."

Max rubbed his hands together like a mad scientist. "Come on, Monkey Girl, I'll invent a new sundae for you. Something with peanuts and bananas. . . ."

Lola grabbed a checkered cloth from a table and wrapped it around her like a blanket. "Lead on," she said.

172

The freezer room was a maze of steel shelf units, each one stacked with tubs bearing handwritten labels.

"So what's your favorite flavor?" Max asked Lola as they walked down the first aisle.

"I don't care. Just hurry. I'm freezing."

He looked at the stack in front of him. "How about Grasshopper Pie?"

"I thought you were squeamish about eating bugs."

Max laughed. "It's just a name. It's green ice cream made with mint and chocolate."

"Here's 'Termite Tamale,'" read Lola. "That must be the San Xavier equivalent to your Grasshopper Pie."

"Tamale ice cream? That's nasty," said Max. "Almost as bad as my mom's idea for pizza-flavored gelato. Did I tell you about that? It's partly why we ended up back in San Xavier. It all started when we were in Venice. . . ."

There was an unreal quality to sound in the freezer, everything muffled by a thick layer of frost. As Max walked along telling his story, he didn't notice that Lola was no longer behind him.

It wasn't until he'd passed Molten Larva, Rocky Toad, and Dung-Beetle Delight, and stopped dead in front of Slugs 'n' Sprinkles to comment to Lola that there was something very off-putting about the names of these flavors, that he realized he was talking to himself.

"Monkey Girl?" he called. "Where are you?"

He was shivering himself now. His clothes, still damp from when the tourist had splashed him, were starting to freeze solid. He needed to get out.

His hands were too cold to carry a tub of ice cream, so he decided to eat whatever was closest to the door. But where was the door? He tried to navigate by remembering which flavors he'd already passed, but nothing looked familiar. Tarantula Truffle? Mealworm Mocha? Cricket Crunch? He definitely hadn't seen any of those before.

He jumped up and down on the spot to shake off his dusting of frost. He was beginning to feel like a piteously underdressed Arctic explorer. Was it possible to catch frostbite in an ice-cream fridge? This was insane. Was it snowing in the fridge? It was like Boston in midwinter. Icicles hung from the ceiling, as sharp as daggers.

"Lola! Where are you?" Snowflakes landed on his tongue as he called her.

And there she was.

Her dark hair flecked with snow, her cheeks flushed pink from cold, and a red-checkered tablecloth gripped tightly around her, she appeared out of the whiteness like a girl in a fairytale.

"I . . . lost you," she said, her teeth chattering uncontrollably.

They huddled together for warmth as they tried to find their way out, and for one crazy moment Max wondered if they might actually perish like this, frozen together like human Popsicles.

"Grasshopper Pie!" yelled Lola. "Over there! That's the way we came in!"

Glowing with relief, she threw a celebratory snowball at Max (her first ever), and he gleefully retaliated.

His aim went high and he hit a large icicle.

With a low moan, the icicle snapped off and fell, cutting straight through the air. It landed at Max's feet, embedding itself in the snow like a butcher's knife. A crack spread through

174

the icy ceiling and set off a chain reaction. Next minute, Max and Lola were dodging a volley of icicles, each one as lethal as a sharpened lance.

They emerged white-faced from frost and terror. In a triumph of hope over experience, Max was clutching a tub of Grasshopper Pie. But, in his heart of hearts, he knew before he opened it that the grasshoppers would be real.

"I'm sure they're very nutritious," said Lola.

Max silently replaced the lid.

The concierge smirked when he saw their frigid faces. "It looks like you made yourselves at home. I trust your hunger for ice cream has been sated?"

"We got lost," said Max. "And we're frozen."

"Here." The concierge threw them some towels. "Wrap yourselves in these and let's get going. We don't want to be late."

"Late for what?" asked Lola as he hurried them back to the elevator.

"Feeding time."

"You mean lunch?" asked Max hopefully.

"You've just had ice cream," said the concierge. "Surely you're not hungry again already?" He turned his attention to Lola. "Have you ever seen a real, live jaguar?"

"Of course I have."

"Up close?"

"With binoculars!"

"Today, on our VIP Backstage Tour, you may approach as close as you wish."

Lola stopped in her tracks. "Don't tell me you have a jaguar in captivity?"

The concierge smiled proudly.

"But they're an endangered species," Lola pointed out. "You're not allowed to catch them."

"Quite so. Normally, we shoot them and sell the pelt. But this fellow is quite possibly the last one in this area. We realized he was worth more alive than dead."

"What a heartwarming story," said Lola sarcastically.

"Thank you," said the concierge. "And our compassion has paid off. He'll be our number-one tourist attraction when he masters the balance ball. How's that for a happy ending?"

Lola mimed clapping her hands. "But what will you do when your number-one tourist attraction dies of old age and there are no more jaguars to replace him?"

"We're ahead of you on that one. We've just bought a lion from a traveling circus. They couldn't afford the meat bill anymore, but that's not a problem for us—with our never-ending supply of tourists."

"You're not going to feed the tourists to the lion?" asked Max.

The concierge looked guilty. "I meant, um, of course . . . a never-ending supply of tourist money," he corrected himself, not very convincingly.

"But wait," objected Lola, "lions are from Africa. You don't get lions in Central America."

"Most tourists don't care. They just want to see animals. And between you and me, Africa's fauna is more exciting than anything you find in San Xavier. Nobody's going to get rich off a cage of spider monkeys, if you know what I mean."

"No," said Lola, "I don't know what you mean." Max could tell that she was working hard not to lose her temper.

"In this business, you've got to think big. Between you and me, we're planning to turn the parking lot into a game reserve. Lions, giraffes, elephants, zebras, maybe throw in a few kangaroos—how do you like that idea?"

Lola chose her words carefully. "I'm speechless."

While the concierge jabbed at the elevator button, Lola hung back to talk to Max in whispers. "Can you believe they've put a jaguar in a cage? We have to rescue him."

"No," said Max. "Please don't do this."

"I've got a plan. I'm going to commune with his spirit."

"Please don't."

"I read about it in a book. If it works, the jaguar will let me pluck out one of his whiskers and we'll be bonded for life. You have to empty your mind of human thoughts and get in tune with the natural world. Then you become one with the jaguar."

"What if the jaguar wants to become one with you by eating you?"

"I'm in big trouble."

"Hurry up!" called the concierge, holding the elevator doors for them. "Feeding time waits for no man—unless that man is the food!"

Chapter Fourteen
THE LAST JAGUAR

"**W**elcome to backstage at the Grand Hotel Xibalba!" The concierge made a grand bow as they exited the elevator on the second floor.

RESTRICTED ACCESS—EMPLOYEES ONLY read the sign on the double doors that blocked their way.

The concierge stabbed a code into a keypad on the wall, and the doors swung open. "This is where the magic is made. On this floor, we have our offices, our kitchens, our storerooms—and, our next port of call, the hotel menagerie."

"Menagerie? You have more animals than just the jaguar?" asked Lola.

"But of course. Tourists expect variety in our shows. We have monkeys, snakes, parrots, a tapir, and we're always looking for more jaguars. You wouldn't believe how hard they are to find."

Lola said nothing, but Max could see her fists clenching and unclenching. He guessed that it was taking all her self-control to keep herself from punching the concierge.

For his part, he was still perplexed. "I don't get it," he said to the concierge. "Why would you keep animals inside the hotel, when the jungle is all around you?"

The concierge looked at him like he was mad. "After a late night in the casino, you can't expect guests at San Xavier's premier hotel to get up at dawn just to catch a glimpse of a monkey's rear end! Mother Nature is too inconvenient and unpredictable. We bring the wildlife to the guests—and teach it to do tricks."

He pushed open another white door.

"Of course, the menagerie is like a locker room. In here, the animals are off duty. I assure you that they are much more interesting when they are performing—some of them even wear costumes."

Max gasped. The room in front of him was the saddest place he'd ever seen. And he wasn't even sensitive like Lola.

Cages lined the walls. And in each cramped cage huddled a bird, mammal, or reptile—each creature radiating unhappiness. Spider monkeys whimpered and hugged themselves. Parrots pecked out their own feathers. And crammed into a cage hardly bigger than its body was a tapir like the one that had run out into the clearing the night Max and Lola had met up at the Black Pyramid.

"Poor thing," said Lola, "it can't move an inch. I mean, it's true that if it could turn round, it would send a spray of pee all over the room, but that's not the tapir's fault. It's a natural defense mechanism."

The saddest sight of all was the big cage at the far end of the room. For there, in an easy-clean environment devoid of grass or trees or soft, sweet earth, paced a jaguar.

You didn't have to be an animal lover to see how miserable he was.

"Behold the eternal dominance of man over beast," exclaimed the concierge with a flourish. He paused for applause that didn't come. "This brute had some fight in it when it first arrived, but we soon showed it who's boss."

"Where did you find him?" asked Lola.

The concierge tapped his nose. "Classified information."

As they got closer to the jaguar's cage, Lola gave a little gasp. "Are those whip marks on his pelt?"

"No one said show business is easy," said the concierge. "But it's a fast learner. We're working up a jaguar-taming act that will be the talk of San Xavier."

Lola put her hands against the cage mesh. The jaguar stopped pacing and came to stand in front of her. Lola knelt down so her eyes were level with his.

"Care to feed it?" asked the concierge. "At your own risk, of course. We cannot be responsible for unattended limbs."

Lola nodded enthusiastically.

"Pepe! Bring food!" called the concierge.

A zookeeper appeared, carrying a tray of raw meat in one hand. His other hand and arm appeared to be missing.

"What happened to him?" Max whispered.

The concierge cocked his head toward the jaguar. "It was a nasty business. Did you know that a jaguar's tongue can part skin from flesh, and flesh from bone? And its teeth are specially designed to pierce the skull and bite the brain—so Pepe here got off lightly."

The keeper regarded the animal with hatred. He passed the tray to Lola and took a leather bullwhip off the wall. Tucking the whip under his stump, he unlocked the metal door. Then he cracked the whip to make the jaguar retreat to the far end of the cage.

He gestured to Lola to place the tray of food inside.

Refusing his offer of the whip, she stepped into the cage.

The jaguar growled.

Max couldn't help noticing how chewy Lola's legs looked. How tasty her arms. How thin her skull—

"Coming, Hoop?"

"Not me; I'll wait out here. Animals don't like me."

"Think of the memories," said the concierge, pushing Max into the cage. "It's part of your VIP Backstage Tour experience. You'll be glad you did it, afterward."

Max heard the door clang shut behind him. He was so nervous, he thought his legs might collapse beneath him.

The jaguar growled louder and licked his chops.

"Just stay calm, maintain eye contact, and don't make any sudden movements," Lola instructed him. "Do what I do."

Lola walked slowly toward the jaguar, holding out the tray.

Max took one step, tripped over an old chewed bone, and landed headfirst not far from the jaguar's front paws. All he could see at that moment were two sets of long, sharp claws flexing in readiness to clamp him down while his skull was pierced and his brain was bitten into.

He smelled jaguar breath.

He shut his eyes.

He heard Lola say something in Mayan.

A rough tongue licked his face.

Max waited for his skin to part from his flesh and his flesh to part from his bones, but it didn't happen. The jaguar was licking him tenderly, as if he were a cub.

"I told him you're a friend," said Lola. "He likes you." She tried to distract the jaguar with the tray of meat, but he wasn't interested. He put a paw on Max's head, pinning him down in the sawdust, and flicked his tail contentedly, like a cat with a mouse.

Lola crouched down. "I will set you free," she whispered.

"Thanks," said Max, "but can you hurry up?"

"I was talking to Bahlam, the jaguar," she said.

"What about me?"

Lola ignored him and carried on crooning in Mayan to her new best friend. Max only had a sideways view of the proceedings as his head was still squashed to the ground, but he could see they were getting along well. Then—what was she doing?—Lola leaned over and—*No, don't do it*—plucked out one of the jaguar's long, white whiskers.

Max winced. *Way to get eaten, Monkey Girl.*

But the jaguar seemed to purr his approval.

She bowed to the animal and stood up. "Come, Hoop, let's leave him to his food."

"Can't move," Max reminded her.

Lola stroked the jaguar's paw and gently lifted it off Max's head. "Not much longer, Bahlam. We will come back."

Max felt a pang of guilt. Much as he hated to see the animal confined to a cage, he knew Lola's rescue plan was doomed. There was no way that two kids could smuggle out a jaguar without anyone noticing.

He tried not to meet the jaguar's eyes as he got to his feet and brushed himself down, but he could feel him watching sadly as he and Lola left the cage. The second they were out and the steel door clicked shut, the creature attacked the hunk of meat, ripping flesh from bone with a ferocity that made Max feel weak at the knees again.

The concierge looked at Lola suspiciously. "What did you say to it? It seemed to like you."

Lola shrugged. "Just baby talk. What can you say to a dumb animal? It's not like it can understand me."

"Quite so. Shall we continue the tour? Where would you like to go next—casino or pizza buffet?"

The World's Biggest Pizza Buffet on the seventh floor was like a huge, poorly lit diner. The booths were arranged around a long central table that groaned under wooden platters of pizza, each one as big as a cart wheel. There must have been fifty different kinds.

"Eat all you like—it's on the house," said the concierge, showing them to a booth. "I must leave you for a moment to finalize some details for the big show tonight. Bon appétit!"

"It's good to get him off our backs," said Lola when he'd gone. "He's so creepy. There's something about his eyes and the way he twitches his nose—"

"You're acting pretty weird yourself today. It's not exactly normal to go around pulling out jaguar whiskers."

Lola took the long white bristle out of her pocket and held it up to the light. Her eyes were shining. "See how beautiful it is? So now I have a jaguar to be my animal guide."

"What does that mean?"

"It means he'll protect me."

"He's stuck in a cage."

"It's deeper than that. It's like a bond between us. And anyway, we're going to rescue him."

"Yeah . . . about that. How exactly?"

"I'm not sure yet. I know we're deep underground, but there must be staircases and emergency exits, don't you think?"

"Absolutely," said Max. "Because this hotel's priority is obviously the safety of its guests."

Lola sighed. "There's no need to be sarcastic."

"I just don't think you've thought this through. I mean, assuming you did spring the jaguar, what would you do with him? You can't set him loose in Limón. And it's not like he can get the bus with us to Puerto Muerto."

"I'll take him back to wherever they caught him."

Max put his head in his hands. "Don't do this, Monkey Girl. We promised Uncle Ted we'd go straight back to the villa."

"You think you'll be safe if you can get to your uncle's house? You must know by now that it doesn't work like that. As long as we have a Jaguar Stone, the Death Lords will come after us. It doesn't matter where we are, or what we're doing."

"That doesn't mean we should act like crazy people."

"It's not crazy, Hoop. You're the one who convinced me that two kids can save the world. Maybe we can start right now by saving these animals."

"Animals? I thought it was just the jaguar?"

She made a sad face at him.

"Are you out of your mind?" he said. "You seriously think we're going to walk out of here with a performing jaguar, an incontinent tapir, a flock of parrots, and an army of monkeys?"

"Don't forget the snakes."

"You're kidding me."

"Come on, Hoop. You know it's the right thing to do."

"I can't think straight. I need food."

Lola smiled at him. "Let's have some pizza. And then we'll work out a plan."

Chapter Fifteen
THE VAMPIRE'S KISS

Max and Lola chewed in silence for a while. A body-language expert might have guessed (correctly) that Lola was thinking about animal welfare, Maya mythology, and the big questions of the universe, while Max was focused solely on the food.

"See this?" He thrust a slice of bubbling, cheesy pizza under her nose. "This is proof that the Death Lords are not running this hotel."

"Oh really?" said Lola. "How's that?"

"Because if the ancient Maya were in charge, that buffet would be all greasy tamales and corn mush."

"It's true that Xibalba is not famous for its wood-fired pizzas," conceded Lola. "Maybe I just haven't stayed in enough big hotels."

As Max lifted the cheesy slice to his mouth, a yellowish brown substance the color and consistency of mustard splattered down on it.

"What the . . . ?"

He looked up to see where it had come from, and instantly lost his appetite.

He pointed to the ceiling. "Bats! They pooped on my pizza!"

"They look like vampire bats," added Lola. "And they're everywhere."

And so they were.

Max realized that what he'd assumed was a decorative brown stripe running around the top of the walls was actually a large bat colony, hanging from a plasterwork ledge. Most were sleeping, but a few flitted about.

As he watched, one peeled away from the rest and landed on the carpet near their table. It was a mouselike creature with shiny black eyes, and it sidled sneakily along on two bony webbed legs toward Lola's bare ankle.

"That's so gross," he said, stamping to make it take flight. "I didn't know bats could walk."

"It's only the vampires." Lola drew her feet up under her on the seat. "That's how they creep up on victims in the night." She waved to a server, and he came rushing over.

"*Ba'ax tawa'alih?*" he asked. "Is anything wrong?"

186

"It's the bats!" said Lola.

"*Uukum Soots'*," said the server, nodding and pointing upward.

"*Uukum Soots'* means 'vampire bat,'" translated Lola.

"I got that," said Max. "But where did they come from?"

The server spoke again in rapid-fire Mayan.

"He says that a crew from Hollywood have been shooting a vampire movie," explained Lola. "The bats were extras and a few of them escaped."

"A few? There are thousands of them." Max was outraged. "Are they just going to let them hang there?"

"The term is *roosting*," said Lola. "He says that if we wait a little, they're planning to release some hawks to catch them. We can watch if we like."

"Seriously? A massacre over the mozzarella? Dead bats in the doughballs?"

Lola shuddered. "Let's get out of here. I thought we could go back up to second and have a snoop around."

"I still don't like this rescue idea," said Max.

"Do you want to wait here for me?" She stood up.

Another splatter of bat guano plopped onto the table.

"No, I'll come with you. But only because I promised Uncle Ted that we'd stick together."

"Not leaving already?" asked a voice that was as brown and silky as the maple syrup Max poured on his pancakes in Boston.

He looked up. The voice wasn't talking to him. It was talking to Lola. And it was wafting out of the handsomest face Max had ever seen.

Lola smiled shyly at the newcomer and sat back down. "Have we met?"

"Only in my dreams."

As the stranger slid, uninvited, into the booth next to Lola, Max took in the rest of his appearance. He was about eighteen years old, tall, with piercing blue eyes and long black hair combed dramatically back from his pale, chiseled face. He wore a frilly white shirt and black jeans. He looked like a poet. From his accent, he sounded English. Something about him seemed vaguely familiar.

The stranger saw Max studying him. "You've recognized me, haven't you? Would you like an autograph, kid?"

"Kid?" Max glared at him. "You're not much older than me."

"Is he your little brother?" the stranger asked Lola.

Lola laughed. "He's not even Maya. You're not very observant, are you?"

"It's been a long day. Trouble with the bats. Why we can't add them in postproduction is beyond me." He switched on a charming smile. "But that's not your concern. You're just here for the magic. And why shouldn't you be? You pay good money at the cinema to see me. I never forget that it's people like you that keep me in designer hair products.

188

I love my fans and I'd like to thank you for hunting me down."

Max broke it to him bluntly. "We're not your fans. We didn't hunt you down. We don't know who you are."

"Really? You don't know me?"

Max shook his head.

The stranger looked at Lola quizzically.

She shook her head, too.

The stranger slapped his hand on the table. "I guess that's my reward for coming to a dump like this. 'Let's do something different,' they said. 'The world's first jungle vampire movie,' they said. I should have known it was a bad idea when the sun dried up all the fake blood on the first day of shooting."

"Who are you?" asked Lola.

"Does the name Ray Love mean anything to you?"

"No," she answered truthfully.

Max narrowed his eyes. "Ray Love? Wait, are you the one they call Loverboy?"

The stranger put up his hands in surrender. "Guilty as charged."

"Well, it was nice to meet you, Mr. Love," said Lola briskly, "but we have to go."

Loverboy pouted and ran his fingers through his glossy black hair. "Don't be intimidated by me. I may be a famous movie star but, underneath the showbiz glamour, I'm a person just like you. Well, much wealthier, obviously. And better looking. And more talented. But my acting coach says it's good for me to mix with ordinary mortals now and again." He smirked at Max. "Go on, kid, say something ordinary."

"A bat just pooped on your head," said Max.

As Loverboy dabbed at his hair with a napkin, Max and

Lola wondered how to escape. Since the movie star was sitting next to her and blocking her exit from the booth, Lola began by saying, "Excuse me. . . ."

Loverboy perked up. "Here it comes. Wherever I go, it's always the same." He puckered his lips, ready to give Lola a kiss.

"What are you doing?" she asked, horrified. "I just want to get past you."

"As in, get over me? You never will. I'm scoring a ninety percent approval rating across the whole females-aged-nine-to-ninety-nine demographic."

"Really?" Lola sounded surprised.

"I know what you're thinking: Why isn't it one hundred percent? But my agent tells me that these things are never accurate."

"I can believe that." Lola leaned against him slightly to get him to scooch along in the booth. "So if you'll just—"

"Kiss you? But of course." He winked at Max. "Get the camera ready!"

Max watched, appalled, as the movie star turned to Lola, drew back his lips to expose two sharp fangs, changed course from her mouth to her neck, and—

"Get off me!" yelled Lola.

"Leave her alone!" shouted Max. For want of a better weapon, he grabbed a plastic ketchup bottle, leaned across the table, and squirted it at Loverboy.

For one mad moment that Max would never forget, he was staring at an angry vampire and a beautiful girl, both splattered with blood-red sauce like the stars of a gory horror movie.

Loverboy's eyes blazed with fury. "You stupid boy! My

director will kill me! What's wardrobe going to say when they see this shirt? It was hand-sewn."

"You should have thought about that before you lunged at Lola!"

"It's my thing. It's what the fans expect. It's called 'The Kiss of the Vampire' after my first movie. It's what I do for photographs, you moron!"

"But your teeth . . . her neck?"

"You didn't think these fangs were real, did you?"

Max shrugged, slightly embarrassed.

"Are you people savages or what?" spat Loverboy. And with that, he was gone.

"Thanks, Hoop," said Lola.

"For saving you from a vampire?"

"No, for covering me in ketchup. I was being sarcastic."

"I'm sorry. But those fangs were very realistic, didn't you think?"

Lola laughed. "Don't tell me you believe in vampires?"

"Well, it's a big thing back home right now. All the girls at my school are reading vampire books."

"Really? They've obviously never had a toe attacked by a real vampire bat in the middle of the night." Lola stood up and picked up her backpack. "I know you don't want to hear this, Hoop, but I'm sensing a pattern."

"Bring on the conspiracy theory."

"Think about it. When the Hero Twins, Hunahpu and Xbalanke, went down to Xibalba, they were set a series of tests. There was dark and cold and jaguars and vampire bats—"

"No! This doesn't count! We were eating pizza and we happened to meet a guy who's playing a vampire in some dumb movie. You can't call that a test!"

"Don't you want to know what comes next?"

"Let me guess. After the pizza . . . the burger and the hotdog?"

"Ha-ha, very funny. But actually, the next thing they face is—"

Max interrupted her. "It's Rat Man!"

"We meet again," said the concierge. "I trust you are replete?"

"We've had enough to eat, if that's what you're asking," said Max.

"So you are ready to resume your tour? For most people, our next stop is their favorite part of the hotel. In fact, guests come from all over the world just to see our latest acquisitions."

"Acquisitions? You have a museum? Maya artifacts?" Lola hopped around excitedly.

The concierge looked appalled. "This is a hotel. People come here for fun. I am referring to the acquisitions in our casino. We pride ourselves on acquiring all the very latest gaming machines. We have slot machines, arcade games, the latest holographic video games. Many of them are exclusive to our casino."

Lola screwed up her face. "Thank you, but I don't think we're interested. I don't even think we're old enough."

The concierge chuckled. "There's no age limit here. All of life is a gamble, is it not?" He handed her a drawstring bag of tokens. "So live a little."

Max looked at her pleadingly. "Couldn't we just check out the holographic video games? I've read about them but I've never seen one in real life."

"I'll do a deal with you. If I come with you to look at your

192

games, then you come with me to look at that"—Lola quickly thought of a code word for the jaguar—"that fur coat I was interested in."

The concierge's eyes lit up. "Madam has a taste for fur? We have a wide range of rare and exquisite pelts in our lobby boutique."

"I bet you do," responded Lola. "So which floor is the casino?"

"It is on eight, our penultimate floor. I will leave you to enjoy yourselves. Be sure to meet me in the lobby in one hour. I have a very special surprise for you."

Chapter Sixteen
PYRAMID OF PERIL 3-D

"**B**e careful," Lola warned Max as they stood in the doorway of the casino. "The Death Lords are notorious for being crazy mad gamblers. If they're hanging out anywhere in the hotel, this is where they'll be. We shouldn't even have come down here. It's too risky."

"I just want to try the new games. I'll be quick, I promise. And then we'll go visit your precious Bahlam."

Max surveyed the room. He'd never been in a casino before, but it looked how he supposed all casinos looked: a huge, windowless space full of slot machines and gaming tables. The only light came from the machines themselves, a few candles on tables in a sitting area, and a scattering of fairy lights on the ceiling.

Lola smiled when she saw them. "It's the Maya night sky. It's what an astronomer would have seen, looking out of one of those old observatories."

Max looked up and realized that the fairy lights were actually a map of the constellations in the Maya cosmos. He even saw a constellation he recognized. "It's the Cosmic

Crocodile! He guided me in Spain the night Lord 6-Dog was shot, and he guided me out to sea when— Whoa!" A fiery comet shot across the sky and Venus, the planet of warfare, rose on its predawn path. "That's so realistic! How do they do that?"

A gentle breeze made all the candles flicker.

"It feels like we're outside," said Lola. "It's so warm and humid in here. It's the first time I haven't been cold in this hotel."

By the time they reached the center of the room, they were engulfed in noise. The screams of anguish and cries of triumph as the patrons lost or made huge fortunes were underpinned by the steady patter of card dealers and the constant clatter of regurgitated tokens from the slot machines.

"Over here," yelled Max, spotting the large screens and inviting white glow of a cluster of video game pods. "Look! They have *Pyramid of Peril!*" he cried in delight. "Zia picked up an old version at a yard sale in Boston. You have to see it. There's a girl in it who looks just like you."

"Really? Is she strong, intelligent, and brave, with lightning-fast reflexes?"

"Of course. Do you want to play?"

"Nah." Lola flopped down in an armchair in front of a low, candlelit wooden table. "I need to work out my rescue plan." She took a pen and paper out of her backpack and moved the candle closer. Soon she was drawing complicated diagrams and scribbling notes like a scientist working out a formula.

Max, meanwhile, was having the time of his life. The game was spectacular. It felt 100 percent real. He wasn't sure how it worked, but all he had to do was stand on a pad and interact with what he saw on the screen. Then somehow the game surrounded him with all the sights and sounds and smells of a network of tombs inside an ancient Maya pyramid.

"Monkey Girl! Look at me," he cried as he battled 3-D skeletons and avoided falling snakes and leapt over unexpected chasms.

"That's what real life has been like lately," observed Lola. "I don't know why you'd want to do it for fun."

"This is different. I know the rules. And I can't get hurt."

"It's a shame the Death Lords don't know the rules."

"What? Sorry, can't talk, coming to a tricky bit. . . ."

He had to sprint down a tunnel, timing it perfectly to avoid falling rocks, and hurl himself under a stone slab at the end before it slid shut.

It took quite a few goes, and Lola had lost interest long before Max finally made it under the slab. So she didn't see that on the other side was a royal tomb, painted blood-red with toxic cinnabar. In the center of the room, surrounded by jade carvings, quetzal feathers, painted pots, jaguar pelts, cocoa beans, spiny oyster shells—all the wealth of a ruler whose trade routes stretched from the oceans to the mountains—was the sarcophagus of an ancient Maya king.

Flip, flip, flip, quick as a whip, a figure came somersaulting out of the corner like a ninja and landed already posed in attack position.

She stood in front of Max with her arms crossed. "I am the guardian. None shall pass."

"Come see! Come see! It's you!" Max called to Lola, who was deep in thought.

She looked up and did a double take. "Wow, you're right—she *does* look like me!"

She stood up for a better look. "Hey, can you pan around a bit? That place looks familiar. What tomb is that? I feel like I've been there."

"It's probably just a mash-up of lots of different tombs. Video game designers go more for atmosphere than authenticity."

"Watch out! Why am I pulling a knife on you?"

"You—what? Aaaargh." Max ducked as the Lola look-alike began hurling a seemingly endless supply of flint daggers at him.

He dodged, he jumped, he ducked, he deflected.

It was exhilarating. This game was so lifelike, he could feel the wind as the daggers whirled through the air, could smell the chalky flint whizzing past, could hear the dull thuds as they hit the tomb wall behind him. One time he even felt the sting of a holographic blade as it grazed his leg.

With a scream, Lola threw herself on top of him, dragging him down to the floor, and rolling with him off the game pad. They crashed into the table, overturning it, and came to a halt against the armchair.

"What was that for?" asked Max.

There was a smell of burning.

"My hair! It's on fire!"

Lola grabbed a pillow from the armchair. Little feathers flew in the air as she hit her head with it to smother the flames.

Now she was jumping on the pillow, which had evidently started to smolder, and simultaneously stamping out sparks on the rug.

Max watched her in a daze, trying to understand what was happening, until he realized that when they'd knocked over the table, a candle had fallen to the floor and caught her thick black ponytail.

Just to be sure that the fire was out, he leapt up, grabbed a pitcher of fruit punch from a passing server, and emptied it on her head.

"Enough!" spluttered Lola. "I am officially extinguished."

"What was that about?" asked Max. "Haven't you ever seen a video game before?"

"I was going to kill you!"

Max smiled. "No, you weren't. It looks realistic, but it's called a ho-lo-gram," he explained, in a patronizing, talking-to-children kind of tone.

"No, you don't understand. I had a dream. I was in that tomb. I was throwing knives at you. It was exactly like your game. Except . . . I killed you. And then your body was eaten by mutant cave spiders."

"It's okay; calm down. Those knives weren't real."

"No? Then look at your leg."

Max looked down.

His jeans were slashed to ribbons.

They sat on the floor, stunned, Max in his shredded jeans and Lola soaked in punch and examining the frazzled ends of her ponytail, amid the upturned furniture.

Max picked an orange slice out of her hair. "Once again," he said, "I must congratulate you on your ability not to draw attention to us."

Lola hit him with the charred pillow.

But the funny thing was that no one else *had* noticed the ruckus.

All the other patrons of the casino were still glued to their games of choice.

Even the server had not batted an eyelid when Max had used the jug of punch as an impromptu fire extinguisher.

Apparently, this casino was used to drama.

"So," he said, "shall we sneak out before anyone notices the damage?"

Too late.

Someone was coming; the lines of gamblers were parting to let him through.

"Not Rat Man," groaned Lola. "I can't deal with him right now."

But it was Eusebio.

"Ix Sak Lol!" he cried. "Are you hurt? Who has done this to you?" He looked threateningly at Max.

"Done what to me?" Then she realized that Eusebio was looking at her ketchup-spotted shirt. "Don't worry, Eusebio, that's not blood. It's a long story. But I'm fine."

Eusebio nodded. "Then, if you do not need me, I will leave you to your silly games."

"Wait, Eusebio, what are you doing in the casino?"

The boatman looked away sheepishly.

Lola's eyes opened wide as she answered her own question. "Now I get it! You're a gambler! You're gambling all your money away! Does your wife know about this?"

"Please, keep your voice down, Ix Sak Lol."

But Lola was on a roll. "So this is why you need money so badly. I was shocked yesterday when you tried to cheat Max's uncle, but now I understand—"

Eusebio looked embarrassed. "I am not a gambler, Ix Sak Lol. I check the slots for tokens. Sometimes the tourists do not pick up all their winnings."

"That's even more pathetic! Have you no pride?"

Eusebio stiffened at the insult. "Have you no respect for your elders?"

"Not when they're grubbing around for pennies in a place like this."

"You are too quick to judge, Ix Sak Lol."

"Tell me then," she challenged him, "if you're not gambling, why are you so obsessed with money these days?"

Eusebio crouched down and looked her straight in the eye. He spoke quietly. "If it is any business of yours, I am collecting money for Little Och's hospital treatment. His parents are working double shifts, but still they cannot hope to pay for it. Do you have the money to pay for it, Ix Sak Lol?"

Lola said nothing.

"No? Then do not sneer at me for raising it in any way I can."

"Here," she said, pushing the drawstring bag of tokens into his hands. "I'm so sorry. How could I be so stupid?"

Eusebio nodded. "Things are changing so fast around here, it makes us doubt each other. I, too, am sorry. You were right to condemn my behavior yesterday. When I saw you stranded on the riverbank, I thought you were another group of rich tourists with more money than sense. Shame on me, I saw my chance and I took it. If I had known that it was Ix Sak Lol, of all people, who needed my help . . ." His voice faded away in shame.

"Actually," said Max cheerily, "you're right about one thing. Uncle Ted *is* rich. But I don't think you have to cheat him. I'm sure he'll pay for Little Och's treatment. He likes children since he met me."

Remembering how unlikable Max had been when he first arrived in San Xavier, Eusebio and Lola exchanged a smile.

Max didn't get the joke, but he smiled, too. It was good to know that, despite all the other depressing developments on the Monkey River, Eusebio was still a good guy.

"What are you two doing here?" asked Eusebio. "Shouldn't you be on the bus to Puerto Muerto?"

"It's the hurricane," explained Lola. "The bus was canceled."

"Of course, of course, the hurricane. They say it is a big one. I saw the ants marching this morning, but I forget about the outside world when I am working in this godforsaken place."

"Is it bad out there?" asked Max.

"Without windows, who can say? But I was glad to cancel tomorrow's blast-fishing trip."

"Blast fishing isn't fishing," said Lola. "They just throw in some dynamite and scoop up the dead fish."

"But they get a lot of fish," Eusebio pointed out. "And that is what tourists want."

"It's those F.A.T.S.O. guys, isn't it?" Lola thumped on the table. "I hate them!"

"They have taken over the hotel for their conference. Which reminds me that I must get back to work. It's all hands on deck today. Everyone is getting ready for the big show tonight."

"So what's the big deal about this show?" asked Max.

"I do not know," replied Eusebio. "It's down on nine. I am working in the kitchens on two, making tamales for intermission."

Lola put a hand on his arm. "Wait, Eusebio, before you go—can I ask you something?"

"Anything, Ix Sak Lol."

"Who owns this hotel?"

"I suppose it is some big company in San Xavier City. Why?"

"Do you ever think that the owners might be evil?"

"We don't get health benefits or paid vacations, if that's what you mean."

"No, I mean seriously evil—like the Death Lords!"

Eusebio shifted uncomfortably.

"I'm right, aren't I?"

"I do not know, Ix Sak Lol. But let us talk back at Utsal. In here the walls have ears." His eyes darted to the security camera that hung above their heads. "So let us change the subject. Have you had a pleasant day?"

"Yes, thank you for asking." Lola, too, glanced at the security camera and looked meaningfully at Eusebio. "We were fortunate enough to see the menagerie earlier, and you can imagine how much I loved it."

Eusebio met her gaze. "Indeed. I know you are an animal lover."

Lola nodded earnestly. "So I was wondering, if you had to evacuate the menagerie for some reason, say an emergency like a fire or something, how would you get all those animals away from here? Would you load them on your boat?"

It seemed to Max that they were talking in code—for the benefit, he supposed, of the ears in the walls—and that a plan was being hatched under his nose.

Eusebio stroked his chin. "In this hypothetical situation, I think it would be better to use a truck like the one currently in the loading bay at the back of the hotel."

"How interesting," said Lola.

Eusebio stood up. "I must get back to the second floor.

Perhaps you would like to meet me later and revisit the animals? Come while everyone is at the show."

"I'd like that," said Lola. She went to give Eusebio a hug.

"One more thing, Ix Sak Lol," he whispered. "Your hair is full of candle wax, feathers, and orange pips. The ketchup on your shirt looks like gunshot wounds. If you do not want to call attention to yourself tonight, you might want to visit our beauty salon on the sixth floor."

And with that, he patted her sticky head and melted back into the throngs of gamblers in the casino.

"Why didn't you tell me?" Lola asked Max as she picked dried wax out of her hair. "I hope they can get it all out."

"It makes a change for you to be the messy one," said Max. "I've seen you walk through mud all day in the jungle and not get a splash on you."

"Another reason for me to hate this place."

Max lowered his voice to a whisper. "I hope you know what you're doing."

"I'm just getting my hair washed."

"You know what I mean. About meeting Eusebio during the show."

She put a finger on her lips. "He said the walls have ears, remember? The Death Lords must be spying on everyone."

"Eusebio did *not* say anything about the Death Lords."

"Come on, Hoop, admit it. How do you explain the last two tests?"

"Not this again—"

Lola counted on her fingers. "Dark, cold, jaguars, bats, then"—she paused dramatically—"knives and fire!" She pointed at Max's shredded jeans. "Knives!" She waved her scorched ponytail. "Fire! See? It all fits!"

He shook his head. "If the Death Lords wanted to test us, don't you think they'd go for something a bit bigger than shredded jeans and singed hair?"

"Maybe they're playing with us?"

"Maybe this is just a really bad hotel."

Lola attempted to run her fingers through her hair. "Time to break out the vouchers, Hoop. I'm going to the salon. Shall I meet you back here?"

"I think we should stick together. We promised Uncle Ted."

"So you *are* getting spooked!"

"No, I'm not. But they had crocodiles in the pool and bats in the buffet. If they have snakes in the salon, you might need a little help."

"Like you could ever rescue me from a snake."

But, funnily enough, that was almost exactly what happened.

Chapter Seventeen

SHAMPOOS, TATTOOS, BAD NEWS

Never having considered the art of beauty from an ancient Maya point of view, Max was unprepared for the sights that surrounded him.

Things he had expected to see in a beauty salon: hair dryers, bottles of gloop, fluffy towels.

Things he had not expected to see in a beauty salon: a terrifying array of Stone Age tools, including flint chisels, saws, and hammers.

A Maya woman approached him. She wore a traditional white cotton dress, embroidered with colorful flowers and birds. Her name badge read KOO.

She saw Max's discomfort at the tools.

"Old things," she reassured him, "like in a museum."

"What were they for?" asked Max.

"Dentistry. The ancient Maya had a lot of fun with it." She pointed at a poster advertising different styles of tooth

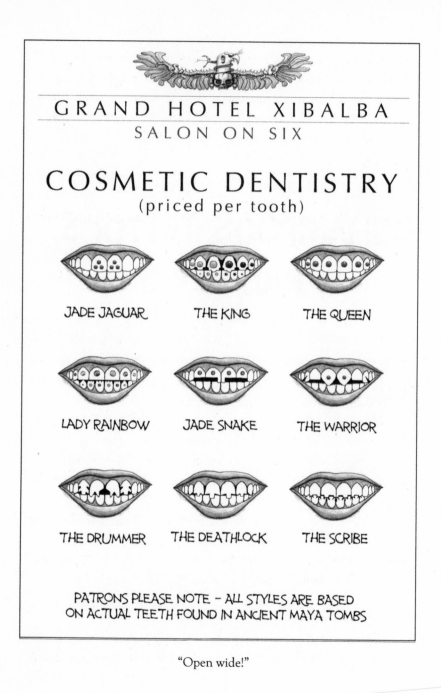

"Open wide!"

embellishment. There were teeth filed into points, and teeth filed into mountain ranges. There were sculpted canines, bedazzled bicuspids, incisors inset with jewels. "You want to try?" Koo grabbed a little stainless steel pick with a mirror on the end and waved it at him. "Open wide!"

"*No!*"

"Sorry," said Koo. "It has been a slow day. I am bored. My only client fell asleep." She gestured at a barber's chair at the far end of the salon. All Max could see of the customer was a pair of legs sticking out from under a pile of towels.

Koo sighed. Then her eyes took in Max's unruly hair. "Is that your natural color?" she asked, with pity in her voice.

Max nodded.

"Never mind, we can work miracles these days." She guided him over to a low shelf behind the sofa in the reception area. It was loaded with beauty products. "Let me give you a makeover."

"No, thank you," said Max firmly. "I'm just waiting for my friend."

He looked around for Lola, but she'd been spirited off into a back room by her stylist, a young Maya girl like herself, who'd been delighted to get her hands on a head of thick, glossy—albeit slightly scorched—hair after a day of styling fine-haired, wispy-curled tourists.

"How about a new haircut?" suggested Koo, " I could do it ancient Maya style, all crazy punk?" She showed him a wig on a mannequin head. The hair was caught up in a high, springy ponytail and embellished with feathers, shells, and beads.

Max shook his head.

"False nose?"

"What?"

She indicated a display of adhesive nose bridges, some

with goggles attached. "To give you the profile of a Maya king."
She selected a huge nose arch and held it in place against his
face. "It suits you."

"I don't think so."

Koo replaced the false nose and picked up a stingray spine.
"A tattoo?" she suggested. "Very trendy."

"No."

Koo was not so easily discouraged. "Warrior face paint?"
She brandished a pot of blue paste.

"Blue is for sacrifice victims; warriors used black," Max
told her.

"How do you know that?" asked Koo suspiciously.

"I've, er, read about it." He could hardly tell her that he'd
been painted blue himself a few times.

"So you know about the Maya, eh? That is good. Many
tourists, they come in here and they tell me that the Maya
have all died out. And I say, What do you think I am, chopped
lizard?"

"Liver," Max corrected her.

"No food here. This is Salon on Six. You ask at buffet on
seven, if you want liver. Maybe they have Liver Pizza."

"No, it's just . . . never mind."

Koo shrugged and looked around for something else to
sell him. "We have a special on nose piercing."

"No, thank you. I'll just sit and read, if that's okay with
you."

He settled on the sofa and picked up a tourist guide to
San Xavier.

Koo sat down next to him and began to file her nails.

She nodded toward the towel-swaddled customer. "That
one, he is like a baby. If he wakes, I must drop everything and

go to him. He has a tantrum if he has to wait even one minute."

Not wanting to talk, Max kept his eyes glued to the tourist guide.

"You like to read? That one"—again Koo gestured to the towels—"he says he has a library in his house. He must be rich, no?"

She looked at Max expectantly.

"I guess," said Max.

"But he is mean. He has a temper like a fer-de-lance. You know what that is?"

"Yes." Out gathering firewood in the forest, he'd once come face-to-face with this deadly pit viper. Lola had told him later that it was the most dangerous snake in Central America.

"So what do you think?" continued Koo. "Can a snake change its spots? Eh?"

Max decided not to point out that the fer-de-lance wasn't spotted, but had more of a diamond pattern. "I don't know," he said.

"You don't think that a good woman could make him change?"

Horrified to be caught in a heart-to-heart with a stranger, Max pretended to be engrossed in an article on shrimp farming.

Koo nudged him. "That girl you are waiting for, is she your girlfriend?"

Max shook his head.

"No? You are single?"

He nodded.

"You are happy to be single?"

"I'm fourteen."

Koo sighed. "When I was fourteen I had big dreams of

marrying a rich man and living in a palace. But I am still waiting." She scrutinized herself in a mirror. "I worry that I will lose my looks."

Max kept his eyes fixed on the magazine.

"Tell me," persisted Koo. "You are a rich tourist. What advice do you have for me?"

Max ignored her.

She nudged him again, hard. "What is your advice?"

Max panicked. His eyes fell on a headline in the magazine. "The key to a successful shrimp farm," he pronounced, "is a good water-filtration system."

Koo narrowed her eyes, trying to understand what he'd just said and ponder its significance to her love life. Luckily, before she could ask any more questions, the heap of towels at the far end of the salon began to stir.

Max watched as the legs stretched out, extending two smallish feet in two shiny, pointy-toed black leather boots.

Max knew those boots.

"I must go back to work," said Koo. "Perhaps we can talk again. Enjoy your reading."

"*Frío! Frío!*" whined a familiar voice. "The towels have gone cold."

Koo tried to soothe him. "Nice hot towels, Koo brings them to you."

Max watched in the mirror as she carefully lifted the old towel from the man's face. Just before she replaced it with a steaming new one, he caught a flash of black hair, a hooked nose, and a thin handlebar mustache.

It was enough to confirm his worst fears.

There, in a barber's chair maybe fifty feet away from him, sat the thuggish Spanish aristocrat who'd been chasing him since his very first day in San Xavier: Count Antonio de Landa.

Landa was descended from the guy who had burned all the Maya books way back in history, and he seemed determined to outdo his ancestor's notoriety. He was brutal, vicious, power hungry, slightly insane—oh, and he'd tried to marry Lola.

Of course, at the time of the wedding, he'd unwittingly been sharing his body with the evil priest Tzelek. But Landa had been collecting photographs of Lola long before that, and his creepiness knew no bounds.

Max's heart was racing. Somehow he had to warn Lola not to come out of the back room. But how to get across the salon without Landa recognizing him?

Slowly he reached up to a hook on the wall and took down a jaguar-patterned nylon cape, the kind hairdressers use to protect their clients' clothes. He draped the cape over his head while he searched the shelf behind him for more items to add to his disguise.

As Max's hand closed around the face paint, Landa launched into one of his tantrums. "Hot? You call this hot? *Idiota!* How will the pores open if the towel is cold?"

"But Don Antonio, your skin is cold like a fish. It sucks the heat straight out of my towels."

"Cold like a fish?" His thin lips smiled. "Cold like a shark, you mean."

Koo shuddered. "So, Don Antonio, are you going to the show tonight?"

"I have no time for such fripperies. I am engaged in an important research project; I am writing a book."

"You are a writer?" She inspected one of his small, bony

211

hands. "Ah yes, I see you have sensitive, artistic fingers."

"Give me a manicure, if you know how."

Koo sniffed to show she was offended. "Trust me, Don Antonio. I am a qualified nail technician."

"Trust you?" he snapped. "You are a woman, are you not? Once I trusted a woman, and she left me on our wedding day."

Koo almost dropped her nail file in surprise. "You are married?"

"She escaped before I could force her to say her vows. She was my one true love, *el amor de mi vida.*"

"For myself," said Koo, "I believe there is more than one woman for one man."

"Then your heart has not been broken."

"More times than I can count."

"Then I see you know nothing about true love."

Koo pursed her lips. "So where did you meet her, this true love of yours?"

"It was destiny that brought us together. Our paths first crossed when she was a child, but I waited for her with patience."

"It was an arranged marriage?"

Landa nodded. "Arranged by the gods, to bring together the Maya kings and the throne of Spain."

Max was electrified. He couldn't stop eavesdropping on Landa's confessions. Was he talking about Lola?

"She was Maya, your girlfriend?"

"She was a royal princess, descended from the Jaguar Kings."

At this point, Koo apparently decided that her client was deranged and moved the scissors out of his reach. Max reached the same conclusion. If Landa was calling Lola a royal princess, he was talking nonsense. Which meant that Max did not have to break it to Lola that the crazy count had stalked her since she was little. All Max had to do was—

No! No! No! What was that mustachioed maniac saying now?

"The old man, the shaman, he paid me to steal her from her mother."

"Trouble with the mother-in-law, eh?"

"He said the mother was a bad woman."

"So you rescued her, like a knight in shiny armor?"

"I left her under a mahogany tree."

Max's stomach flipped.

"How romantic," said Koo, evidently never dreaming that he could be talking about abandoning a little baby. "If she is your destiny, perhaps she will find you again?"

Landa let out a groan. "*Me odia.* She hates me."

"Poor man, how you have suffered." Koo put down the black nail polish she had selected for him, and began to massage Landa's temples. "But you know what they say, Don Antonio: there are plenty more fishes in the sea."

Landa sprang up, sending the manicure tray flying. "How dare you say that? There is no one else for me. She is the one."

Koo tried to calm him down. "Please, Don Antonio, the polish, it needs to dry—"

"Have you understood nothing? I am a broken man. Every day I wait for a sign from the gods. I would give everything I own just to see her again. . . ."

Catching sight of his own reflection, Landa picked up the barber's chair and hurled it at the mirror, like a rock star trashing a hotel room. Max froze where he sat, but the angry

213

aristocrat had no eyes for him, nor for anyone who was not the girl who had broken his heart. He threw some coins at Koo and swept out, twirling his salon cape around him like a matador.

The noise brought Lola's stylist running out of the back room.

"Are you all right, Koo?" she asked, looking at the mess. "Who did this?"

Koo picked up the coins and looked at them sadly. "He is just another gambler. But he has placed his bets on the wrong woman."

"Forget about him," said the other stylist. She admired herself in the cracked mirror. "Let's close up early and get ourselves ready for the show tonight."

Lola emerged from the back room. "Hoop?" she called. "Where are you?"

"I'm over here."

She followed his voice to the reception area. "Is that you under there?"

The figure she addressed wore blue body paint; a false nose with goggles; an elaborate wig complete with feathers, shells, and beads; and a jaguar-patterned nylon cape.

"How do you like my new look?" asked Max, who had loaded on the Maya finery to disguise himself from Landa.

"What are you doing, Hoop? Was it you making all that commotion?"

"Me? No."

"So who was it?"

He looked at her through his ridiculous goggles. Her hair was straight and glossy; she wore a new T-shirt; she was all clean and shiny again. But Max knew that, with one name, he could reduce her world to ruins. That name was Antonio de Landa—or Toto, as Lola had called him.

Should he tell her what he had overheard or not?

"Just let me take this stuff off and clean myself up."

Playing for time, Max slowly dismantled his disguise and wiped his face with a towel, all the while wondering how to handle this unwelcome development.

Landa was a stalker, a dangerous madman, a psychopath to be avoided at all costs. But if Lola found out what he'd been saying, she was sure to want to confront him. It could only make a bad situation even worse.

"So who did this?" Lola asked again, indicating the broken mirror and the upturned furniture.

Max looked where she pointed. He crossed his fingers behind his back. "That? Oh, that was me."

"What? Why did you smash up the salon?"

"It was an accident. I tripped. It was the goggles."

"You *tripped*? But—"

Koo came out with a broom and Max waved at her.

She waved back sadly.

"See," said Max. "It's fine. We're cool."

Lola narrowed her eyes. "But why—"

"There you are!" squeaked a voice. Max was saved from further interrogation by the arrival of the concierge, who scurried in wheezing and panting, as if he was out of breath. He didn't even notice the mess in the salon. "I've been looking everywhere for you two! It's time to go down for the show."

"We have to get out of this if we're going to rescue Bahlam," Lola whispered to Max. "Follow my lead!" She slumped on the sofa and groaned. "I don't feel good. I think it was the pizza."

Max slumped next to her. "Me, too."

215

"What's this?" asked the concierge.

"Your Guano Special at the pizza buffet has made us sick," explained Lola.

"Too sick for the show," added Max, clutching his stomach.

The concierge's nose was twitching furiously, as if he could smell bad acting. "What do you mean, too sick for the show? You have VIP tickets."

"We'd like to take a rain check," said Max, "if it's all the same to you."

"No," replied the concierge, "it is not all the same to me." His eyes were flashing pink with anger and his voice rose to a squeak. "You have partaken of our hospitality, you have eaten and drunk your fill, you have availed yourselves of all our facilities, and you have left behind a trail of destruction. All I ask is that you fulfill your duties as our VIP prize winners and make an appearance at the show. If you refuse, I will have no choice but to charge you for your stay at the Grand Hotel Xibalba. And believe me, with damages, that is one bill you cannot afford to pay."

Max and Lola went into a huddle.

"Eusebio will be waiting," whispered Lola. "We need to sneak the animals out while everyone else is at the show."

"So we do what Rat Man says. We just make an appearance. We'll take our seats, wave at the crowd, and when the lights go down, we'll slip away."

Lola bit her lip. "Okay. I guess we have no choice."

They turned to the concierge. "We are feeling a little better," said Max.

"A wise decision," said the concierge. He wiped his brow with a handkerchief, as if a crisis had been averted. "Follow me."

He led them out of the salon, through a set of "Employees Only" doors, and into a dark, narrow corridor that led to a single elevator.

An elevator without a call button.

"This is the VIP elevator," explained the concierge, taking a jade-colored passkey out of his pocket and sliding it through a slot in the wall. "It goes straight down to nine."

Inside the elevator, the doors closed silently and they dropped so fast that Max's ears popped. "The ninth floor must be pretty deep," he said. "Feels like we're going to the center of the Earth."

Eventually, with a squealing of brakes, they came to a bumpy stop. The lights flickered, then fizzled out altogether. The only sound in the darkness was a scratching noise like the claws of a small animal.

"I don't like this," said Lola.

Max said nothing. He was trying not to have a panic attack.

Then—and relax!—the doors slid open, and they emerged into a brightly lit corridor.

Something shot out between Max's feet.

"It's a rat! There was a rat in the elevator! Maybe it chewed through the— Wait, where's the concierge?"

The concierge was nowhere to be seen.

Max's and Lola's eyes met. But before they could discuss their suspicions, a small, round Maya woman—the first ugly Maya woman Max had ever seen—came to greet them. She wore the traditional white embroidered dress, and she held a clipboard.

"Good evening," she said. "You must be the Hero Twins. We've been expecting you."

Chapter Eighteen
SHOWTIME

"**W**e are not the Hero Twins," said Lola. "There's been a mistake."

The woman checked her clipboard. "A mistake? I don't think so. You are on my list. You are the VIP guests, are you not?"

"But who made the list? Who gave it to you?"

"I am just an usher," said the woman impatiently. "Please follow me. The show is about to start." She turned and strode off briskly, her sandals slapping the stone floor.

"Wait!" Lola called after her. "Why did you call us the Hero Twins?"

The usher turned. "It is not important."

"It is to me," said Lola stubbornly.

The usher rolled her eyes. "This way, please."

"Better do as she says," whispered Max, "if you want to get back to meet Eusebio."

"But Hoop, you don't understand—"

"Don't tell me—it's a Maya thing."

"The way she called us the Hero Twins . . . something very bad is about to happen."

"Please!" called the usher from farther down the corridor. "You will not have time for your preshow refreshments if you do not hurry!"

"Or," said Max, "it's just a cute way of referring to their VIP guests. Now let's get our preshow refreshments."

Security cameras high on the wall swiveled to track them as they followed the usher down a long, curving concrete tunnel.

She stopped in front of a large steel door.

"This is the control room," she explained. She tapped a code into an entry system, and the door swung open. Another Maya woman—tall, thin, even uglier than the usher, and wearing the same uniform of embroidered white dress—stepped out. "Welcome to the show," she said, sticking out her hand. "We are so excited to have you here."

Max shook her hand.

Her grip was uncomfortably strong.

She smiled, looked directly into his eyes, and would not let go.

Her teeth were black.

Unnerved, Max pulled back. With a loud squelching noise, the woman's forearm detached from her body—her hand still firmly gripping his.

"Ew! Ew!" In shock, he hurled the limb down the corridor. It came scurrying back on its fingers and pawed at him like a cat wanting to be fed.

"What have you done?" screamed the woman. Her face turned purple, her eyeballs shot out of their sockets, and her mouth opened so wide that it ripped the sides of her cheeks.

"What have you done?" echoed the usher. She clutched her stomach as if she had a pain, then threw open her hands as her intestines burst out of her body and writhed about like snakes on the floor.

Max turned in horror to Lola, but she was standing there, hands on hips, looking completely unfazed.

"Oh puh-lease," she said. "Not the exploding-intestines trick again?"

As the two women howled with laughter, their bodies morphed into their real Death Lord selves, Scab Stripper and the Demon of Pus.

"Why am I not surprised to find you two down here?" asked Lola. "Now suppose you tell us what's going on? What's with all the Hero Twins references?"

"If you want to pick my brains, Ix Sak Lol, I'll make it easy for you," said Scab Stripper. He pulled off the top of his skull like a cap, to reveal a tangled mass of worms where his brains should be.

"You guys are sick," said Max, his heart still pounding from shock.

"We'll take that as a compliment," replied Pus, holding open the metal door. "Come on in, the boss is waiting."

It was a control room out of a movie set, with more gleaming technology than Max had ever seen in one place. On every wall giant screens pumped in information in a visual overload of news feeds, maps, charts, diagrams, video surveillance. On several screens giant slow-motion close-ups showed Max's horrified face as he'd grappled with the breakaway arm.

All around the room were rows of workstations where operators analyzed and edited the flow of footage. And dominating the room from the comfort of a large leather armchair suspended from the ceiling by a robotic arm was Ah Pukuh himself.

Instead of his usual ancient Maya garb, the god of violent and unnatural death had squeezed his corpulent body into an expensive-looking modern business suit. His hair was short, spiky, and bleached white. With his headset mic and earpiece, he looked every inch the trendy TV producer (albeit with a bad case of plague boils).

As Max and Lola stared at him in amazement, his high-tech chair brought him zooming toward them.

"Ah, the Hero Twins! So glad you could make it!" he said in a voice that tried to be charming but merely came off as creepy.

"I see you've finally got too fat to walk," said Lola.

"I will treat that remark with the contempt it deserves." Ah Pukuh lifted an enormous buttock and let loose a toe-curling blast of gas.

"Why are we here?" asked Lola, waving away the smell.

"Why are any of us here? It is a good question. But please try not to worry about it, as I will soon be bringing your miserable lives to an end. But first, let's have a little fun. I believe you have a gift for me?" He waggled his fat fingers expectantly.

Lola spat in his hand.

"You will regret that, little girl. Give me the White Jaguar."

"We don't have it," lied Lola.

"Must we play games? It was all going so well."

Ah Pukuh jabbed at a control pad in the arm of his chair, and the steel door burst open to admit a squad of heavily armed security guards. Before Max knew what was happening, a few had peeled off to restrain him, while the rest surrounded Lola.

Strong hands held him tight. He watched helplessly as Lola kicked and struggled but couldn't prevent the goons from taking her backpack and passing it to Ah Pukuh.

The god of violent and unnatural death soared out of reach in his mechanical chair, then plunged his greedy hands into the bag and pulled out the football-shaped object. "Come to Daddy," he crooned as he pulled away the deerskin wrapping to reveal the alabaster jaguar head.

Seeing the villain sitting smugly in his high-tech HQ, stroking a white cat, reminded Max of an old James Bond movie he'd watched with his father. What was it with international criminal masterminds? Why did they never take their limitless resources and use them for good? Or at least for fun?

Ah Pukuh held up the Jaguar Stone tenderly. "Welcome home, my beauty! It's time for a family reunion." He clicked his fingers. "Where is the jaguar priest?"

A man stepped forward, carrying a large pot of smoking incense. The pot was decorated in a jaguar pattern, as was the man. Every visible inch of his skin was painted in jaguar spots. He wore a jaguar-pelt cape over his shoulders, the head of a jaguar over his own head, and a jaguar-pelt loincloth. The only non-jaguar-patterned thing about him was a large deerskin shoulder bag worn across his body.

He bowed low to Ah Pukuh.

The god of violent and unnatural death lowered his chair to be level with the priest. He stroked the stone on his knee and blew it a little kiss. Then he placed the stone reverently in the priest's deerskin bag, and watched as it was carried out with an escort of security guards.

Ah Pukuh leered at Max and Lola. "And now, on with the show."

He jabbed at his control pad again.

A wall of giant video screens rose silently into the ceiling to reveal an expanse of plate glass windows overlooking a big sports stadium. It was like being in the press box at Fenway.

Despite the direness of his predicament, Max whistled in admiration. "How did you construct all this underground? It's incredible!"

"It was no problem for my Maya architects," replied Ah Pukuh. "We have always built the impossible."

"Excuse me," said Lola to Max, as she hugged her empty backpack, "but can you stop making nice with him? He has just robbed us of the White Jaguar. He is our mortal enemy."

Ah Pukuh's chair came to rest right in front of her. "Make that your immortal enemy. You would be well advised to make nice with me, too. Soon I will rule all Middleworld. Wouldn't you like to have friends in high places?"

Lola spat at him again.

A posse of guards ran forward, but he motioned them away.

"You are an enigma to me, Ix Sak Lol. You act all high and mighty, yet you expectorate like a street urchin. You profess to support the Maya, yet you have no admiration for my glorious deeds. Soon I will make the whole of Middleworld sit up and take notice of the Maya. I will reassert our dominion." He gestured to the stadium, where the seats were rapidly filling up. "See how they flock to my pleasure dome, one and all."

Max surveyed the audience. "I wouldn't call it one and all. It's hardly a representative cross section."

Ah Pukuh stared at him. "You sound like my marketing department."

"See for yourself," said Max. "You have skeletons and corpses on one side. And a lot of beardy guys in plaid shirts on the other."

"So half the audience are from Xibalba," guessed Lola. "And the other half is from F.A.T.S.O.?"

"Can I just say," said Ah Pukuh testily, "that we did not pronounce that acronym out loud before we chose it and we will be voting on a name change very soon. But yes, my esteemed colleagues from the world of strip-mining and logging are here for their annual conference, and tonight's show is in their honor."

"There's the poncho family!" Max pointed into the audience. "They look a bit confused."

"Idiots! How did they get in here?" Ah Pukuh muttered.

"Don't hurt them," Lola pleaded. "This is not their fight. They're just innocent tourists."

"That concept is an oxymoron. But they are about to have the touristic experience of their lives. They will never forget what they see tonight. Not even years of therapy will erase it."

"What's going to happen?" asked Max nervously.

"A better question would be," said Ah Pukuh, "*what is* not *going to happen?* Because tonight we are attempting to make history. We are presenting something that has never been done before: Maya myth brought to life in a spectacular live-action show that pits immortals against mortals in the never-ending circle of life and death."

"So it's a ballgame," guessed Lola.

Ah Pukuh clapped. "Yes, indeed, the game of the gods."

Max wondered how long a game lasted. Maybe it was like British cricket, which he'd heard could go on for days.

Lola narrowed her eyes. "I think I know where this is

going. Could it be a Hero-Twins-versus-Death-Lords grudge match, by any chance?"

Ah Pukuh smiled at her. "Clever girl."

"So we can win back the White Jaguar?"

"In your dreams."

Max looked anxiously between the two of them. "Will someone please explain to me? So it's a reenactment of some old ballgame. But the Hero Twins are played by actors, right?"

Ah Pukuh ignored him and talked just to Lola. "It will be an inaugural game for my state-of-the-art ball court. How do you like it?"

She looked down at the ball court and surveyed it critically.

Max tried to see it through her eyes.

The playing area was shaped like an uppercase I with a long, narrow center span and wider end zones.

"What's the playing surface?" asked Lola.

Ah Pukuh puffed out his already corpulent chest with pride and popped several buttons off his suit. "It's rubberized for extra bounce. Made from the sap of my very own rubber trees. We also have electronic boundary monitors and an automatic scoring system—both totally biased to the home team, of course. Best of all, we have embedded video cameras to capture all the action—with instant replays from every angle, projected in high definition onto giant screens." He pointed to the massive pod of video screens, speakers, and stage lights that hung from the ceiling over the center of the court. "And, essential for spectators in Xibalba, we have digital betting consoles in every seat for continuous gambling throughout the game. Ka-ching!"

A troop of monkeys dressed in little tunics and feathered headdresses ran out, and began doing acrobatics.

"Looks like the show's starting," said Max.

Lola pressed her nose against the window. "It's Bahlam," she whispered.

The last jaguar of the Monkey River was crammed into a wheeled cage pushed out by the one-armed zookeeper.

The arena went quiet as the cage was unbolted.

The jaguar sprang out and paced around the floor, as if he was looking for someone in the audience. Then he threw back his head and roared with all the pain and anger and hopelessness of a wild heart in captivity.

Lola banged on the glass. "Bahlam! I'm up here!"

"Stop that," said Ah Pukuh. "The glass is soundproof. And you're making smudges."

The monkeys rolled on a huge, brightly striped rubber ball.

The one-armed zookeeper cracked his whip, and the video screens zoomed in on the hatred in the jaguar's green eyes. The zookeeper cracked his whip again, this time across the jaguar's back. With a howl of pain, the animal jumped onto the ball and attempted to keep his balance, while all around him the monkeys juggled bananas.

"You call that entertainment?" said Lola in disgust.

"I agree," sighed Ah Pukuh. "Boring, isn't it? I wanted something more like the Roman Colosseum, with wild animals ripping apart human victims, but the focus groups didn't go for it. Apparently, today's audiences are too squeamish for that sort of thing. I suggested that we do it anyway and feed the focus groups to the animals!" He laughed at his own joke and nudged Max. "Whaddya say? Shouldn't the Maya be more like the Romans? They knew how to entertain a crowd."

"If you want to be more like the Romans," said Max,

"maybe you should concentrate on building aqueducts and straight roads."

"Oh, we have plenty of those already—piece of cake—but we prefer to focus on the fun stuff. The Romans are so misunderstood. In truth, they were as productive as the Maya in the field of violent and unnatural death. In my humble opinion, I don't think they get enough credit for it. We'll be teaching a different kind of history when I'm in charge."

Max and Lola weren't listening to his rambles. They were watching the progress of the White Jaguar as the jaguar priest and his warrior escort entered the arena, crossed the ball court, and walked up the steps of a square platform on the far side. An honor guard on the platform parted to reveal a stone altar composed of five jaguar heads arranged to echo the five points of the Maya compass: north (white), south (yellow), east (red), west (black), and center (green).

Lola nudged Max. "The real White Jaguar is still in the priest guy's bag, so the white one on the altar must be the dummy Hermanjilio carved from a gourd. It's such a great replica, you can hardly tell the difference. But somehow we have to steal the real one back."

"Not a chance," said Max.

The jaguar priest was making a big show of lifting up the fake White Jaguar to exchange it for the real one. Lola groaned. "He's making Ho Hool Bahlam, the legendary Five-Headed Jaguar, the source of ultimate power. We'll never get any of the Jaguar Stones back now."

"Feast your eyes." Ah Pukuh zoomed down behind them in his chair and put his head between them. His breath and body odor, a tangy combination of rotting flesh and raw sewage, hit them like a tidal wave, and they reeled back and gasped for air. "Giddy? It is understandable. For the first time in mortal history, the five Jaguar Stones are reunited. All they need now is mortal blood to fire their power. And when I activate them after the ballgame, all that power shall be mine."

Max rolled his eyes. "Can I ask you something?"

"About what?"

"Criminal psychology."

Ah Pukuh blasted him with his unholy halitosis. "My specialist subject! Ask away."

"Well, I just wondered why the bad guys always feel compelled to explain their evil plans to the good guys?"

"So you can marvel at our genius."

"But why waste time talking about it? Why not activate the Five-Headed Jaguar right now?"

"Whose side are you on?" murmured Lola.

"The boy asks an excellent question, and I will be delighted to answer it. To activate the mighty Five-Headed Jaguar requires blood. But not just any blood. To launch the new age of Ah Pukuh, I require the most precious blood of all: the blood of the famous Hero Twins." He listened to a voice in his headpiece. "Speaking of which, they are ready for you. Shall we go?"

Chapter Nineteen

THE SUPERHERO TWINS

There was nowhere to run and all exits were blocked. Max and Lola had no choice but to fall into line. Directly ahead of them, leading the parade, was Lord Kuy, the owl-man. Behind them, bringing up the rear, marched a full contingent of security guards.

Ah Pukuh was clearly taking no chances in conveying his VIPs from the control room to the arena.

As he walked, staring at Lord Kuy's back, Max noticed that the normally restrained and solemn owl-man had a little spring in his step, and his feathers looked freshly groomed for the occasion.

Lola, on the other hand, trudged along, her eyes fixed on the ground, as if she was in a funeral procession. Which, as it later turned out, she kind of was.

"So, am I right in thinking we're not VIP guests anymore?" Max asked her.

"We're the Hero Twins," she said. "And we're playing ball tonight."

"The Maya ballgame? But I don't know how to play."

229

"It doesn't matter. We could be the best ballplayers in the world, and they wouldn't let us win. This version of the game is strictly ceremonial, like a ritual. The forces of good and evil battle it out for control of the cosmos. And I think we can be pretty sure that evil will win today."

"So it's like a performance?"

"Except it ends with the losers getting sacrificed."

"Approaching backstage area," reported Lord Kuy into his headset.

A door swung open, and Max and Lola were ushered inside.

"This is the green room," said Lord Kuy. "Just pop those on"—he pointed at two deerskin tunics hanging on a hook— "and make yourselves comfortable."

Since the room was completely bare, save for the tunics, a hard wooden bench, and security cameras that moved whenever they did, making themselves comfortable was easier said than done.

"You can't force us to play," said Max.

"Die now or die later, it's all the same to me," said Lord Kuy. He opened the green-room door to show the ranks of armed guards waiting outside.

"But then you won't get your ballgame."

"There is a family in ponchos who can be forced to play in your place." The owl-man rotated his head smugly. "No one is indispensable."

Lola stepped forward. Wearing the deerskin tunic, she looked like a figure from a Maya stone carving. "But *they're* not the Hero Twins, are they? And that's what this is all about, isn't it? Way back in the mists of time, you lost a ballgame to the Hero Twins, and now you want revenge?"

Lord Kuy's owl eyes blinked rapidly. "It is more than that. The ballgame between the Hero Twins and the Death Lords marked the start of this creation. So what better way to usher in Lord Ah Pukuh's reign? For once, our marketing department has come up trumps. We are all very, very excited."

"Did you build this hotel just to lure us here?"

"Don't flatter yourself, mortal; that would be excessive even by Ah Pukuh's standards. This place is to be his new base of operations. He wanted something a little more high-tech than the Black Pyramid. It was an intern who realized you'd be in the area. Apparently the video will go viral."

"What video?" asked Max.

"You're going to be movie stars," replied Lord Kuy enigmatically.

Lola found the nearest camera and spoke into it. "So you want a rematch, do you, Xibalba? Well, get ready for another humiliation. I am Xbalanke the Undefeated, and this is the mighty Hoop, short for Hunahpu. The Hero Twins have returned!"

Max heard her voice piping through the corridors of the hotel, booming out of loudspeakers in the stadium, surely even echoing down to the halls of Xibalba itself. He looked at her with pride and nodded his support.

"Call off this ballgame now," she continued, "or we will *crush* you. You do not stand a chance against our magic. You never did and you never will!"

Lord Kuy spread his winged cape across the camera to cut her off. "Save it for the ball court."

"Oh, we will," said Lola. "You have made the biggest mistake of your featherbrained life to bring us here tonight. Because what you don't know is that we are ballgame champions, just like the original Hero Twins. And we have been studying magic. We will literally *slay* you! Get ready for humiliation."

Lord Kuy put a clawed finger to his tufted ear and winced in pain, as if people were yelling into his earpiece. "Excuse me for a moment," he said, sweeping out the door.

"What was all that about?" whispered Max.

"Game talk. I was trying to psych them out."

"You've psyched me out. We're toast."

"I know."

"And we didn't even rescue the jaguar."

Mention of Bahlam seemed to kick-start Lola. "Get your tunic on and start warming up. We can do this. We are lucky. We have always been lucky. With a little help from the Jaguar Kings, we can totally win this thing."

Max was still shaking his head in disbelief when there was a soft knock at the door and in walked one of the street photographers, the one with the sloth. This time, in place of the sloth, he held a large envelope.

"Your VIP gift," he said, bowing and presenting the envelope to Lola, "compliments of the Grand Hotel Xibalba."

"Thank you." Lola opened it and pulled out a folder marked *Souvenir Photograph*.

"Here, Hoop, you look."

So he did.

And there it was, the truth of the matter.

The truth that Lola had been trying to tell him all day.

The photo showed Max and Lola posing in front of the hotel with the sloth, the parrot, and the snake, completely surrounded by the Death Lords—who were making faces and doing rabbit ears.

"I should have listened to you," he said. "You warned me

about this place. And now we're going to die."

"Wait, there's something else," said Lola, shaking out the envelope. A piece of paper fluttered to the floor. She picked it up and carefully unfolded it. "It's a map of Ixchel, the site of the White Pyramid! And there's a cross and the word Bahlam!"

She turned excitedly to the photographer. "Is this where he was found? Is this Bahlam's territory?"

The photographer nodded. "You have friends here," he whispered, before he slipped out of the door.

Lola's eyes were shining. "We may have lost the White Jaguar, but if we get out of here alive, at least we can save our real jaguar and get him back to his home."

Max made a face. "To Ixchel? That's where my parents jumped into the cenote and ended up imprisoned in Xibalba. That's what started this mess."

"We won't get involved in anything like that, I promise," replied Lola. "We'll just set Bahlam free and say good-bye to him." She carefully refolded the map and put it in her backpack. "Some good has to come of this day."

"Places, people!" Lord Kuy swept in again. "Hero Twins, listen for your cue. On my signal, you will start dancing."

"Dancing? You mean this is a dance-off? It's not a ballgame?" Max was half relieved that the game was off, and half terrified about dancing in public.

"No, Hunahpu the Halfwit, I mean that you will dance onto the ball court. The Hero Twins danced, and so shall you. It is the respectful way to approach Lord Ah Pukuh and his retinue. The audience expects it."

"Can this day get any worse?" groaned Max.

Lord Kuy raised a winged arm.

"Three, two, one . . . action!"

He pointed at Max and Lola expectantly.

A minion opened the doors to the arena, and a roar went up from the crowd.

An orchestra of wooden trumpets, conch shells, and drums began to play.

Max hung back, not even pretending to be brave.

The security guards pushed him forward.

"It's okay, Hoop!" Lola whispered. "Just do what I do!"

But when she started moving in short rhythmic steps, Max found it impossible to copy her—mainly because she was graceful and lithe and dancing in perfect time to the music. He, on the other hand, jigged around jerkily like a child at a wedding reception, and tried not to meet the eyes of anyone in the audience.

On one side were the Xibalbans, a mass of twisted, jeering faces that gave new meaning to the phrase *an ugly crowd.* They had rotting skin, bones sticking out of wasted sinews, dangling eyeballs, and skulls sprouting little tufts of hair. Yet for all their physical repulsion, they were colorfully dressed in rich arrays of exotic feathers, jaguar pelts, woven fabric, shells, and jade jewelry.

Facing them, on the other side of the arena, the strip miners sat grim and dour in their plaid flannel lumberjack shirts.

Lola had danced her way down to the end of the ball court, where the Five-Headed Jaguar awaited its transfusion of blood. Max hung back, at the end where Ah Pukuh and the Death Lords sat in a courtside box, flanked by a platoon of bodyguards armed with flint-tipped spears. Ah Pukuh had changed into his ceremonial finery. Gone were the suit and the spiky bleached hair. Now he wore a heavily embroidered loincloth, an intricately woven necklet of eyeballs and optic nerves, and a massive headdress of shrunken heads, human bones, and sharp flint blades. The heads and eyeballs jiggled along to the music.

For still it played.

And still Max and Lola danced.

For Max, the worst thing was that his every move was broadcast on the video screens over the center of the court. And he'd run out of moves approximately five seconds after the music started.

After what felt like an eternity of self-conscious twirls and random leaps, he was relieved to see Lord Kuy striding onto the court with a microphone.

Finally, the music stopped and Lord Kuy addressed the audience. "On behalf of His Heinous Highness, Ah Pukuh, and Their Malevolent Majesties, the Death Lords, it is my pleasure to welcome you on this very special occasion. Thank you for joining us as we celebrate Ah Pukuh's forthcoming accession to the throne of Middleworld and the better days that lie ahead. For too long, we have had to sit idly by and watch the erosion of all that we hold dear. Abominations such as kindness"—boos from the audience—"recycling"—more boos—"and charity"—outraged boos and catcalls—"have run rampant in the mortal world. But even as I speak, the seeds of hopelessness have been sown. Soon, soon, the dark days will come again. So put your hands together, ladies and gentlemen, for the malefactor of the moment and the boss of the *bak'tun* . . . let's hear it for Lord Ah Pukuh and his new age of evil, suffering, and naked greed!"

As Ah Pukuh took a bow, the F.A.T.S.O. miners and loggers leapt to their feet and cheered.

Lola looked around in disgust. "The world is in big trouble, Hoop, if this lot are taking over. Even without the power of the Jaguar Stones, they could do a lot of damage."

"Lord 6-Dog says that good always triumphs over evil. Eventually."

"We may not have time for eventually."

Lord Kuy waited for the applause to die down, then signaled for Max and Lola to join him in the center of the ball court. The lights in the arena dimmed, until the three of them stood in a single spotlight. As the owl-man talked, scenes from ancient Maya paintings appeared on the giant video screens.

"Many moons ago, at the start of creation, two upstarts from Middleworld were summoned to Xibalba to play ball against the Death Lords. Their names were Hunahpu and Xbalanke, the Hero Twins. Before the ballgame could begin, the twins were tested in other ways: by deadly trials of darkness, cold, jaguars, bats, knives, and fire. The twins somehow survived . . . and by unfair means went on to win the game. Long have we tasted the bitterness of that defeat. Now, at last, our day of vengeance is here."

The audience went wild. Motioning for them to calm down, Lord Kuy pushed Max and Lola forward. "Tonight the role of the Hero Twins will be played by two more upstarts from Middleworld who have tried—and failed—to outwit the Death Lords. Ladies and gentlemen, representing Hunahpu and Xbalanke, I give you the *New Hero Twins!*"

Blinded by the spotlight, Max and Lola shielded their eyes, and tried to turn away as the audience booed and jeered and showered them with chewed corncobs.

The band started up, the monkeys did cartwheels across the court, and the audience gave Ah Pukuh a standing ovation. In close-up on the giant screen, his fat chins wobbled with pleasure, like the blubber on a sea lion.

"*Let the games begin!*" he roared.

The video screens began running a cartoon sequence of Max and Lola, like the titles to a cheesy game show. "And now," came an announcer's voice, "while our Hero Twins get ready for the ballgame, let's watch some hilarious highlights of their day at the Grand Hotel Xibalba. As you'll see, they had quite a testing time! Let's see how they got on. . . ."

A night-vision shot of Max's head filled the screen. His eyes glowed white in the infrared beam.

"The party started in the Dark House," said the commentator, "with an uninvited guest."

Max seemed to be talking to himself in the empty room. The audience went wild as a cockroach crawled up his chin and tipped itself into his open mouth.

"Next came the Cold House, where hell literally froze over and our VIPs received a frosty reception!"

And there were Max and Lola dodging icicle spears in the giant ice-cream freezer.

"But never fear, a visit to the Jaguar House soon had them hot under the collar."

Max winced as he saw his head crushed in the sawdust under the jaguar's paw.

"In the Bat House, they said 'Fangs for the Memory' to the star of stage and screen Mr. . . Ray Love."

Now it was Lola's turn to cringe, as she and Loverboy filled the screen, he baring his vampire fangs and both of them soaked in blood-colored ketchup. The audience oohed and aahed, impressed by this macabre brush with celebrity.

"When our dynamic duo descended to the casino,"

"Score!" roared the crowd, leaping to their feet.

continued the announcer, "they faced the tests of knives and fire."

The audience roared with laughter to see Max's jeans being sliced by holographic knives and Lola holding her burning ponytail in horror.

"So how was *your* day?" asked the announcer, a question that was evidently his catchphrase. "And now lords and ladies, friends and fiends, give a big Xibalba welcome to the *Hero Twins!*"

"Los-ers! Los-ers! Los-ers!" chanted the audience, now whipped up to a frenzy.

All this time, Max and Lola were standing stock-still, like racing cars at a pit stop, while the Death Lords' minions quickly fitted them with padded headbands, padded wristbands, kneepads, and thick padded belts around their waists.

A conch-shell trumpet sounded.

"And playing for Xibalba," announced Lord Kuy, "put your hands together for the all-time champions of the underworld, those down and dirty cheats, One Death and Seven Death!" The crowd went wild as the two Death Lords came running into the arena. Like Max and Lola, they wore thick padding. What flesh they had was covered in red war paint.

Just like that, with another blast from the conch shell and a furious drumroll, it started.

Boom!

The heavy rubber ball hit the court hard and bounced directly toward Max's face. Instinctively, he launched himself to the right to avoid it, shielding his face with his arm. The ball whizzed past, almost grazing his cheek, and landed far behind him.

"Score!" roared the crowd, leaping to their feet.

"You're supposed to return the ball, not run from it," shouted Lola. "Get ready for the next one!"

"I don't want to play!"

"You have to play!"

"We can't win, so what's the point?"

"The last Hero Twins tricked them, and maybe we can, too!"

"So tell me the rules!"

"Two teams—like doubles tennis, but no net and no rackets. Use your hips; no hands, no feet. Got it?"

Max pointed at a stone ring high up on the side wall. "Is that the basket? Because that looks impossible!"

"No, that's just a marker. Think tennis, not basketball. You score if the other side can't return, or if they hit out—"

Her voice was drowned out by the trumpet and drums. The crowd picked up the rhythm, and the frenzied stamping of their feet echoed through the ball court.

Lola gave Max a thumbs-up sign and bounced on her toes, ready for action.

A skeleton in a crimson tunic, evidently the referee, stepped onto the court, holding the next ball. At a signal from Lord Kuy, he lobbed the ball toward them.

Lola sprang forward into the path of the ball.

Just before impact, she turned at her waist and hit the ball square and hard with her right hip. The ball shot low and deep into the opposite side.

One Death planted one arm on the ground, pivoting

his body and swinging his hip under the ball. He connected with a satisfying thud, and the ball flew in a high arc directly toward Max.

"Go for it!" shouted Lola.

Max paused to gauge the trajectory, then jumped up, thrusting his hip toward the ball. He misjudged the angle and it smashed him in the chest, hard as a cannonball. Winded, he flew backward and hit the ground flat on his back like a deflated balloon.

"Score!" yelled the crowd.

The boos of the crowd were deafening. Tamales, fruit, and corncobs rained down on Max as he lay there. Ah Pukuh, the Death Lords, and the shrunken heads were wiping away tears of laughter.

Lola helped Max to his feet. He winced as a hard-shell taco hit him between the shoulder blades. "Come on, Hoop! You're a gamer; can't you pretend this is a video game?"

"No," he said. A mango bounced off his head. "We're doomed."

Lola's optimistic façade drooped. "I hate losing to these bullies."

The referee walked on court with a new ball.

"Wait!" Max gripped Lola's arm. "Maybe video games are the answer!"

Lola brightened up. "Tell me!"

"What we need are . . . special powers!"

Lola's shoulders slumped again in disappointment. "Oh. I thought for a moment that you'd actually had an idea—"

Max was running down the court, waving his arms. "Time out! Time out!"

The crowd reacted angrily to this delay, and the volley of missiles increased. Dodging a bunch of bananas and skirting the skeleton referee, Max didn't stop until he was standing in front of Ah Pukuh's throne.

The god of violent and unnatural death was drinking a gourd of foaming hot chocolate. He paused, and held up a bloated hand to bring the crowd to silence. "Have you come to surrender?"

Max shook his head.

"No? I am sorry to hear that. Because this is the dullest ballgame I have ever watched. I, for one, would like to stop right now, and move on to the main event."

"What's the main event?" asked Max.

"Your slow and painful death," replied Ah Pukuh.

The crowd erupted in cheers.

"I think you're going to like my idea," said Max. "Have you ever played a video game?"

A dreamy look came into Ah Pukuh's eyes. "Yes, in Spain, on the tour bus with the band."

"Remember how in games you unlock special powers to use against opponents?"

Ah Pukuh nodded enthusiastically. "My character had X-ray vision!" The shrunken heads chattered excitedly at this thought. "I was unbeatable!"

"So," continued Max, "let's give the crowd what they want! A ballgame of mythical proportions. We're playing by Xibalba rules now, so anything is possible. Why play against a couple of kids when you can play against great ballplayers like the real Hero Twins! Allow us to unlock special powers, and we'll give you a game to remember!"

A murmur of excitement went around the crowd.

Ah Pukuh passed his empty drinking gourd to an attendant. Hot chocolate dripped down his jowls. With his powdery white skin, stained by rivers of chocolate the color of old blood, he looked like a zombie at a feast. He wiped his mouth with the back of his hand and let loose a loud volley of gas that echoed through the ball court.

The entire audience covered their noses.

Max clamped his hand over his face and tried not to retch.

Ah Pukuh summoned Lord Kuy and the skeleton referee. "Shall we allow this?" he asked them.

The referee looked worried. "Might they not outplay our champions, One Death and Seven Death?"

"Impossible, it is pure theater," said Lord Kuy. "There is no chance of the Hero Twins winning. The game is fixed. But this twist would vastly increase gambling revenues."

"More beans in the coffer, eh?" Ah Pukuh drooled at the prospect of augmenting his fortune of cocoa beans.

The crowd were roaring and chanting now with enthusiasm for the idea.

Lola stood by Max. "Good thinking, Hoop."

"At least it will buy us more time," he whispered.

Ah Pukuh stood up to address the crowd. "Citizens of Xibalba, the decision is yours. Should we kill these wretches now? Or should we transform them into worthy opponents? Stand up to vote for sacrifice. Stay seated if you want the game to continue."

No one moved.

"Very well," said Ah Pukuh. "We start where we left off: the score is two–nil to Xibalba."

"That's not fair—," began Max.

"Deal!" said Lola.

It was straight out of a video game. Max watched himself on the video screen as his body transformed from an ordinary kid into a brawny athlete.

Lola giggled. "Wow! You're ripped! I'll have to stop calling you Hoop—no one could say you look like a matchstick now!"

"What about you? You look like Wonder Woman!"

Lola stared—now with hawklike super vision and enhanced spatial awareness—at her bodybuilder muscles. "This is crazy. We're the Superhero Twins!"

"We're like avatars. We have no feelings, we can't get hurt . . . nothing is impossible. Maybe we can even win this game!"

While Max and Lola adjusted to their physical transformations, minions swept up the trash that had rained onto the court, and the crowd worked themselves into a frenzy of gambling. The Death Lords were giving odds and placing bets on every aspect of the match.

"One thousand cocoa beans on the home team to win!"

"Two thousand beans on a dismemberment!"

"Five thousand beans on One Death to score a hat trick!"

Max couldn't help noticing that no one was betting on a victory for the Hero Twins.

When play resumed, excitement was at fever pitch.

Ah Pukuh gave the signal.

Once again the conch-shell trumpet sounded, the drummers beat on their drums, and the crowd took up the rhythm with their feet. The referee lifted a new ball above his head and lobbed it into play.

They were off.

Max and Lola were all over the court, leaping, diving, pivoting their new swivelmatic hips.

The heavy ball shot back and forth across the court in intense volleys.

Each point was fought over long and hard.

Fortunes in cocoa beans changed hands with every twist and turn of the game. By match point, the teams had been playing solidly for two hours, with neither side able to gain a convincing lead.

Now with one last play, it was winner take all.

"We can do this," said Max, still admiring his new muscles.

"Stay focused!" yelled Lola. "The Death Lords are plotting something. Did you see that last cheat of theirs?"

The drums pounded, the crowd chanted, and the ball was thrown into play on the home side.

Seven Death took a flying leap and sent it spinning toward Max.

"I've got this one," he called to Lola.

He aligned himself up for the smash of his life, a speed-of-sound midarc slam from his steel-hard hip that no one, not even a Death Lord, would be able to return.

Piece of cake.

He bounced into the air on superbendy knees.

The ball came thundering toward him.

And then it all went wrong.

"Nooooooo," he screamed.

With a split second to go, he felt his special powers draining away until he was just an ordinary kid again—a kid suspended directly in the path of a rubber ball the size and weight of a cast-iron watermelon.

The impact sent spasms of pain through his body.

"I've got it!" Lola sprang halfway across the court with catlike agility and tried to take the shot before it hit the floor. She might have succeeded if the ball hadn't changed course to avoid her and zoomed around in a wide arc.

Max, Lola, and the ball landed with three ignominious thumps.

As Max lay sprawled on the floor, wretched and in pain, the ball rolled along until it was in front of his eyes. Then it split open, like a hatching egg, to reveal its core. Underneath all the layers of rubber was a decomposing severed head.

It winked at him. "Game over," said its mouth.

Victory to the Lords of Death.

The crowd went wild as One Death and Seven Death pumped the air and strutted round the ball court.

A squad of security guards marched over, and pulled Max and Lola roughly to their feet, binding their hands behind their backs.

"*Sac-ri-fice! Sac-ri-fice! Sac-ri-fice!*" chanted the crowd.

Chapter Twenty
THE TAPIR'S REVENGE

A h Pukuh heaved himself to his feet and held out his arms to the crowd. They clapped and cheered. The F.A.T.S.O. contingent threw their caps into the air, while the Xibalba side threw body parts. The guards dragged Max and Lola over to Ah Pukuh and prodded them with spears to make them kneel.

"Speech time," said Lord Kuy to Ah Pukuh, passing him a folded bark-paper scroll.

The cameras zoomed in as Ah Pukuh unfolded the paper, cleared his throat, and addressed the crowd. "Citizens of Xibalba and esteemed guests, at this moment, history begins again! For over twelve *baktuns* in the Maya calendar and five thousand years by the reckoning of Middleworld, we have waited for this glorious day. What better way to mark the beginning of my dominion over Middleworld than by sacrificing these meddling mortals?"

The crowd roared their approval.

"Prepare the victims," commanded Ah Pukuh, summoning the jaguar priest to daub them with blue body paint.

"Here we go again," muttered Lola. "Sacrificial sapphire, my least-favorite color."

The guards forced them to lie down, flat on their backs, their wrists and ankles bound with leather ropes to iron rings embedded in the end zone floor.

"Remember this day, citizens of Xibalba! Today we sacrifice the Hero Twins! Not with the usual obsidian blade, which is disappointingly painless in its speed, but with a weapon far more terrible. In homage to the creative geniuses of ancient Rome, the Hero Twins will be mauled and eaten by wild animals."

The atmosphere in the arena was electric as everyone waited for more details of the gruesome spectacle to come. (Except for the terrified poncho family, who had their hands over their ears.)

"First to the feast will be a noble cat," continued Ah Pukuh, "the king of the jungle."

Max's guts unclenched. Bahlam was the only cat in the menagerie and if he was to be their nemesis, Max was fairly sure he would refuse to eat them. Thanks to Lola's bonding with the jaguar, they were safe. He almost smiled to imagine Ah Pukuh's reaction.

"Even as I speak," continued Ah Pukuh,

"we are taking delivery of a ravenously hungry African lion. *Let loose the beast!*"

Max's insides knotted themselves into a ball, and rolled into the farthest corner of his stomach to hide.

"Fanfare!" commanded Ah Pukuh.

There was a blast of conch shells and a fierce beating of drums, and the floor shook beneath their heads. Max turned enough to see a trapdoor opening at the opposite end of the ball court. He could hear the gears grinding as a platform juddered upward through the floor, conveying the hungry lion to its dinner date.

He closed his eyes.

He heard the audience gasp.

He heard a spine-chilling roar followed by a squealing of brakes.

He knew these sounds.

He opened his eyes.

Whatever nightmare creature the audience was expecting to rise up out of the trapdoor, it certainly was not a howler monkey riding on a tapir.

"Lord 6-Dog!" cried Lola.

For it was he—mounted on the hotel tapir and attempting to make it rear up on its hind legs, like a simian Lone Ranger on a stunted hippo.

With Lord 6-Dog urging him on, the tapir leapt off the platform and galloped down the court toward Ah Pukuh. The death god's face was a mask of terror but, wedged as his enormous bulk was in his chair, he had no time to get out of the firing line as the tapir turned around, aimed its hindquarters with care, and let fly a super soaker with all the volume and pressure of a fire hose.

The platform under the trapdoor had made another trip and was now rising with a new cargo. This time, Bahlam the jaguar sprang out, as well a horde of monkeys.

Drenched to the skin and smelling even worse than usual, the god of violent and unnatural death rose in rage. "Catch them!" he bellowed, but his voice was lost in the chaos as the hall was rocked with explosions. The shock wave from the blasts caused him to lose his balance and, when Ah Pukuh fell, his blubbery mass took down the Demons of Jaundice, Pus, and Filth with him.

What followed was total mayhem.

The guards who'd been watching Max and Lola leapt forward to tackle the interlopers. As his tapir charged toward them, Lord 6-Dog pulled a stick of dynamite out of a saddlebag lashed to his trusty mount's back.

He jabbed at the timer, and threw the dynamite.

Kaboom!

The bad guys were falling like flies.

On one side of the court, Bahlam was terrorizing the security guards, while on the other side, the monkeys lobbed missiles at the Death Lords as fast as automatic artillery launchers.

Another load through the trapdoor had disgorged a cargo of snakes.

Immediately, Lord Kuy was attacked by a huge boa constrictor with a taste for owl, while the smaller snakes got to work on the F.A.T.S.O. delegation.

The Xibalba crowd roared and stomped their feet, thinking this was a new twist to the evening's entertainment.

Although they were still tied to the floor, Max and Lola began to take hope.

While a couple of Death Lords heaved the battered Ah Pukuh back onto his feet, he issued a steady stream of orders: "Protect the Jaguar Stones! Shoot the howler! Kill the Hero Twins!"

Hearing this last command, the jaguar priest ran toward Max and Lola, brandishing a razor-sharp obsidian knife. He knelt down at Lola's side and raised the blade.

Max screamed.

"Keep screaming," said the priest. "That is good."

"Eusebio!" cried Lola. "What are you doing here?"

"Explanations later," he said, sawing through the ropes. "Keep screaming, so no one notices that I am setting you free. We need to get out of here."

Max lay there, screaming obediently and looking around to take stock of the situation. Across the arena stood Ah Pukuh, surrounded by his bodyguards. His face was purple with rage. He was foaming at the mouth and shrieking an incoherent mixture of commands, curses, and animal howls. The shrunken heads were wailing like a Greek chorus, and the eyeballs in his necklace were popping like corks under pressure.

Lord 6-Dog was standing on the back of his tapir, fending off guards and hurling dynamite. Explosions were going off all around the arena. A platoon of spider monkeys had scampered up the cables to the central video pod and were disconnecting all the cameras.

Half the crowd—the half that realized what was happening—was on its feet screaming and panicking. The other half, who thought everything was scripted, was on its feet hooting and cheering.

It was pandemonium.

"Let's go!" yelled Eusebio.

Lola looked longingly at the Five-Headed Jaguar, still surrounded by a ring of security guards.

"Thou hast thirty seconds to effect thine exit, and that's an order!" Lord 6-Dog shouted to her as he rode by. He charged across the court, lighting another stick of dynamite to intercept reinforcements of security guards entering from the other end.

Max pulled her away and, dodging skeletal arms and flying missiles, Eusebio steered them both back to the trapdoor. The platform was now resting five feet below the level of the ball court, and it was the same distance again down to the floor of the staging area underneath.

At Eusebio's whistle, the spider monkeys came running, and sprang through the trapdoor. The boatman whistled again, and the sleek form of Bahlam followed noiselessly. Lola and Eusebio jumped down.

"Come on, Hoop!" called Lola.

Standing on the platform, the top of his head just sticking out above floor level, Max took a last look around the arena.

"Lord 6-Dog!" he called.

"Go, young lord! Look after Ix Sak Lol!"

Brandishing a fistful of dynamite in each hand, Lord 6-Dog was attempting to hold back the guard while the rest of them made their getaway.

It reminded Max of that terrible night in Spain when the brave monkey-king had taken a bullet trying to protect him. On that occasion, Max had been forced to abandon his lifeless monkey body in the gutter.

He ran to Lord 6-Dog's side. "Lola's fine!" he yelled. "She's with Eusebio. I'm not leaving you!"

Left: The eyeballs on his necklace were popping like corks under pressure.

"But young lord—"

"I'm not leaving you," repeated Max.

Lord 6-Dog nodded. "Then let us make mayhem!"

Max helped Lord 6-Dog light the explosives and hurl them into every corner. His last thought before fireworks, smoke, and chaos rocked the room was that the sizzling dynamite he held in his hand was imprinted with the F.A.T.S.O. logo. He would have raised his eyebrow at the irony if he hadn't been blown off his feet.

A series of explosions took out the supports of the central video installation, and the entire unit plummeted to the floor. The enormous pod of lights, speakers, and scaffolding was next to come crashing down.

Max was caught in a tangle of electrical cables, and the more he struggled, the more entangled he became. He was a sitting duck.

A thick stingray spine embedded itself in the wood floor beside him. He looked to see who had aimed it and met the eyes of Koo from the beauty salon. She waved to him from her front-row seat. "Cut yourself free," she called, "and fly on the wings of love."

In the event, he flew on the wings of a tapir.

Just as he'd sliced through the cable, Lord 6-Dog's strong tail had wrapped around him and pulled him out of the chaos and onto the tapir's back. Then they were racing through a shower of debris and throwing themselves, somehow, through the trapdoor.

As soon as they landed in the staging area, Eusebio sent the platform jerkily sparking and fizzing back to ground level.

"Follow me," he said, and led them to a huge freight elevator, which was being held for them by the sloth man.

Besides him and his sloth, it was filled with snorting mammals, squeaking reptiles, and squawking birds. Plus Lola and Bahlam.

Eusebio slid the steel mesh door closed and pressed the up button.

They held their breath, unsure if it would work.

They let out a collective breath when the elevator lurched into motion.

"I must warn you," said Eusebio, "that we are about to make our daring escape in the slowest elevator known to humankind."

"At least it's moving," said Lola, "and Bahlam is with us." She knelt down by the jaguar and stroked his pelt.

Max leaned against the wall to take stock. "Thank you, Lord 6-Dog," he said. "You saved my life."

"Back at thee," said the king. "Tonight thou didst act like a brave Maya warrior."

Max could feel himself blushing. It was probably the best compliment he had ever been paid. "Well, you know, I owed you one, after that night in Spain," he mumbled.

But Lord 6-Dog wasn't listening. He was gazing with admiration at the tapir. "Of course, it is my steadfast steed that we should both be thanking."

The tapir gave a snuffle, and raised its tail slightly. Everyone panicked and tried to get out of the line of fire, but it was a false alarm.

"I think he's just happy," said Lola.

"It's a she," Lord 6-Dog corrected her.

Lola smiled. "How did you two meet, anyway?"

"When I arrived at this place, Eusebio was unloading boom sticks from a conveyance—"

"Wait; boom sticks?" queried Lola.

255

"It's what he calls the dynamite," explained Max.

Lord 6-Dog continued. "My host monkey, Chulo, recognized Eusebio and gave me the sense I could trust him. So I went over and introduced myself."

"Way to go, Chulo!" cried Lola and Max, waving to Lord 6-Dog's inner monkey.

Eusebio laughed. "I have to admit that I was surprised to see Chulo talking, but I had only to look into his eyes for Lord 6-Dog to convince me of his true identity." He bowed in Lord 6-Dog's direction. "Middleworld is honored to have a new champion."

Lord 6-Dog returned the bow with a flourish. "The honor is mine."

"So that's when the two of you worked out how to sabotage the ballgame?" asked Max.

"Exactly, young lord. My new friend Eusebio briefed me on the situation and showed me the boom sticks."

"So where did the boom sticks, I mean dynamite, come from?" asked Lola.

"Thank F.A.T.S.O.," said Eusebio. "I ordered it for their blast-fishing trip."

"Ha! So we used their weapons of mass destruction against them," said Lola.

"It is a most exciting innovation," enthused Lord 6-Dog. "With one case of boom sticks, I could have rewritten Maya history."

"You rewrote our history tonight," said Max. "There's no way we could have got out of there alive."

"Here." Eusebio passed Max a cloth. "Clean off your sacrificial paint."

Max ripped the cloth and passed half to Lola. "Are you going to say it?"

She wiped her face. "Say what?"

"*I told you so.* You were right about the hotel and the Death Lords and everything."

"But I was wrong about Eusebio."

Hearing his name, the boatman smiled at her across the tapir. "It sounds like we are finally reaching ground level. I hope no ghouls are waiting for us."

The elevator screeched, juddered, and jerked to a halt.

Eusebio cautiously slid open the steel mesh door.

"Hold it right there!" shouted a burly security guard.

A man stepped out of the shadows and made a little tweeting sound. Max recognized him as the hotel photographer who'd carried a parrot. His call was like a siren song to the captive birds in the elevator who—glimpsing the moonlight and sensing forest—flocked out in a flurry of beaks, wings, and claws, and attacked the guard who stood between them and their freedom. He took off running.

"There's our getaway vehicle." Eusebio pointed to a beat-up panel truck.

The third photographer, the one with the snake, was waiting by the truck, impatiently opening doors and urging them to get inside.

"Where's your snake?" Max asked him.

"I set him free, where he could make the most trouble," answered the photographer.

They heard screams coming from inside the hotel.

"Let's load up," called Lola.

"You can't put a jaguar in with a tapir," Eusebio pointed out. "That's like trusting Max Murphy to sit next to a pizza and not eat it."

"Bahlam understands the situation," said Lola. "He is my

257

animal companion and I trust him with my life. But it's your choice. We can load him in the back with the tapir, or he can sit up front with us."

"In the back," said Eusebio without hesitation.

"What happened to the African lion that was going to eat us?" asked Max.

"I intercepted the delivery and refused to sign for it," said Eusebio. "It's on its way back to the circus."

"Poor thing," began Lola. "Couldn't we—?"

"No! Don't even think about it!" said Max. "Can we just save this lot first?"

When the animals had staked out their corners in the truck, and Max and Lola had wiped off the last of the blue paint, Eusebio started the engine.

"*Ko'ox!* Let's go!" said Lola, She opened the cab door. "Hey! Look what I found!" She tossed an unused stick of dynamite to Lord 6-Dog. "Another boom stick!"

The monkey-king grabbed it, and Max ran with him back to the elevator. He ignited the dynamite, waited for the doors to open, pressed nine, and tossed in the explosive.

Max pulled the door shut, and, with a whine of electric motors, the elevator began to descend.

Max and Lord 6-Dog ran for the truck. Eusebio had the motor running and took off the second they leapt into the cab. It was a tight fit with Eusebio at the wheel and Lola, Max, and Lord 6-Dog all squeezed into the passenger seat.

The parking lot was scattered with branches and detritus from the hurricane, but the wind seemed to have died down. Now only the parking lot barrier lay between them and freedom. "It takes exact change!" yelled Eusebio.

"Ram it! Ram it!" chanted Max and Lola.

But the barrier soared up airily as they approached, and the poncho family, who were crammed into the booth, waved good-bye and flashed a thumbs-up. The normally moribund poncho children were whooping with excitement.

As the truck turned out of the parking lot and onto the road, Max heard the muffled boom of an explosion. "Nobody will be using that elevator for a while," he said with satisfaction.

"It will delay them," warned Lord 6-Dog, "but it will not stop them. Ah Pukuh will not rest until he has tracked us down."

From the outskirts of Limón they headed north on a highway that had recently been built to take tourist buses to Ixchel. At this late hour, there was little traffic, but their progress was slowed by fallen trees and other debris from the hurricane.

Fortunately, Eusebio was an expert driver and he always found a way through. The old truck was less resourceful and struggled every time they climbed a hill.

At first no one talked.

They were just enjoying the sensation of being out and being alive.

When they'd put some distance between themselves and the Grand Hotel Xibalba, Lola broke the silence. "I hope Bahlam's okay back there. I don't hear any fighting."

"That poor tapir must be scared to death," said Max.

"She has her secret weapon, don't forget," said Lola. "It was pretty effective against the Death Lords."

"It's going to take more than tapir pee to save the world from Ah Pukuh," Max pointed out. "He has all five Jaguar Stones."

"On that subject," said Eusebio, "I have good news. Here,

Ix Sak Lol, please take the wheel a moment." Lola grabbed the steering wheel and kept the creaking truck on the road, while Eusebio felt around on the floor of the truck. He pulled up Lola's backpack.

Taking the wheel again with one hand, he passed it to her. "You left this in the green room."

"Thank you, but—" She frowned at the unexpected weight of the bag. "What's in here?"

"Is it food?" asked Max hopefully.

Lola opened the bag wide to reveal a deerskin cloth. Then she folded back the cloth to reveal a Jaguar Stone of white alabaster.

Max and Lola cheered and hollered and stamped their feet.

"I can't believe my eyes!" cried Lola. "I really thought we'd lost it this time! I was dreading telling Hermanjilio! You've saved my life!"

"And the lives of the seven billion inhabitants of planet Earth," added Max.

Lola carefully wrapped up the stone. "It's like magic, Eusebio! How did you get it away from Ah Pukuh?"

Eusebio's eyes were twinkling. "I made sure there was plenty of smoke. And of course, I only pretended to switch the stones."

"But the Five Headed Jaguar?"

"Ah Pukuh's White Jaguar head is still a carved gourd." Eusebio chuckled. "Unless the tapir ate it."

Chapter Twenty-one
ACROSS THE ABYSS

So once again, the White Jaguar had been spirited away from under Ah Pukuh's nose. Once again, just when he thought he'd amassed all five Jaguar Stones, his fiendish plans had been thwarted by a couple of kids and a talking monkey.

As they put more and more miles between themselves and the hotel at Limón, Max and Lola considered this fact and couldn't help smiling. But when they allowed themselves to picture their last glimpse of Ah Pukuh, his normally ashen face puce with rage as his shiny new ball court collapsed around him, their smiles gave way to nausea.

They knew he'd be out for vengeance.

And they knew it wouldn't be pretty.

"We're toast," groaned Max.

"I've made up my mind," said Lola firmly. "I'm not going to think about it."

"Thou canst not ignore the reality of thy situation," Lord 6-Dog chided her. "The White Jaguar has slipped from Ah

Pukuh's grasp yet again, and his fury will be redoubled. This time, he will take the ultimate recourse."

"Which is . . . ?" asked Max nervously.

"He will awaken the Undead Army in its merciless entirety."

"We beat Skunk Pig," said Lola with bravado. "Who says we can't beat the rest of them?"

"I do," replied Lord 6-Dog.

"Thanks for the vote of confidence," muttered Max sarcastically.

"I will not give thee false hope. The warriors in the Undead Army are the most terrible fighting force in the history of Middleworld. Once awakened, they must battle to the death. And since they cannot die . . ."

His words trailed off and Lola finished his thought for him: "It is always their opponents' death."

"You mean we're going to have a pack of moldering corpses on our heels for the rest of our lives?" Max groaned. "It will be like living in our own private, never-ending zombie movie."

"About that, Hoop. Do the good guys usually win in zombie movies?"

Max grimaced. "They usually become zombies themselves."

"Great." Lola sounded depressed.

"Forget I said that. I'm sure there are lots of zombie movies where the humans win."

"Name one."

"Um . . . *Zombie Wipeout*."

"You just made that up, didn't you?"

Max nodded sheepishly.

Lola rolled her eyes. "I wish we could end it, once and for

all. We're good at winning battles, but I'm not sure we can win the war."

"It is the battles that decide the war," said Lord 6-Dog. "We must keep fighting."

"Count me in!" exclaimed Eusebio, who'd been listening to their conversation as he drove. "I am proud to fight by your side, Lord 6-Dog. But I never thought I would look to a howler monkey to save the world."

They drove through the night, heading for Bahlam's old hunting grounds near the White Pyramid of Ixchel. It was a new road, still unpaved, and fallen trees from the hurricane were everywhere. Often they had to stop and clear the road.

It was slow going for the old truck.

The sun was rising by the time they entered the high country around the ancient city of Ixchel. Struggling up a particularly steep hill, the vehicle started to lose power. Eusebio spoke to it in Mayan, urging it along. In reply, the engine whined and clanked, and white smoke poured out from under the hood. When even Eusebio's sheer force of will was not enough to propel it along, the truck shuddered to a complete stop.

Everyone else had been dozing, but now the absence of engine noise woke them up.

They piled out into the rainforest dawn and looked around.

They were on a lonely stretch of narrow road bounded by walls of foliage and shaded by low-hanging branches. Insects swarmed around them, and within seconds Max was scratching like a dog with fleas.

Eusebio lifted the hood to inspect the engine. "It does not look good."

Lord 6-Dog peered over his shoulder at the mass of wires, tubes, belts, plugs, valves, and greasy cylinder heads. "Dost thou have the sorcery to deal with it?"

"I have a tool kit," replied Eusebio, "but it will take time. We must free the animals, before it gets too hot."

Half dreading what kind of carnage they might find in there, they opened the back of the truck and let down the ramp.

The jaguar lay sprawled asleep, seemingly without a care in the world.

The tapir was squashed against the truck wall, her eyes two tiny orbs of terror, trying to stay as far away as possible from her most feared jungle predator. The spider monkeys were under and behind the tapir, using her barrel-like body as a shield.

She gave a little whistle and waved her snout at Lord 6-Dog.

"Ah, my trusty steed," he said, patting her neck. "I hope our paths will cross again."

The tapir brushed his monkey cheek with her snout.

"Go now, find thy family."

She ambled down the ramp and disappeared into the rainforest.

The monkeys chattered in terror, unsure of what to do next.

"Go!" Lola called to them, waving her arms. "You're free! Go now!"

But having been mistreated by their handlers at the hotel for so long, they were too scared to move.

Lord 6-Dog took a deep breath, and allowed his massive howler monkey voice box to produce an earth-shattering roar that echoed in the valleys all around. Within two seconds, the truck was clear of monkeys. They ran down the ramp, flew up the nearest trees, and proceeded to pelt Lord 6-Dog with fruit, twigs, and, in one case, a small lizard.

Back in the truck, the jaguar woke up.

He surveyed his freedom and yawned lazily.

"Come, Bahlam," called Lola. "We are close to Ixchel. I am sure you can find your home from here."

As if he understood her, the jaguar got to his feet and padded out of the truck. But instead of vanishing into the forest, he rubbed against her legs like a gigantic house cat.

"You have to go," said Lola. "Go back to Ixchel and find your family."

The jaguar sat down in front of her. His green eyes held her gaze.

The sound of a far-distant conch shell floated from the south.

"And so it begins," said Lord 6-Dog. "The Undead Army is massing."

Max started darting about in a panic. "What should we do? Where should we hide?"

"Calm down, young lord. Let us assess the situation."

"The situation is that we're about to be mown down by the Undead Army. We can't just stand here waiting to die—"

"Look, Hoop!" interrupted Lola. "Why is Bahlam staring at me like that? He's trying to tell us something. I think he wants us to go home to Ixchel with him!"

The jaguar stood up and growled softly.

"He can look after himself," said Max. "We have our own skins to save."

"But Bahlam is my animal guide," Lola continued. "He *is*

trying to save me." She pulled open her backpack and rooted inside. "Let me look at that map."

"I trust this creature," said Lord 6-Dog. "He has a noble soul."

"I don't want to go to Ixchel," argued Max. "That's where all the trouble started."

"It is a good idea," Eusebio told him. "Out here in the jungle, we are sitting ducks. In a few hours' time there will be tourists at Ixchel. You can get a ride with them."

"Are you coming with us?" asked Max.

"No, I will stay with the truck."

"But the Undead Army—"

"It is not me they seek." Eusebio pulled a machete from behind the seat of the truck. "Here, take this to . . . to clear your path."

"But Ixchel is still miles away," complained Max, "on the other side of that mountain. Can't we wait for you to fix the truck?"

"Too risky." Eusebio was adamant. "What if I cannot fix it? Better to start walking. Go now."

"Look!" Lola jabbed a finger at the map. "The road must wind around the mountain, but the map shows a trail that cuts straight through the jungle."

She held it low to show Lord 6-Dog.

"Leave it to me," he said, leaping into the nearest tree. "I will find it."

"This is good news," said Eusebio. "You will get there faster on the trail, for sure."

"I see it!" called Lord 6-Dog from farther up the road. "I have found the trail! It starts at this ceiba tree."

"Good-bye then." Lola hugged Eusebio. "I hate to leave you."

"You forget that I still have my camouflage," he joked, holding out an arm to show her the faded jaguar spots from his disguise as the jaguar priest.

Lola took a deep breath. "Okay, Hoop, let's go."

"Can I just say that I don't like this plan one bit?"

"Objection noted," replied Lola. "But it's all we've got. Just remember the drill. Look where you're walking, watch out for snakes, and don't touch anything, especially tree trunks. Most of them are covered in spikes, or poison, or biting ants."

"I know all that. Don't treat me like an idiot."

Max instantly tripped over a tree root and narrowly missed cutting off his own leg with the machete.

With Lola carrying the machete, Bahlam guiding them on the ground, and Lord 6-Dog scouting through the trees, they soon found themselves deep in the forest.

"Notice how quiet it is?" whispered Lola.

"Yeah," replied Max. "I don't like it. I feel like I'm being watched."

Lola laughed. "You are being watched. That's the Bahlam effect. When a jaguar walks by, the forest goes silent. All the other creatures are frozen with fear."

"What I don't understand," said Max, "is why they sent the road to Ixchel all around the mountain, when they could have just sent it through here?"

"It must be protected land. You often get wildlife reserves around Maya sites."

But that, as it turned out, wasn't the reason at all.

The chasm, when they came to it, was two hundred feet deep and fifty feet across, a gaping gash in the jungle floor that cut across their path and dropped straight down to a sluggish, rock-strewn stream. In the distance, on the other side, they could see the pyramid of Ixchel rising above the rainforest canopy.

"We were so close!" groaned Lola in frustration.

"It might have been helpful," said Max, "if they had marked this on the map."

Lord 6-Dog peered into the gorge. "This was not here in my day."

"So we know it happened in the last twelve hundred years then," said Max sarcastically.

Lord 6-Dog ignored him. "An earthquake," he opined.

"We'll have to go back to the road," said Max.

The jaguar had been pacing around impatiently. Now he turned and roared at them, his tongue bright pink and his teeth creamy yellow against his spotted fur.

Max backed away. "He looks hungry."

"If he didn't eat the tapir, he's not going to eat us." Lola crouched down. "What's wrong, Bahlam? Have you seen something?"

The jaguar made a soft, throaty growl, then disappeared into the undergrowth.

"Maybe he was saying good-bye," said Lola, talking to herself as much as to the others. "It had to happen, sooner or later. He's a wild animal, after all."

She shaded her eyes with her hands and pretended

to be interested in the view of the pyramid.

"He's back," said Max.

And sure enough, the jaguar's head was peering through the bushes. He roared at them and licked his lips.

"I think," said Lola, with a big smile, "that he wants us to follow him again."

The jaguar led them along the edge of the cliff for about half a mile.

And then they saw what he wanted to show them.

A tree trunk had fallen in a storm and formed a natural bridge: a naturally narrow, slimy, potentially rotten bridge, with no guardrail or posted weight limit, across what now looked like a bottomless abyss. It had fallen toward them, branches on their side, massive roots on the other bank. A colony of vultures perched hopefully midway, encouraging them with hungry eyes to try and cross.

"Seriously?" said Max.

The jaguar put one paw on the tree trunk, and the vultures took flight. Bahlam padded easily to the other side. When Max and Lola didn't follow, he came back across and roared at them.

"Here goes nothing," said Lola, handing the machete to Lord 6-Dog.

A vulture hovered above her, waiting for breakfast.

Max watched in horror as she edged out on her stomach, her backpack strapped tightly to her back, crawling along like a snake. It took an age, but she made it.

"Come on, Hoop! Your turn!"

"I can't do it," said Max. "You guys go ahead; I'll go back to Eusebio. We'll meet you at the White Pyramid."

"No, young lord," said Lord 6-Dog, "we stay together. The Undead Army is on our trail. To separate now would be suicide."

Max had watched enough horror movies to see the sense in his argument. But the bridge looked like suicide, too.

"I will go ahead of thee," offered Lord 6-Dog. "If thou hast need of it, hold my tail. Look straight ahead. Do not look down." The distinctive blast of the conch shell echoed over the forest, much nearer now. "There is no time for hesitation, young lord. The enemy is at hand."

Max swallowed.

Lola had done it. He could do it.

"Art thou ready?"

Max nodded.

The surface of the tree was wet and slimy and rotten in patches. The slipperiness made it harder to hold on to, but easier to slide his body over—that is, if he could ignore the slugs and larvae that were living—and pulsating—in the rotten wood. As he pulled himself across, the log groaned ominously under his weight, but he kept going. Inch by inch, he focused on the black fur of the howler monkey in front of him, the hard little pads of his feet, the way he waved the machete like a buccaneer, the way his tail swished around for balance.

"Nearly there, young lord," called Lord 6-Dog.

In reality, Max guessed, they were about halfway.

A column of ants marched toward him, their antennae

waving in excitement. He tensed. He'd been crossing a log bridge in the jungle once before when ants had bitten him and made him fall off. That time he'd landed in a few inches of muddy water; this time, he would plummet to certain death.

Lord 6-Dog sensed his terror. "It is just a patrol of army ants. Pay them no heed," he coaxed.

"*Army* ants! Dad said they can dissolve a wild pig in two hours, snout to tail."

"The Undead Army works faster than that," Lord 6-Dog reminded him, trying to squash as many ants as he could. "Move, young lord. *Move!*"

Max edged forward. He could feel ants crawling under his shirt. He was sure he could feel his skin dissolving.

Slowly, slowly, he reached behind him to brush off the ants.

And *crack!* The tree trunk underneath him splintered, bending down in the middle.

Max screamed as the center of the trunk dropped down several feet. He found himself at the midpoint of an increasingly U-shaped tree trunk. It was still weighted on the bank by its massive buttress roots but in a quick, desperate glance back, he saw that there was very little of the trunk now resting on the other side.

It was only a matter of time before this log, the one thing between Max Murphy and certain death, split in two.

The vultures swooped lower, waiting.

Out of the corner of his eye, Max could see the rocky riverbed, far below.

Far, far below.

Lord 6-Dog came back to him. With creaking and popping noises, the trunk splintered more and dropped lower.

"I can't move," gasped Max, his knuckles white from gripping the tree trunk.

"Grasp my tail," urged Lord 6-Dog, "I will hold thee."

"But what's supporting you? This tree's going to fall."

There were more blasts of the conch shell, louder now, and Max could hear the war cries of the Undead Army. He didn't dare turn round to look, but he sensed that the vanguard was arriving at the other edge.

An arrow hit the tree trunk and fell to the stream.

Lola threw a rope to Lord 6-Dog and, miraculously, he caught it.

"I will tie this around thee. Do not move, young lord." (A spurious command, as Max was frozen with terror.)

An arrow flew over the howler's head.

Having tied the end to a large tree, Lola looped the rope around Bahlam, and the jaguar heaved with all his might.

"Stay low, young lord"—another entirely unnecessary command—"and keep moving. Thou canst not fall."

Max severely doubted the accuracy of the statement, but he clawed his way forward as bravely as he could.

Ducking arrows, Lord 6-Dog bounded back to help Lola.

As Max pulled his legs up behind him, a flurry of arrows embedded themselves in the place where his feet had just been, cracking the tree trunk further and sending large splinters into the gorge.

"Nearly there," urged Lola, holding out her arms.

With one last push, Max grabbed her hand and made it, unharmed, to solid earth. He gave silent thanks that his traveling companion was a girl who always had a rope in her bag and knew how to tie slip-proof knots.

As soon as Max was safe, Lola crawled back out on to the

tree trunk and began chopping at it with the machete.

"Come back," shouted Lord 6-Dog.

"Come back!" screamed Max.

Bahlam growled, evidently saying the same thing in jaguarspeak.

"Just give me a moment," called Lola. "If I can weaken it a little more, it will break when they run across."

"Come back now!" commanded Lord 6-Dog. "That is an order."

Max watched in horror as more and more undead piled onto the bridge, pushing and jostling. A few of them fell into the abyss, but their fellow zombies didn't seem to notice or care. They walked across slowly like tightrope walkers.

Still Lola hacked at the wood.

An arrow pierced her arm.

She let out a cry of pain and dropped the machete. It fell to the river below with a silent splash.

Max could see the fear in her eyes as she slumped down onto the tree trunk.

"She's going to fall," said Max.

But even before the words had left his mouth, Bahlam had padded out and grasped the collar of her shirt in his mouth. Lord 6-Dog went to his aid and, with arrows raining down around them, they half carried, half dragged her back to land and laid her in a thicket for cover.

Bahlam gently licked her wound.

"How are you?" Max asked her. "Does it hurt?"

She bit her lip and nodded.

"We need to keep moving; they are almost upon us," muttered Lord 6-Dog as he dressed her wound with a long thin leaf and a piece of vine.

"Will she be okay?" asked Max.

"This soursop leaf should hold off infection. It will not, alas, hold off the Undead Army."

Bahlam watched with anxious eyes, then turned and bounded back onto the log bridge. He positioned his heavy, muscular body at the weakest point, the spot where Lola had been cutting, and faced the advancing army.

Lola opened her eyes. "Bahlam! No!"

When the jaguar roared, the zombies froze in their tracks.

There was a loud, horrible cracking noise. The trunk split in two under the jaguar, and both parts crashed to the bottom of the chasm, where they lay across the river, as tiny as matchsticks to Max's eyes.

Bahlam and the zombies fell with them.

Stunned and grief-stricken, Lola dragged herself to the edge. "Where is he?"

Max looked over. "I don't see him," he said. "There are so many zombie bones down there, it's like a skeleton scrapyard."

"Ix Sak Lol!"

Max had never seen Lord 6-Dog so angry.

"I'm sorry, I'm sorry, I'm so sorry," cried Lola. "Poor Bahlam. Do you think he could survive that fall? It was all my fault—"

"Aye," said Lord 6-Dog.

"You think he survived?" Lola's eyes were full of hope.

"I think the fault was thine. Thou didst imperil us all. And brave Bahlam has paid the price for thine insubordination."

Lola nodded sadly. "It would have been better for him if I'd left him at the hotel. At least he would still be living."

"Thou canst not call that living." Lord 6-Dog's tone was softer now. "Better that he smelled the forest one last time."

Lola stared mournfully into the chasm. "We should say some words."

"Bahlam wants not thy words. He wants thee to live. That is why he died. Let us not squander his sacrifice. The bridge is destroyed, but the Undead Army marches on."

Max looked across to the other side. For each zombie warrior that had fallen, a hundred more lined the cliff edge, hurling spears and shooting arrows. Some of them had begun climbing down the rock face, intending to cross the hard way.

Max stood up, but Lola remained sitting. She looked drained of life, like a rag doll. "I can't go on," she said. "I feel so tired."

Lord 6-Dog put a hairy hand on her forehead.

"What is it?" asked Max. "What's the matter with her?"

"I fear that the arrow was dipped in the secretions of the poison dart frog."

"A poison arrow?" Max swallowed. "Is there an antidote?"

Lord 6-Dog didn't answer.

"It is what I deserve," whispered Lola.

Suddenly, Lord 6-Dog wheeled around. "Where is thy pack? Thou hast the White Jaguar?"

"Is that all you can think about?" asked Max in disgust. "Lola is wounded, and you're worried about a stupid Jaguar Stone?"

"We can use it to save her," replied Lord 6-Dog.

"We can?" Max looked confused. "It's . . . it's in her backpack. But how . . . ?"

"We must make haste to the White Pyramid and use the stone to summon the goddess Ixchel. Among her many talents, she is a patron healing. She alone can save Ix Sak Lol."

"But she cannot save Bahlam," murmured Lola sadly.

"Rally thyself, Ix Sak Lol. What is done is done. Now thou must honor the memory of Bahlam by fighting the poison in thy veins. Wilt thou do it? For Bahlam?"

Lola staggered to her feet.

"Prithee, look after her," Lord 6-Dog instructed Max. "Keep her walking and talking. Do not let her rest. This trail will take thee straight to Ixchel. I will go ahead to make preparations. Give me the backpack."

They watched as Lord 6-Dog swung away through the trees.

"Can you walk?" asked Max.

She took a step. "Do you hate me? I hate me." Her voice sounded slurry.

"Bahlam died trying to protect you—that's what he was supposed to do, right? That's what he would have wanted."

"But I was stupid. I endangered him. I should have listened to Lord 6-Dog."

"You can't always be perfect."

"I miss him."

Max missed Bahlam, too. He'd been the symbol of everything they were fighting for, the one good thing they had to show for all the horrors of the past two days. Now he was gone. The last jaguar of the Monkey River had given his life for theirs, and Max wasn't sure it was a fair trade-off.

"Let's just get to Ixchel," he said.

"I'm so sorry. I know you don't want to go there. And we'll have to use the Jaguar Stone, after I promised you that we wouldn't use it. I gave you my word."

"It's okay. No big deal. Let's just get there."

"I broke my promise to you and I broke my promise to Bahlam." Tears rolled down her face.

"Just promise you'll keep walking."

Lola trudged along in a wretched silence, her pace getting slower and slower.

Remembering Lord 6-Dog's instruction to keep her talking, Max began to ask her questions. "So remind me, who is Ixchel?"

"She's the moon goddess. She has a companion, a rabbit."

"The moon rabbit? I remember now. My mom told me about him. I used to wave at him from my bedroom window. But what does Ixchel do exactly?"

"She sends floods when she's angry."

"That's it?"

"She's the patron of motherhood, healing, and weaving."

"She sounds busy."

"She's also mythical."

"I think we blurred that line a long time ago. So tell me about the White Jaguar."

"Do we have to talk, Hoop? I have a headache."

"I need to know this stuff."

Lola sighed. "The kings of the Monkey River took the White Jaguar to Ixchel to commune with their ancestors."

"And how did they do that?"

"There was something called the vision serpent, like a big snake. You see it in old wall paintings. It's like the ancestors would appear in the vision serpent's mouth."

"But what about—"

"Enough, Hoop; I'm tired. Can we sit down for a moment?"

"No!" Max was fairly sure that if she sat down, the poison would not allow her to get up again. He cast around for a topic that would interest her. "Hey, Monkey Girl, I just had an idea! Maybe you can talk to your ancestors at Ixchel!"

"That's not funny, Hoop. You know I don't have any ancestors."

"Everyone has ancestors. You just don't know who yours are."

Lola looked at him, her eyes suddenly wide. "You mean, this could be the day I find out who I am?"

"Why not?" Max felt bad giving her false hope, but the thought was making her walk faster, and he was anxious to catch up with Lord 6-Dog.

With Lola now pushing herself on, they covered the distance to the ruined city and soon emerged in the main plaza of the archaeological site. Apart from the main attraction—the soaring white pyramid of the moon goddess—very little of the site had been excavated. Most of the structures were just large green mounds covered in trees.

An overgrown path to the main pyramid led them by the cenote, its water green and inviting.

As Max skirted the edge, he tried to imagine that terrible day when his parents had been working at this site. With a little help from the White Jaguar, that innocent-looking pool had become a gateway to the underworld. Under attack and panicking, his parents had jumped right in and found themselves taken prisoner by the Death Lords.

Max tried to remember if there was a cenote anywhere at the Black Pyramid. He hoped not. He hoped his parents were keeping out of trouble. They seemed to have a knack for unleashing the forces of chaos and leaving their son to clear up the mess. And this mess was still a long way from cleared up.

"This is it," he said to Lola, "the place where all this trouble started."

"I'm sorry to make you come here. But something good is going to happen today. I know it."

Her face looked yellow and waxy, like melon rind, and tinged with sweat.

"How do you feel?' he asked her.

"My arm hurts. But it's worth it to meet my mother. I'm so excited, Hoop!"

"Whoa! What's this about your mother?"

"I thought it through on the trail. Ixchel is the goddess of motherhood. Why else would Bahlam have brought me here?"

"Perhaps you shouldn't get your hopes too high." But Max could tell from her feverishly glittering eyes that she wasn't listening.

"We better hurry," he urged her. "Lord 6-Dog will be—"

"I will be what, young lord?"

Max jumped out of his skin as Lord 6-Dog dropped down from a branch above their heads. "I was about to say that you'd be waiting for us."

"Indeed," replied the howler monkey. "I have done what I can to prepare for the ritual. All is ready at the top of the pyramid. I came down to look for blood."

"Blood?" echoed Max weakly.

"We might summon Ixchel without candles and incense, but we must have blood to charge the Jaguar Stone."

"What, you mean we have to kill something?" asked Max, horrified.

"Why not?" came a voice from the undergrowth. "It is a good day to die."

Chapter Twenty-two
THE VISION SERPENT

An old man stepped out of the bushes. He carried a large woven bag across his shoulder. The shawl around his head had come unfolded, and his long white hair fell free. It had bits of leaf litter caught in it, as if he'd spent the night in the forest.

"Grandfather?" said Lola weakly. "Is that you?"

Chan Kan's milky, almost sightless eyes were filled with fear. "Who are you? Are you a spirit come to seek my punishment?"

"Don't you know me?" Lola looked like she might faint at any moment.

"Don't get upset," Max whispered to her. "He's crazy, that's all. You know that." Remembering Landa's words in the beauty salon, he gave Chan Kan a look of contempt.

Chan Kan turned to the sound of his voice. "Are you her husband?" he asked.

"No," said Max coldly. "You're confused."

Chan Kan waved an ancient finger at him. "You are wrong. For the first time in many moons, I am not confused."

"What are you doing here?" Max challenged him.

"I have come to see Ixchel, to make an offering before I die."

"An offering?" cut in Lord 6-Dog. "Art thou a shaman? Hast thou blood for the ritual?"

"The howler monkey talks?" asked Chan Kan in astonishment. "Is this Xibalba? Am I dead already?"

Lord 6-Dog rolled his eyes impatiently. "Hast thou blood?" he repeated.

Chan Kan nodded fearfully. "If you please, Lord Monkey, these days we use a mix of chili powder, copal, and palm oil. I also have candles, matches, and incense." He patted his bag to show that everything was inside, and provoked a squawk of protest like the one Max had heard at the dock in Limón.

Lola's eyes lit up at the sound.

"Wait, is that—?" began Max, as Chan Kan opened his bag and pulled out a small bamboo cage containing a mangy, almost bald, little chicken. "It is! It's Thunderclaw!"

It was the first time Lola had smiled since they lost Bahlam. She gripped Chan Kan's arm. "You're not going to sacrifice him, are you?"

"We are old and tired and battle-scarred. The end is near for us both."

Lord 6-Dog peered into the cage, then jumped back in alarm. "The Chee-Ken? He is here?"

Max winced. He had once cowed the Maya king and his mother into submission by threatening them with tales of the terrible deeds of Thunderclaw, the Chicken of Death, the Fowl of Fear, who terrorized all of Xibalba.

All nonsense, of course.

"He's on our side now," said Max.

"The Chee-Ken is thy familiar, venerable lord?" Lord 6-Dog asked Chan Kan.

"He is my only friend."

Lord 6-Dog stared at the old man. "I feel that we have met before."

"I know that my memory has failed of late, but I think I would remember a talking monkey."

"I am Ahaw Wak Ok, a great Maya king, but this body belongs to the howler known as Chulo."

Chan Kan looked around nervously. "Is this a dream? Or have the torments of the afterlife begun?"

"Fear not," Lord 6-Dog assured him, "we are well met. Surely the mighty Chee-Ken can quell Ah Pukuh's hordes. What sayest thou, venerable lord? Will the Fowl of Fear fight for us and be our champion?"

"He is unbeaten," said Chan Kan proudly.

The old man was, of course, referring to the bird's former career as a fighting cock. But Lord 6-Dog heard it as a testament to the creature's supremacy in the halls of Xibalba. "With the Chee-Ken on our side," he said, "we cannot lose."

"Should I tell him the truth?" Max whispered to Lola.

She didn't answer. She was leaning against a tree. Her eyes were closed. Her arm had swollen up horribly.

"Lord 6-Dog! We need to hurry! Lola's worse!" Max cried.

"The poison is taking hold! Help her to the top, young lord."

Max shaded his eyes and looked up at the pyramid. The steps were steep and high. "You need to walk," he said to Lola. "I'll help you. Lean on me and put one foot in front of the other."

Lola groaned and slid farther down the tree.

Max realized that he would have to carry her. He'd never carried a girl before.

He took a deep breath and picked her up.

She was heavier than she looked.

By the time he'd staggered across the plaza, his arms were aching, his knees were shaking, and they hadn't climbed a single step yet.

"Help!" Max called to Lord 6-Dog. "I need you!"

But the monkey-king didn't hear him. He'd taken Chan Kan's bag of tricks and raced ahead with it. Secure in his new strength as a howler monkey who could swing through the trees all day and support his own weight with his prehensile tail, Lord 6-Dog had overestimated the muscle power of a teenage human.

And it was no use asking Chan Kan to help. He could barely lift his own feet.

Max sank down on the stones. He couldn't do this. She was too heavy. Even if he could carry Lola's weight, he was scared of overbalancing on those steep, narrow steps.

"Come back!" he called again to Lord 6-Dog. "I can't do this on my own."

He felt so helpless. After everything they'd been through together, Lola was going to die in his arms because he wasn't strong enough to save her. He closed his eyes to fight back the tears.

A rough tongue licked his face.

He opened his eyes and met the gaze of a green-eyed jaguar.

"Lola! Lola! It's Bahlam! He's here, he's come back!" He took her hand and ran it over the jaguar's head.

Lola struggled to open her eyes, but from her contented smile, he knew she understood.

Bahlam stood meekly while Max loaded Lola onto his back. Instinctively, she buried her head in his fur and wrapped her arms around his neck.

"Take care of her," Max told him. "She's all yours now."

As if he understood their plan, Bahlam set off up the pyramid. Max noticed he was limping and realized that, to have survived the fall into the gorge, the creature must be badly wounded. But Bahlam gave no sign of pain. He seemed to think only of the precious cargo on his back, trying not to jolt her as he negotiated the daunting tower of steps.

"The girl rides a jaguar?" marveled Chan Kan. "It is a day of portents."

Max breathed out, relieved.

All he cared about was that Lola would make it to the top.

He wasn't so sure about Chan Kan.

"Can you make it?" he asked him. "Do you need help?"

"I must make the ascent alone. It is part of my penance."

Watching his tired old legs heave his tired old body from step to step was torture.

"It's just that we're in a hurry," said Max. "Lola has been poisoned. We need to get things started. We can't wait for you."

"Then . . . start . . . without . . . me," wheezed Chan Kan. "I . . . have . . . my own . . . ritual . . . to . . . perform."

"What's this all about? I saw you get off the boat at Limón yesterday. Why didn't you tell Lola you were coming here today?"

"It . . . is . . . my . . . last . . . journey."

"Do you know Antonio de Landa?"

But Chan Kan was wheezing so much, he was starting

to sound like Darth Vader. Max wondered if he would even make it up the pyramid.

"I'll take Thunderclaw," he said.

When Chan Kan passed over the birdcage, his hand was so cold and dry and bony, it felt more dead than alive. Max shuddered and climbed up the pyramid steps faster than he ever had before.

By the time he reached the top, incense was billowing in pungent clouds. The White Jaguar sat ready at the base of the altar, and Lord 6-Dog was using melted wax to stick down dozens of tiny colored candles in an honor guard around it.

Through the smoke, Max saw Lola and her animal guide lying side by side like dead bodies on a battlefield.

"How is she?" he asked Lord 6-Dog.

"Only Ixchel can help her now. I pray we are in time."

"Can you believe that Bahlam came back? Does Ixchel heal animals, too?"

"I am sure the gods will recognize his bravery. Here, set the Chee-Ken down and finish these for me." He handed Max a bag of candles.

Max studied Lord 6-Dog's handiwork. "What's the pattern?"

"Set them in rows," instructed Lord 6-Dog as he looked in Chan Kan's bag for more supplies. "Blue for Heart of Sky, brown for Heart of Earth, green for the mountains, tallow for the ancestors, red for an answer, black for the darkness, yellow to protect adults, white to protect children."

"Fourteen counts as a child, right?" asked Max, setting out more white candles.

"Not in my world. I was crowned king at thine age."

Max heard his own voice in his ears. *We're not children,*

Uncle Ted, he'd said at Utsal. *We can look after ourselves*. Feeling very much in need of looking after, Max set out more yellow candles, too.

As Lord 6-Dog spread Chan Kan's fake-blood mixture around the niche in the altar, its creator arrived on the top platform. Speechless with effort, the old man sat down by the birdcage and mopped his face with his scarf.

Next to him, Thunderclaw was also in distress. The little fowl was emitting hoarse coughing noises, and his pink eyes looked watery and even pinker than usual.

"I think the smoke is getting to him," said Max.

He looked around for Chan Kan's now-empty bag and gently placed the birdcage back inside. "You might want to take a nap," he whispered to Thunderclaw. "It's you versus the zombies later."

Lord 6-Dog bowed to the altar. "Let us begin!"

Max's stomach flipped—whether out of fear or excitement, he wasn't sure.

A noise far away caught Lord 6-Dog's attention. He stood stock-still, listening.

Lola flinched in her sleep.

Bahlam growled.

Only Chan Kan ignored it and continued to fuss over the candles.

Max looked out across the forest to see if he could see where the noise was coming from.

And what he saw froze the blood in his veins.

Because that was the exact moment that Max Murphy of Boston, Massachusetts, discovered that five hundred skeletons on the march make a dry crunching sound like a battalion of tanks rolling over a field of cornflakes.

As rapacious as leaf-cutter ants, the zombies were slicing through the rainforest, felling any trees that stood in their way. Max could clearly hear roots being ripped out, and the sickening thuds as tree after tree crashed to the ground.

"Pass me the Jaguar Stone!" Lord 6-Dog commanded.

Max obeyed, then took a step backward and watched as the monkey-king, standing on his monkey toes, reached up to push the White Jaguar into its niche in the altar. As soon as the stone came into contact with the blood mix, it seemed to leap out of his hairy hands and click easily into place.

Lord 6-Dog began chanting in Mayan.

There was a rumble from deep inside the pyramid.

The alabaster Jaguar Stone glowed white-hot as the wispy curls of incense smoke that danced around it began to thicken and solidify.

Max couldn't help but think about the day his parents had stood on this very spot and witnessed this same thing. No good had come of activating the White Jaguar that day, only terror and disaster.

"Beware!" Lord 6-Dog whispered. "Here come the snakes!"

Oh yes, the snakes. How could Max have forgotten about the snakes?

"They are not real," Lord 6-Dog reminded him. "Do not be afraid."

Snakes of all sorts and sizes were appearing in the smoke.

They looked real.

Horribly real.

"Remain motionless," called Lord 6-Dog. "Let the snakes flow around thee."

Max braced. *It's just a trick of the light*, he told himself, *like that rattlesnake that appears for tourists at Chichen Itza.*

But these snakes were not mere shadows.

Their scales glinted in the sunlight. Their tongues darted out to taste the air.

Fat and thin, big and small, striped and plain, they slithered down to the floor, until the platform was a writhing, scaly mass.

Max couldn't even see Lola and Bahlam underneath them.

He tried to go to them, but Lord 6-Dog held him back. "She will not be harmed, young lord. Stand firm!"

And then the serpentine intruders were gone, over the edge of the pyramid, gone to who knew where, and in their place was just one snake, the biggest snake Max had ever seen, a snake the size of a townhouse, looming out of the smoke.

It towered over the little people on the platform.

"Behold the vision serpent!" announced Lord 6-Dog. "Let us bow down."

Max obediently bowed his head, but Chan Kan just stood there, mesmerized. "Am I alive or dead?" he mumbled. "I only came to light some candles."

Lord 6-Dog stepped forward. "Greetings to thee, Great Serpent. I am Ahaw Wak Ok, Lord 6-Dog, son of the mighty king Punak Ha and his queen, Ix Kan Kakaw."

The snake lowered its head until it was level with the monkey's face. Slowly it opened its mouth again, dislocating its jaw to create a massive aperture. As the monkey and the humans watched in awe, a man—a Maya man—appeared. He looked out between the snake's fangs, as if he were looking out of a window.

It was the most bizarre thing Max had ever seen.

It would have been comical if it hadn't been so knee-shakingly terrifying.

"Father!" cried Lord 6-Dog with joy. He bowed his head respectfully.

"Stand up straight, Son, let me see thee." Punak Ha had a magnificently high Maya forehead and a large, sloping nose, but Max was most fascinated by his eyes. He'd expected the great king to be cold and haughty, but these eyes were kind and gentle.

Lord 6-Dog remained bowed low. "I come before thee in the guise of a brutish howler monkey. I am ashamed for thee to see me."

"I see no howler monkey. I see a boy who lost his father all too young; a brave warrior, tall and strong in his jaguar-pelt armor; a mighty king who ruled with wisdom. I see my son who has made me proud every day of his life."

Lord 6-Dog's brown monkey eyes were watery. "I have missed thee, Father. My heart swells to talk to thee again."

"And mine to talk to thee. Hast thou come to Ixchel, like kings of old, to seek advice from thine ancestors?"

"Thine advice is worth more than jade or cocoa beans, and I am moved beyond words to see thee. But, in truth, Father, I have come to seek the healing powers of Ixchel for a fallen comrade."

"Then I will summon her for thee. But know that I love thee, Son."

"Wait! Father! The day thou died, I was out hunting. If only I had been by thy side . . ."

"My death was not thy fault. It was written in the stars, just as it is written that thou wilt take revenge against my killer, Tzelek. Win my final battle for me, Little Dog."

"The forces of evil approach, Father. Is Tzelek with them?"

"This is not the battle, Son. This is not the day."

"I will not rest until I have avenged thy death, Father."

"May it go well with thee. And please tell thy mother that I miss her tortillas."

Lord 6-Dog smiled. "They are still the best."

Chan Kan, who'd been watching this exchange with great interest, stepped in front of Lord 6-Dog. "Ixchel! Ixchel!" he called, "I am Chan Kan . . . shaman of Utsal. I beg thee as the patron of motherhood to hear my request for forgiveness."

Lord 6-Dog turned on him angrily. "What is the meaning of this? Dost thou seek to usurp the ritual?"

"I seek only forgiveness. Ixchel knows why."

The snake roared.

Then it looped its neck up and placed its head flat on the platform. When it opened its mouth, an old woman stepped out.

A very angry old woman.

She was Maya, obviously, but hideously ugly, with an enormous hooked nose and broken teeth. Her choice of outfit did nothing to soften her appearance: there was a writhing green snake in her hair, while human bones dangled from her woven dress.

Chan Kan got down on creaking bones and prostrated himself on the platform.

The old woman put her hands on her hips. "How darest thou come to my temple, Chan Kan of Utsal? None here will speak to thee. Thine own ancestors have disowned thee. Even the lowliest creature in the jungle is worthier than thee."

The air went cold, and black storm clouds covered the sun. It was as dark as evening.

"Forgive me, I beg thee," groveled Chan Kan. "My intentions were noble."

"I judge thine actions, not thine intentions. And as the goddess of motherhood, I condemn thee to eternal torment."

Thunder crashed, lightning flashed, and the rain pelted down. The burning incense spluttered and sizzled.

"Please, dear lady," said Lord 6-Dog, "whatever the old man has done to incur thy wrath, do not punish his granddaughter. She has been struck by a poison arrow and will surely die if thou dost not deign to save her."

Ixchel, moon goddess, patron of motherhood, weaving, and medicine, turned to look at the howler monkey that had just addressed her. The snake on her head turned, too.

"Hello, handsome," she said.

And just like that, she changed from an ugly old crone into a shimmeringly beautiful young woman. Gone was the creaking voice and archaic diction, and in its place was a girlish lilt. "You're Lord 6-Dog, aren't you? I've heard a lot about you. I always hoped I'd meet you one day."

The sun came out and the sky went from black to cloudless blue.

"Charmed," responded Lord 6-Dog, bowing to her. "And thou, I take it, art the new moon?"

"That's right," she said, with a tinkling laugh. "People sometimes think that we're mother and daughter, but it's all me. I can be old and grumpy, or new and lovely. It's just my phases. All women have moods, don't they?" She looked over at Lola. "Is that the girl who needs my help?"

"Aye, dear lady. And next to her is her animal companion."

Ixchel winked at him and put a finger to her lips.

In the jungle sky, the daytime moon shone brighter than the sun.

And then . . .

"What's happening?" asked Lola, sitting up and stretching. "I fell asleep! What did I miss?" The jaguar woke up and rolled onto his back for her to tickle him. "Bahlam! It wasn't a dream! You're here!"

Forgetting that he was in the presence of an ancient and terrifying goddess, Max high-fived Lord 6-Dog and ran to sit with Lola.

"How do you feel?" he asked. "I was worried about you."

"I feel . . ." As she groped around for words, she looked down at the rainforest spread out below them. "I feel . . . on top of the world!"

Ixchel smiled indulgently to watch the two teenagers laughing together. "They make quite a pair," she said. Then, batting her eyelashes at Lord 6-Dog, she added, "Is there anything else I can do for you?"

Lord 6-Dog thought for a moment. His eye came to rest on Chan Kan, who was now slumped, weeping, in a corner. "Perhaps thou couldst show mercy to the old man?"

Chan Kan lifted his eyes hopefully to the goddess.

Ixchel looked at him with scorn.

For a split second, her face darkened and her nose seemed to grow and a ringlet in her hair formed into a little snake. Then the thundercloud passed, and she laughed her tinkling laugh again. "He has one chance to redeem himself, and one chance only."

Chan Kan sobbed his thanks.

"Don't thank me," said Ixchel. "Thank your handsome friend."

Lord 6-Dog smiled at her. "Thou art as merciful as thou art beautiful."

She smiled back. "We should get to know each other better. You should come up and meet my friend, the moon rabbit, some time."

"I would like that," replied Lord 6-Dog.

Ixchel winked at him and turned to Lola. "Hello, Ix Sak Lol. At last we meet in person."

Lola gasped in surprise and scrambled to her feet. "You know me?"

"I know you well. I am Mother Moon. Many nights I have shone down on you, and tried to send you comfort."

"I have felt that," said Lola in a small voice.

"Do not be sad, child. There is someone here who wants to speak to you."

Lola's face lit up like a shaft of sunlight. "Mother?"

She was trembling with excitement as the serpent opened its mouth.

It was a woman, to be sure.

"I am sorry, Ix Sak Lol. I am not your mother."

Lola tried to hide her disappointment. "Hello, Princess Inez. How nice to see you again."

"I came to tell you that I am safe. I escaped the Death Lords' lair and found my beloved Rodrigo. Nothing can part us again."

"I'm happy for you. We have much to thank you for."

Princess Inez, who'd married Rodrigo Pizarro, a conquistador and one of Max's ancestors, had guarded the Yellow Jaguar in a Spanish castle, until Max had set her free. In return, Inez had taken Lola's place on that fateful shark ride down to the Maya underworld.

"And I thank you, on behalf of all who hate the Death Lords, for making this stand. My Rodrigo says—"

Inez disappeared abruptly.

"What's happening up there?" asked Ixchel.

She beckoned to the vision serpent to pick her up, and it moved to obey, then froze, hissing and retching as if trying to eject something.

A rope flew up out of its throat and lassoed one of its fangs. After some huffing and puffing, a head popped up. A head in a pith helmet. The rest of the body followed, rappelling its way up the snake's gullet.

Under the pith helmet was a young man in spectacles—a good-looking young man, with floppy bangs and movie-star stubble. His white open-necked shirt was rolled up at the sleeves and showed off his California tan.

"Be with you in a jiffy!" he exclaimed.

They watched openmouthed as he used a long blowpipe to prop open the snake's mouth and tested it to see if it would hold.

Pleased with his ingenuity, he doffed his pith helmet to the audience. "Sylvanus

Griswold Morley at your service. *The* Sylvanus Morley."

He looked at them expectantly.

They looked back blankly.

He tried to jog their memories. "Vay Morley? Excavator of Chichen Itza? Translator of Maya glyphs? Undercover agent for the US navy—?"

"I know you! I'm named after you!" Max burst out.

"Now you've got it! Not many chaps called Sylvanus these days, so I've taken a bit of a shine to you, young Murphy. You're an adventurer after my own heart! So I've come for a good old chin-wag."

"Are you dead?" Max asked warily.

"Yes, sirree. Kicked the bucket in New Mexico aged sixty-five, but I was the bees knees in my prime, so that's how I like to present myself to the world. Or should I say, the afterworld?"

"Excuse me, sir," said Ixchel, "but you're not authorized to be at this vision ceremony. You'll have to leave."

Sylvanus Morley gave a low whistle. "Well, hell-o there."

"Control yourself. I am a goddess."

"Yes. You. Are." He blew her a kiss.

"We do not have time for this impertinence," snapped Lord 6-Dog. "The lady has asked thee to leave."

Sensing a situation brewing, Max tried to get rid of the flirtatious archaeologist. "It was nice of you to drop in, Mr. Morley, but we don't have time to chat. The Undead Army is chasing us and we need to plan our getaway."

"That's why I came to help you. I've been in a few tight

spots myself, so I know my onions. One time my team and I were stuck in quicksand, like ants in honey. It took some nifty thinking on my part, but I whipped off my pith helmet and . . ."

He noticed the look of agony of Max's face.

"Sorry, sport, I can see you're in a mad dash, so I'll spill the beans. I came to tell you that my old jalopy is hidden in a cave behind the cenote. She's yours for the taking!"

"Jalopy? That's a car, right?" asked Max. "Will it still work?"

"Don't see why not. She has solid rubber tires and a spare tank of gas. Had a feeling she'd be needed one of these days. Here—catch!" He threw Max a bunch of keys.

At that moment, the snake worked itself free, spit out the blowpipe, and clamped its jaws shut. There was a muffled, echoing scream as the archaeologist was swallowed by the ancient Maya vision serpent—handsome smile, spectacles, pith helmet, and all.

Ixchel shook her head despairingly. "Archaeologists! They're like children sometimes." Max nodded in agreement. "Well, I better go and check on him. It was nice meeting you—most of you anyway." She directed a disapproving look at Chan Kan. "Good-bye!" She flashed a final smile at Lord 6-Dog. "Don't be a stranger."

The snake lowered its head, and Ixchel climbed into its mouth. Then, like a cherry picker transporting a rock star above a stadium crowd, it raised her up high.

"Farewell, dear lady," called Lord 6-Dog.

"May the moon light your way through the darkest night! Until we meet again, Lord 6-Dog!"

And just like that she was gone.

And the snake was gone.

The morning air felt cold.

Bahlam paced along the edge of the platform.

Then he turned and roared a warning.

Max and Lola came and stood behind him.

When they looked down, what they saw, massed at the bottom of the White Pyramid, was the entire Undead Army.

Chapter Twenty-three
ATTACK OF THE ZOMBIES

"For twelve hundred years, three hundred *baktuns*, have I longed to hear the voice of my father again. Little did I dream that this would be the day. Like balm on a wound, it has healed my pain and reinvigorated my being. In truth, I feel like a new monkey."

"Cool," said Max dully. "But the zombies are here."

"Fear not, young lord. Didst thou not hear my father? He said this is not the battle."

"Just because *you* get to live another day, it doesn't mean *we're* safe. Besides, technically speaking, you're dead already."

Lord 6-Dog considered the problem. "I believe," he said, "that we are under the protection of Ixchel for as long as the White Jaguar works its magic."

"So we just stay on this pyramid for the rest of our lives?"

"That is not an option, young lord. When the candles burn down and the incense runs out, the ritual will be over."

Max eyed the tiny mound of incense left on the altar and the ranks of sputtering candle stubs. "How long do we have?"

"A warrior measures time not by the passage of the sun, but by his victories in battle."

Max looked down at the Undead Army. There was a echoing click of ancient vertebrae as five hundred zombies turned their heads to stare back up at him.

"Either way, I think our time is up."

"We have the mighty Chee-Ken."

"Yeah, about that . . . ," began Max.

Lola shushed him. "Thunderclaw will fight for us tooth and nail."

"Chickens don't have teeth," Max pointed out. "Or nails. This one doesn't even have feathers."

"You know what I mean," said Lola, "so why waste time trying to be clever? We need to band together . . . like them." She pointed down to where the Undead Army was taking up battle positions. "I've been watching them. Ixchel's protection is like a force field around the pyramid. They can't get through it, but they keep on trying. Every time they get knocked back, they just regroup and attack again."

Lord 6-Dog stroked his hairy chin. "What they lack in intelligence, they make up in stamina. The question is, How can our militia out-think them and outflank them?"

Max took stock of their so-called militia. Two kids. One talking monkey. One tame jaguar. One scabby chicken. And an old man sobbing in the corner.

"We're doomed," he said.

"Stop it, Hoop! You're not helping."

"What should I do?"

"Go talk to Chan Kan. He won't talk to me. Whatever was between him and Ixchel, he's really taken it to heart."

"He's not talking to me either. He won't talk to anyone but Thunderclaw."

At ground level, those zombies that still had vocal chords

let out a bloodcurdling scream, and the army rushed forward.

Ixchel's protection stopped them in their tracks.

Although they couldn't step onto the pyramid, it didn't prevent them from trying. They threw themselves at the steps, often dislocating their own bones in their efforts to climb up. Flights of arrows and spears hurtled through the air, but turned to vapor as soon as they came close.

Max and Lola watched this performance with mixed feelings, glad to be safe for now but horribly aware that this magical shield would soon be gone, and then nothing would stand between them and these skeletal maniacs.

Bahlam continued pacing up and down, snarling and growling at the zombies. He walked in circles around Lola, Max, and Lord 6-Dog, as if to tell them that he would protect them with his life. But he kept his distance from Chan Kan.

The zombies began to shout angrily in Mayan, punctuating their words with wild chopping, stabbing, and slicing motions.

"What are they saying?" asked Max.

"You don't want to know," replied Lola. "But they have some very inventive ideas for what they are going to do to us."

Max flinched as one of the zombie warriors acted ripping out his eyeballs and stuffing them down his throat.

"If only we had more boom sticks," mused Lord 6-Dog.

"If this was a movie," said Max, "Uncle Ted would have fixed his plane and he'd arrive in the nick of time and airlift us out of here."

Right: "The zombies are here."

They looked up and scanned the skies.

All was blue and clear and entirely devoid of air traffic in any direction.

"He better hurry up," said Lola.

"As I understand it," Lord 6-Dog pointed out, "Lord Ted does not know we are here."

Max and Lola sat and watched the incense smolder into ashes and the last few candles burn down.

"I'm sorry you didn't meet your mother," Max said, "but I'm sure you're related to Princess Inez. You look just like her."

"Me? Related to royalty?" Lola snickered. "Hardly."

"Why not? It could be true."

"Princesses don't get abandoned in the forest."

Max remembered Landa's confession in the salon at the hotel. He'd said that Lola was descended from the Jaguar Kings. But was he a genealogist or a lunatic?

Chan Kan let out a pain-racked groan. Ever since Ixchel had berated him, he'd sat slumped against a wall, hugging the bag with Thunderclaw and muttering to himself.

Lola ran over and sat next to him. She tried to wrap his shawl around him, but he pushed her away.

"Grandfather, I know you don't want to talk to me, but maybe you will listen. Whatever you have done, Ixchel was too hard on you. Please don't get so upset. I'm sure her rules don't even apply anymore. I mean, she's the ancient Maya moon goddess, and we're in the twenty-first century."

"The moon still rules the tides," said Chan Kan. "And when Ixchel is angry, she still sends storms, floods, and tidal waves."

"Actually," Max called over, "I think you'll find that's global warming—"

"Ixchel was right," interrupted Chan Kan.

"Right about what, Grandfather?"

He flinched to hear her call him that. Suddenly he took her hands in his dry-as-dust hands and focused his blank eyes on her bright eyes. "My life flows by like a river rushing to the sea. I see the sun crossing the sky but I have no sense of time passing. I can remember a day many years ago, but I cannot remember yesterday." A tear rolled down his cheek. "And you, I have forgotten your name."

"It's Ix Sak Lol."

"No, that is not your name."

Lola stared at him. "What *is* my name?"

He sighed. "What does it matter? What are names but words? I know who you are."

"Who am I?"

"You are the girl who played with crystals by the river."

Lola shook her head sadly.

"No? Then what do you remember?" asked Chan Kan.

Lola sighed. "I remember the stories you told me. All the legends and myths of our people."

"One day, perhaps you will tell stories of your own."

Lola said nothing. Max guessed she was thinking that her chances of surviving long enough to tell anyone a story were extremely slim.

Somehow Chan Kan guessed that, too. "Those ghouls down there, what do they want? Is it the Jaguar Stone?"

"Yes," said Lola, surprised at his perspicacity. "It's the Jaguar Stone, it's us, it's everything. They want to uproot and trample every living thing on this planet."

Chan Kan's mind seemed to wander off again. "When you tell the story of this day, make it about a fool who was blessed with great treasure. But he was so scared of losing it, he destroyed it in his greed. One day a goddess came down, and gave him one last chance to redeem himself. Maybe that is the name of the story. 'One Last Chance.'"

A jungle breeze blew across the top of the pyramid, scattering the last black ashes of the incense.

The last candle, a white one, sputtered and went out.

In the altar, the White Jaguar stopped glowing. In one smooth movement, it ejected itself and sat half in and half out of the niche.

With the barrier gone, the Undead Army gave a mighty shout and surged up the steps of the pyramid.

Bahlam ran down to meet them.

"No!" cried Lola.

Chan Kan climbed wearily to his feet. "I wish you happiness and long life."

Lola, Max, and Lord 6-Dog watched openmouthed, one eye on the advancing enemy, one eye on the old man, as Chan Kan shuffled over to the altar and took out the White Jaguar.

As the stones of the pyramid juddered beneath him, Chan Kan seemed to shake off the long years of near blindness and the troubles of old age, and he stood there for a moment as a young shaman, like a tall, straight tree in the rainforest, his eyes clear, his long black hair flowing down his back, his bag looped across his body, cradling Thunderclaw like a baby in a sling.

He held the White Jaguar above his head for all to see.

The Undead Army froze in its tracks.

"Is this what you want?" he asked the zombies. The old man's raspy voice floated down, as the voice of the king had once floated down to the crowds below. "It is the Stone of

Wisdom, a virtue I have lacked. But what I have lacked in life, I will embrace in death. This stone is my one last chance."

"Grandfather!" cried Lola.

But it was too late. Chan Kan could no longer hear her voice. He heard only the voices in his head. His whole being was focused on his final sacrifice, the one that would atone for all the lies that had seeded and sprouted and grown wild and rampant, like a strangler fig, around his heart.

Clutching the White Jaguar to him, he ran as nimbly as a young man to the edge of the platform and, like a pouncing cat, leapt off.

Below him the green water of the cenote danced and bubbled and opened a gateway to Xibalba.

Thunderclaw squawked all the way down.

When they hit the surface, all three of them—Chan Kan, the chicken, and the Jaguar Stone—vanished in a flash of light.

And that was it.

In one dramatic and misguided gesture, Chan Kan had blown the last chance of everyone in Middleworld.

Just like that, everything they'd been fighting for was lost.

All five Jaguar Stones were now in Xibalba.

Thanks to Chan Kan's spectacular own goal, Ah Pukuh had everything he needed to begin his new age of chaos and destruction.

It was over.

Pure and simple.

And there was nothing that Max Murphy or anyone else could do about it.

Chapter Twenty-four
FACING THE MUSIC

Max watched as the waters of the cenote closed over Chan Kan's head, just as they had closed over his parents all those weeks ago.

Lola and Lord 6-Dog stood silent and openmouthed, unable to believe their eyes.

The Undead Army remained motionless, while their rancid brains computed what to do next.

Mosquitoes stopped buzzing, parrots stopped flying, spider monkeys stopped chattering in the trees. Time seemed to be suspended, as if the world itself had stopped turning.

Then, as if a hypnotist had suddenly clicked his fingers and told them to wake up, all hell broke loose.

Lola screamed Chan Kan's name.

Lord 6-Dog took up a fighting stance to face the coming onslaught.

Max grabbed Chan Kan's discarded walking stick to use as a weapon, and said mental good-byes to his parents.

The warriors of the Undead Army looked around as if seeking agreement with each other.

Any moment now, thought Max, *any moment now.*

He gripped the walking stick with two hands and held it in front of him like a kung fu master, at the same time being painfully aware of how pathetic it must look: a kid with a bamboo cane against an army of killer zombies.

The Undead Army raised its weapons.

Max tightened his grip on the cane.

With another mighty cheer, the army rushed forward.

But instead of racing up the pyramid, the zombies ran to the side and leapt into the cenote, one after another, like kids jumping off a dock.

The cenote flashed and consumed them all.

And everything was quiet again.

"They've gone," said Max. "They followed the Jaguar Stone." He threw his head back in relief. "We're safe."

"Chan Kan saved us," said Lola. "He gave his life for us."

"Chan Kan has condemned every man, woman, and child in Middleworld to certain death," Lord 6-Dog pointed out.

"It's not like *you* had a better plan," Lola muttered.

"My plan was not to serve Middleworld to Ah Pukuh on a platter."

"It wasn't his fault. How could Chan Kan have known that Ah Pukuh had the other four stones?"

"He was a shaman. He should have known."

"He was old and confused, but he meant well."

"That does not excuse him."

Lola changed the subject. "Has anyone seen Bahlam?"

"Once again," commented Lord 6-Dog, "thy lack of awareness astounds me."

Lola turned on him. "What have I done? Why are you being so mean to me?"

"Bahlam threw himself into the ravine to cover for thy headstrong behavior."

"I know that," said Lola. "And I said I was sorry."

"No creature could survive that fall."

Lola stared at him. "But Bahlam came back. He carried me up the pyramid."

"He is thine animal guide. Some instincts are stronger than death. He came back in spirit to help thee."

"You mean, he died at the ravine?" She sat down heavily and buried her head in her hands.

With a roar that might have been pity or regret or fury, Lord 6-Dog leapt for the nearest overhanging branch, and disappeared into the trees.

After a while, Max and Lola walked down the pyramid.

"Cheer up," said Max. "Don't blame yourself. Bahlam was doing his job."

Lola said nothing.

At the bottom, a smell of fast food wafted over.

"Are you hungry?" Max asked. "The vendors have arrived. The site will be opening soon."

Lola shook her head. Her eyes were full of tears. "Chan Kan, Bahlam, Thunderclaw . . . I need to say good-bye to them."

Trying to ignore the tempting aromas and look mournful, Max walked with her over to the cenote, its green water now opaque black.

Lola stared into its depths for a few moments, then ran into the forest and returned with an armful of white flowers.

"It's not mahogany," she said. "But it will do."

She threw the white blooms one by one into the water, chanting Mayan words that sounded like a prayer.

Soon, the surface of the cenote was flecked with white petals.

Max nudged her. "Tourist alert!"

A middle-aged couple strode toward them. They wore matching flowered shirts, khaki shorts, comfortable shoes, and nylon backpacks. The woman walked ahead, waving a map, while the man lagged behind with a large video camera.

The woman ignored Lola and went straight to Max. "Is there a show today? Our tour guide said the natives sometimes burn candles and make offerings in these old places." She looked warily at Lola. "Can you ask the Indian girl?"

Max made up some gobbledygook. "Ish kish mishy mashy pock pock?" he asked Lola, trying to keep a straight face.

"Ish kish pish," she improvised in reply.

"She says no," said Max.

The woman curled her lip. "This place needs to get its act together. At Disneyland the shows are twice a day on the dot."

"Have you been to the Grand Hotel Xibalba in Limón?" suggested Max. "I think you'd like it there."

"Does it have proper food?" asked the man.

"The world's biggest pizza buffet."

"Sounds good to me," said the man.

"But I can't wait. I'm hungry now," complained his wife.

And so, with the ancient pyramid soaring behind them and the stones of a lost civilization under their feet, the couple went off in search of a hot dog cart.

"I can see why Eusebio hates tourists," said Lola.

"Actually," said Max, "I'm starving. Do you think there is a hot dog cart?"

"Forget about food for a moment!"

"But we missed dinner last night. And we haven't had breakfast."

"We need to talk about how we're getting back to your uncle's house."

"What about Sylvanus Morley's jalopy?"

"One, it won't be there. Two, if it is there, it won't work. And three, I can't drive—can you?"

"I've driven a boat—"

Max was interrupted by a hand tapping him on the shoulder. "Excuse me?" said a voice. "Have I missed the show?"

Max rolled his eyes, irritated. "Look, there's no—"

"Eusebio!" cried Lola. "I am so happy to see you."

"I feel a little self-conscious," said the boatman. "Tourists keep taking my picture."

"I'm not surprised," said Max. Eusebio was still sporting the jaguar-pelt loincloth and jaguar-painted skin that he'd been wearing when they escaped the hotel.

"Where's Lord 6-Dog?" asked Eusebio. "And what happened to the Undead Army? I expected to find a pitched battle in progress."

"Lola will tell you everything," said Max. "And while you two catch up, I'm going to find some food."

When he came back, loaded up with tamales and corn on the cob, Max found Lola and Eusebio still sitting by the cenote, deep in conversation. From Lola's red eyes, he guessed they were talking about Chan Kan.

"He was a man with many secrets," said Eusebio. "But in the end, he proved how much he loved you, Ix Sak Lol."

"Hey buddy," said a voice, "will you take our picture?"

A group of tourists was lined up expectantly.

"Let's get out of here," said Max, gathering up his food. "Did you bring your truck, Eusebio?"

"No, I left it on the road, and got a ride on a tourist bus. The driver was a cousin of my brother-in-law's sister. I am sorry that I cannot drive you home."

"Oh, but you can! We have a jalopy!"

"What is a jalopy?" asked Eusebio.

Lola stood up and rearranged her hair to cover as much of her tear-stained face as possible. "It is a word for an imaginary car in an imaginary cave."

"There is a word for that?" Eusebio looked impressed.

In fact, Lola's definition was wrong, because the jalopy was not imaginary. It was exactly where the dead archaeologist had said it would be. A vintage Bentley, covered in a tarp, hidden in a cave.

Eusebio's eyes lit up. "It is in better condition than any car I have ever driven. Help me push it out, and I am sure I can get it started."

Max and Lola sat in the shade and watched as Eusebio tinkered with the jalopy.

Lola held Bahlam's whisker. "I keep hoping he will come." She drew in the dirt with a stick. "If I knew how to read Chan Kan's crystals, I think they would tell me that today is a day for no happy endings."

"I'm sorry about Chan Kan," said Max. "And Bahlam."

Lola wiped her eyes with the back of her hand. "Let's talk about something else."

Max took a deep breath. "Do you ever think about Toto?" he asked.

Lola looked up. "Toto? You mean Antonio de Landa? Why do you ask?"

"Just wondering," said Max, as casually as he could.

She shuddered. "I hope I never see him again. It's a terrible thing to say, but I hope he drowned in the ocean that last night in Spain. Except I know that he didn't."

Had she seen him at the hotel? Max turned to her sharply. "How do you know that?"

"He's a survivor. He's like a cockroach. He could probably survive for a week with his head cut off." She lay back against a rock and closed her eyes.

They didn't speak again until Eusebio had coaxed the jalopy back to life.

"All aboard!" he called.

Max went back to the plaza to look for Lord 6-Dog.

Now that the site was crawling with tourists, he was surprised to see how jolly it all looked. No one would guess that a mythic battle for the future of the Earth had taken place on these very stones just hours ago.

Nor that the Earth had lost.

"Ow!" A wild plum bounced off Max's head.

"Psst!" He looked up to see Lord 6-Dog peering at him out of a tree. "Thirteen apologies, young lord," he whispered. "I did not mean to hurt thee. But I am in hiding from the tourists. Every time they see me, they start to howl at me and expect me to howl back. It has given me a powerful headache."

"Eusebio has fixed the car. We're leaving."

"Thou dost know my thoughts on the infernal combustion engine. If I am not needed to ride with thee, I will swing by my tail to thine uncle's house. Last one there is a dung-beetle!"

Eusebio and Lola were waiting for Max in the jalopy.

He jumped into the backseat, and they were off.

"Which is the best way?" asked Eusebio as he drove out of the site entrance, past a surprised guard at the gate. "I have never been to Puerto Muerto."

Max rifled through the old papers in the seat pocket. "There are some maps back here. They're kind of old, though."

"Go right," commanded Lola. "I saw a logging camp from the pyramid. Wherever there are loggers, there are roads."

Her voice was flat, weighed down with sadness.

The landscape they drove through matched her mood.

"I hope Lord 6-Dog doesn't come this way," muttered Max. "His tail won't find much to swing from."

Mile after a mile of bare black earth and dead tree stumps. A silent wasteland with no birds, no monkeys, no wildlife of any kind save for the swarms of yellow butterflies that flitted hungrily through the ruins of the forest.

"Fools," muttered Eusebio. "Have they learned nothing from history? Once the rainforest is felled, it is gone forever."

"Even the ancient Maya didn't learn," said Lola. "They cut down trees to build fires to make plaster. And when the drought came, instead of scaling down, they built more pyramids and made more plaster."

"But they did not have chain saws," Eusebio pointed out.

"Please!" Max begged them. "Can we lighten up?"

But what was there to say?

They were all thinking the same thing.

The loggers' handiwork would be nothing compared to the devastation that Ah Pukuh had in mind. Very soon, he would be putting into action his plans to lay waste the whole of Middleworld. And no one would care about saving trees or animals when they couldn't save themselves. Now that

Ah Pukuh and the Death Lords had all five Jaguar Stones, the whole world would soon be cut down as easily as the last rainforests.

What made it worse was that—if you didn't count talking monkeys—only Max, Lola, and Eusebio knew what was coming.

And they did not look forward to spreading the news.

When they arrived at the Villa Isabella late afternoon the next day, a brown howler monkey was sitting on the gates waiting for them. She was wearing a little white embroidered apron. "Welcome home! I've been watching for you all day! It's so good to see you!"

"Lady Coco! This is our friend Eusebio," called Lola. "Eusebio, meet Lady Coco. In her human life, she was queen of Itzamna."

Eusebio bowed his head in greeting. He didn't think twice about meeting a Maya queen in the body of a monkey. After what he'd seen at the Grand Hotel Xibalba, he knew that anything was possible.

Lady Coco scanned the jalopy's passengers anxiously. "Where's 6-Dog?"

"He'll be here soon," said Max. "He wanted to swing through the jungle, what's left of it."

The monkey-queen smiled with relief. "I was worried about you. So was Lord Hermanjilio."

"Is he here?" asked Lola. She sounded nervous.

"Yes, he is here," boomed Hermanjilio from the front door. "And I think we need to talk, young lady."

"Time to face the music," said Lola grimly.

Without greeting any of the rest of them, Hermanjilio strode over to Lola. "Where is it? I entrusted it to you."

"I'm sorry."

"Where is the White Jaguar?"

"Xibalba," she whispered.

"*What have you done?* I cannot believe that I risked everything to smuggle the White Jaguar out from Xibalba and now it's right back there again."

"It wasn't Lola's fault," said Max. "It was Chan Kan."

"Then Chan Kan is an idiot!" yelled Hermanjilio.

"He's dead!" Lola yelled back. "Does that make you happy?"

"What—?" began Hermanjilio, but Lola jumped out of the car and ran inside. A door slammed somewhere upstairs.

"Chan Kan jumped into the cenote at Ixchel," Max explained.

Lady Coco put on her best hostess smile. "Won't you come inside, Lord Eusebio, and partake of some refreshments?"

Eusebio looked at Max and Hermanjilio. They were staring at each other, with faces like thunder. "Yes, I'd like that very much," he said.

When they were alone, Hermanjilio cross-questioned Max angrily. "Why were you at Ixchel? Ted said you were coming straight back here."

"It's a long story. But the Undead Army was chasing us. And Lola got hit by a poisoned arrow. She would have died if we hadn't taken her to Ixchel and asked the moon goddess for help."

"Presumably the Undead Army would not have been chasing you if Lola hadn't stolen the White Jaguar from me."

Mile after mile of bare black earth and dead tree stumps.

"She did it for me. The Death Lords were blackmailing her. Please go easy on her, Hermanjilio."

"Go easy on her! She has just imperiled the entire human race! She had no right to touch the White Jaguar!"

"The Death Lords drove her to it. They messed with her head."

"What do you mean?"

"They taunted her about having no family. They made her feel worthless. It was like all the fight had gone out of her. Then I persuaded her to stand up to the Death Lords. And everything went horribly wrong."

Hermanjilio sighed. "I might have known they'd get to her that way. I should have seen this coming. I was the one who found her, you know. I was walking through the forest on my way to meet Chan Kan for the first time. He wanted to talk about starting a village school. And there she was, sleeping in a basket under the mahogany tree. It's not the best start in life, is it? Left out in the jungle for wild animals to eat? Who would do such a thing?"

"You must have some clue about Lola's parents?"

"None at all. I asked in villages for miles around, but no one was missing a baby. The Maya love children far too much to just abandon them. So, in the end, we had to assume that her parents were dead. To this day, no one has ever asked about her. But luckily for her, Chan Kan stepped forward right away to offer her a home with his family. Everyone says he couldn't have loved her more if she was his real grandchild."

"Hermanjilio, I have to tell you something," Max blurted out. "It's something I overheard at the hotel in Limón. Antonio de Landa was there, and he was talking about how an old man, a shaman, paid him to steal a baby away from its mother. He said the baby grew up to be a beautiful girl and the love of his life, but she left him on their wedding day. He had to be talking about Lola!"

"Did you tell Lola about this?" asked Hermanjilio.

"No, I wanted to talk to Uncle Ted first. But you'll do."

Hermanjilio was staring into the forest. "So you think the old man was Chan Kan? And he paid Antonio de Landa to kidnap Lola from her own mother? Why would he do that? And why did Lola's mother never look for her baby?"

"Chan Kan told Landa that the mother was a bad woman."

"But to steal a child? And to let the child think she's an orphan? That's brutal. And anything could have happened to her in that forest. What if I hadn't come along?"

"Maybe Chan Kan and Landa set it up?"

Hermanjilio stared at him. "Now I think about it, Chan Kan was very precise about fixing that meeting. He told me which trail I should take to the village. I remember him telling me to look for the mahogany tree. And he said it was important to be on time—which is not something you hear much in San Xavier."

"So he made sure you'd find her and bring her to the village with you?"

"Where he was waiting to step in and officially adopt her?" Hermanjilio ran his fingers through his hair. "But why would he do such a thing?"

"I guess we'll never know."

"Promise me this, Max. The first chance you get, you sit down with Lola and you tell her everything you know. You cannot keep this a secret from her."

"I'll ask Uncle Ted to do it. I don't want to give her more bad news about Chan Kan. It's not like it solves the mystery of who her mother is. Or was."

318

"It needs to come from you."

"You tell her then. You're a professor. You know the right words to use. I'm no good at that stuff."

"You're good at being her friend, Max. That's what she needs right now."

All this time, Max and Hermanjilio had been sitting in the car.

The first colors of sunset were streaking the sky.

Max glanced toward the house. Three heads immediately ducked out of sight at the window. He guessed that Lady Coco, Eusebio, and Raul had been watching them, no doubt wondering what they were talking about.

Lord 6-Dog landed, with a thump, on the hood of the car. "How now, my lords?"

"You made it!" said Max. "Lady Coco will be happy to see you—she's been worried about you."

"Tonight, all mothers have cause to worry. Word in the forest is that Ah Pukuh is crowing about his victory and preparing to march on Middleworld. The end, I fear, is nigh for us all."

Max had been imagining this moment ever since he'd first got conscripted into the Death Lords' search for the Jaguar Stones. He always feared there would come a day when they'd have to admit defeat and let the bad guys have their way.

Life, Max Murphy had learned, was not like a video game. Scenes did not reload; revenge was not sweet; no one played by the rules.

But the fact that planet Earth was about to be overrun by a megalomaniac Maya god and his hellish hangers-on seemed less important at that moment than the fate of one stolen baby who would never know her mother.

Chapter Twenty-five
NO MORE SECRETS

After that, all Max could do was wait. Wait for his parents to come back from the dig. Wait for Uncle Ted to come back from San Xavier City, where he'd been keeping an eye on Little Och. Wait for Ah Pukuh to declare war on the mortal world. Wait for Lola to come down to breakfast, so he could break it to her that pretty much everything Chan Kan had ever told her was a lie.

It was a beautiful morning, and Raul had laid out an epic spread of eggs, bacon, pancakes and waffles on the terrace, but for once in his life Max wasn't hungry. He just sat there throwing crumbs to the birds and rehearsing in his head how to tell Lola what he'd overheard in the salon.

A toucan croaked in the tree above him.

"Shhh," Max hushed it. "I need to think."

"Were you calling me?" asked Raul, bringing out a jug of fresh mango juice. "Do you need more waffles?" He took in Max's untouched plate and frowned. "Is something wrong? I hope you're not getting sick."

"I'm fine. Just not hungry."

Raul poured out the juice. "Are you worried about something?" he asked, gently. "Is it your parents?"

In reality, with everything else that had happened, Max had forgotten to worry about his parents. But not wanting to tell Raul about Lola, he nodded sadly.

"I am sure they will be back soon. Your uncle called last night, and said to tell you that your parents are in San Xavier City right now, filing paperwork about a suspected looting." Raul sighed. "I sometimes think this country runs on paperwork."

"How is Little Och, did he say?"

"He is astounding the doctors with the speed of his recovery. Your uncle's been sleeping at the hospital to keep an eye on things, but he promised to get here tonight to see you and Miss Lola." Raul looked as excited as a child before a birthday party. "Lady Coco and I are planning a big dinner to celebrate."

"Sounds like fun," said Max, without enthusiasm.

Lola came out, muttered her good mornings, and slumped in a chair.

Raul shook his head. "My, my, I hope you'll both be feeling more energetic at the dinner tonight." He looked pointedly at Lola. "Jaime Ben is planning to join us."

"Who's he?" asked Max.

"You probably know him as Lucky Jim," replied Raul. "That's your uncle's nickname for him, but his real name is Jaime Ben. You'll see quite a change in him—won't he, Miss Lola?"

Lola gave a little nod. Something about this exchange set Max on alert. Feeling slightly jealous, he made a mental note to keep an eye on the new, improved Jaime Ben.

Lady Coco came out with a large tray. "I've come to get food for 6-Dog and Lord Hermanjilio. They've been up all night, poring over history books and old Maya texts, trying to predict what that evil Ah Pukuh might do next."

She loaded up the tray with good things, and Raul carried it out for her.

Max and Lola sat in silence for a while.

"So how are you this morning?" he asked her.

Her face told him how she was. Her eyes were red from crying. She looked like she hadn't slept. "As well as can be expected," she said, "given the mess I've made of things."

"It was my fault, too. I dragged us into that hotel."

Lola shrugged. "Whatever."

He hesitated. Then, figuring she couldn't feel much worse than she did right now, he took the plunge. "There was a guest at the hotel . . . in the beauty salon . . . he said something. . . . It was about Chan Kan."

"Don't, Hoop. I know you didn't like him. But it's wrong to speak ill of the dead."

"This is about you, too. About the day you were found."

"You better tell me then," she said dully.

So he told her what he'd overheard: how Chan Kan had paid Landa to kidnap her, how he'd arranged for her to be found by Hermanjilio, how he'd said that her real mother was a bad woman.

While Max talked, Lola stared blankly out to sea.

"So, that's it," Max finished up. "That's all I know. I'm sorry I couldn't find out the name of your mom."

It was a while before Lola spoke.

"You know what, Hoop, I'm done with family. I've always felt like an outsider, and that's just how it is. I can't believe I've wasted so much time on even thinking about this stuff."

"So you're okay?" Max was relieved it was over. "Do you want to play a video game or something?"

"No, it's such a nice day. I think I'll sit out here and read."

Max went inside to see if the Internet was working.

As the rest of the day passed, he couldn't help noticing that, whenever he looked out of the window, Lola's book lay untouched on the table. And for someone who said she'd already wasted too much time on thinking about stuff, she seemed to be very deep in thought.

Apart from Lola, who was still subdued, dinner that night was a rumbustious affair. It started late because Raul insisted on waiting for Uncle Ted, who was flying in from San Xavier City. He'd called to say he was bringing a surprise guest with him, which Max assumed would be his father or his mother, or maybe Little Och. But when the front door finally flew open, it was his family's housekeeper from Boston who walked in with Uncle Ted.

"Zia?"

She crushed Max in a bearhug. "I have missed you," she said. "I have not seen you since Spain." She looked around. "Where is Lola?"

"Oh, she's probably reading a book somewhere. You'll see her at dinner."

Uncle Ted clapped his hands together. "Then let's eat!"

Raul had made a special feast of Spanish paella, a rice dish with chicken and shrimp. The table was covered with little side dishes, all fragrant with saffron, rosemary, garlic and the sweet smell of almonds.

"*Viva España!*" called Zia, twirling her hands like a flamenco dancer.

Max laughed. "You were amazing in Spain," he said. "The way you rescued us in Santiago. Lola and I can never thank you enough."

"It was my pleasure." She turned to Uncle Ted who was sitting next to her. "I know your mother was Spanish, Teo, but did you ever visit Spain? I don't remember."

Teo? She already had a nickname for Uncle Ted?

"Once or twice," he replied. "But I'd like to go again with you." He looked at her lovingly. "Or anywhere."

What? Uncle Ted and Zia were a couple? That was insane.

"So tell me again how you two met up in San Xavier City?" Max asked them.

"I have been on vacation in San Xavier since I brought Their Majesties home," explained Zia. "I came here to surprise you, Max, but you'd left for the Black Pyramid with your parents." She glanced at Uncle Ted.

"On that occasion," he said, "we did not click."

"But love and hate are two sides of the same coin," observed Zia.

"And we flipped the coin," added Uncle Ted. "But to answer your question, Max, I was in San Xavier City with Little Och. . . ."

"And I came to visit your parents. . . ."

"And that was the day before yesterday—"

"And we have been together ever since."

Max looked from his housekeeper to his uncle in amazement. Just a few days ago, Uncle Ted had borrowed a plane to get away from Zia. Now they were finishing each other's sentences like an old married couple.

He looked down the table to get Lola's reaction, but she hadn't heard any of it. She was deep in conversation with Lucky Jim, or Jaime Ben, as Max had to get used to calling him.

He almost hadn't recognized Uncle Ted's former right-hand man. He was wearing a shirt and jeans instead of his usual black business suit. His hair was longer and covered the intimidating scar on his face. He looked younger, thinner, happier.

And—except for Uncle Ted, who still called him Lucky—everyone in his new life as a student teacher called him Jaime. Max decided to carry on calling him Lucky, too.

He saw Max looking and smiled. "I was just telling Lola how much my little brothers and sisters have missed her. She babysat for them when I was in Xibalba, and I almost think they're sorry I got out! They made me promise to ask her to come visit."

"I'd love to," she said, giving Lucky a big smile.

Max's invisible antennae were going crazy, trying to analyze the situation. Was there something going on between Lucky and Lola too? Did he just see them exchange a glance? He wished Lady Coco hadn't put so many candles on the table. The candlelight made even Lord 6-Dog look romantic—until, that is, he took the flowers out of the vase and ate them.

"I am sorry that thy parents could not be here, young lord," said the howler, spitting petals.

Zia nodded. "They are sorry, too, Max. They really wanted to be here tonight, but they are having trouble with paperwork—the authorities are making things difficult for them over permits and such. They can't leave San Xavier City at the moment."

"They haven't been arrested, have they?" asked Max.

"Perish the thought," said Uncle Ted—which, Max noted, was not the same as saying no.

"Hey, Hoop," called Lola, "let's go back to San Xavier City with your uncle tomorrow. I could visit Little Och and you could see your parents—"

"It might not be the best time—," leapt in Uncle Ted.

"They are tied up—," agreed Zia.

"Are they in jail?" Max asked bluntly.

"That's such an ugly word," said Zia.

"Let's just say that they are not allowed visitors at the moment, Max. The situation is a little delicate."

Truly, thought Max, they were the worst parents in the world.

"Come with me anyway," said Lola. "I am going to report my kidnapping."

All eyes were on her.

"You poor girl," said Zia. "When did this happen? Are you all right?"

"I'm fine; it happened years ago. I just found out that Chan Kan paid Antonio de Landa to take me from my mother when I was a baby. I don't know why or how. But if I press charges, I am hoping that Landa will have to tell the full story."

Zia dropped a large serving plate of fruit salad, and Lady Coco ran in to clear up the mess.

"I hope this is not a joke, Lola," snapped Uncle Ted angrily, "because it's not funny."

Lola looked confused. "Why would I joke about something

like this? Max overheard Landa talking about it in the Grand Hotel Xibalba."

"Antonio de Landa?" Uncle Ted's face filled with hate. "You can't believe anything he says. I'm sorry, Lola, but he's just out to make trouble."

"I don't think so, not this time," said Max. "He didn't know that I heard him."

Lola nodded. "I think it's true. Chan Kan was acting so strangely when we went to Utsal. He kept apologizing to me. He said he regretted what he'd done and that he wanted to put his life in order. He had something really big on his conscience. But it was like he kept confusing me with someone else. He kept talking about my husband."

Uncle Ted put his arm around Zia, and she sobbed against his shoulder. "How can you be so cruel, Lola?"

"What did I say? What does any of this have to do with Zia?"

Zia wiped her eyes. "It is okay. You just hit a sore spot."

"You don't have to talk about it," Ted soothed her. "It's too painful."

"No, it's time I faced up to it, Teo." She cleared her throat and looked around the table. "Chan Kan was my father."

Max and Lola stared at her uncomprehendingly.

She continued, "I shut him out of my life many years ago. Fifteen years ago, to be precise. That was when my daughter died. She was twelve months old. Chan Kan came to the funeral, and I never saw him again. Or ever wanted to. And now, now you are telling me that he bought another child to replace his own dead granddaughter? Words fail me. I bear you no ill will, Lola. But I will never forgive Chan Kan. He was an evil man."

327

Lola looked like she'd been slapped. "I'm so sorry."

Eventually Hermanjilio broke the silence. He spoke softly. "So, Zia, straight after your daughter died, Chan Kan adopted a girl baby of the same age?"

Zia nodded.

"I don't want to raise your hopes," continued Hermanjilio, "but there is another possibility. Chan Kan was a skilled medicine man, was he not? I have heard of potions that mimic death."

"No." Zia shook her head vehemently. "I held my baby in my arms till she grew stone cold. She had no pulse."

Uncle Ted's face was ashen. "I know Chan Kan had strong views, but surely he was not capable of that."

"Oh yes, he was," said Zia in a small voice.

"So what if my hunch is right?" insisted Hermanjilio.

"There is one way to find out." Zia looked at Lola and asked gently, "Do you have a birthmark under your right ear?"

As silent as a sleepwalker, Lola got up from her chair and walked around the table to Zia. Then she crouched down and flicked back her hair.

"You do! You do! I've noticed it before!" yelled Max excitedly.

Zia stared at Lola's neck. "I cannot believe it," she whispered. "Is this really happening? Have you really come back to me?" She burst into tears and hugged Lola close.

"Wait! I don't underst–," squeaked Lola, but Zia was holding her so tightly she couldn't speak.

Max tried to clarify the situation. "So Lola is Chan Kan's real granddaughter? And Zia's real daughter? But why would Chan Kan have faked his own granddaughter's death?"

Zia looked up. "He did not approve of my choice of

husband. He wanted me to marry a Maya man, a villager, and stay close to home. He had my life planned out for me."

Lola extricated herself from her mother's embrace. "But, so, wait . . . I have a father, too? Who is my father?"

"That would be me," said Uncle Ted.

Max literally fell off his chair.

"I don't understand," said Lola.

"My brother Frank and I met Zia—or Tooki as we called her back then—at school in Limón. It was soon after our mother had died and our father had sent us away so he could grieve alone. I'll never know how Tooki persuaded Chan Kan to let her go to school, but once she arrived, she was determined never to go home. She never spoke much about her family, and I guess—with the narcissism of youth—we were never curious enough to drag it out of her. All we knew was that she was Maya, that her father was strict, and that she herself had more progressive views. She became like a sister to us, one of the gang. In fact, she was with us when we found Landa's journal. . . ."

Something clicked in Max's brain, like an itch being scratched. He recalled Uncle Ted telling the story of the day they found the journal—*we were camping with a friend*—and he'd always meant to ask the identity of that third person.

"Then Tooki and I did the one thing Chan Kan could never forgive. We fell in love."

"That's why he called you a bad woman?" Lola asked her mother.

Zia nodded.

"What's so bad about marrying a Murphy?" asked Max indignantly.

Uncle Ted laughed. "It wasn't because I was a Murphy, it

was because I wasn't a Maya. Chan Kan believed that he was descended from the Jaguar Kings and he didn't want to sully the royal bloodline."

Max clapped his hands. "So the Monkey Girl is actually a princess! It's like a fairy tale!"

"More like a fantasy," said Zia. "There is no Maya royalty anymore. But Chan Kan refused to let go of the past. After I married Teo, I never saw my father again until, until . . ."

"Until our daughter's funeral," Uncle Ted finished for her.

"Had I been ill?" asked Lola. "What did you think I died of?"

"We thought you'd been murdered."

"Murdered? Why would you think that?"

"You'd been kidnapped. The ransom note said they wouldn't hurt you as long as we didn't go to the police. So brave Teo tried to rescue you himself."

"It was a stupid idea," said Uncle Ted. "I took the money to the meeting place in the forest. I had a gun. . . . There was a shoot-out. . . . It all went wrong. But I swear I heard Antonio De Landa's voice. Next day, my daughter's lifeless body was left at our door."

Zia took over the story. "Chan Kan came to Puerto Muerto straightaway. He screamed at me that I had killed my daughter by marrying outside of our community. He said the gods had punished me." Her face contorted with pain. "And then, he demanded to be left alone with her little coffin to conduct his rituals. . . ."

She folded Lola in her arms again. "And that must have been when he stole you away from me. And he made it so he could legally adopt you, and we would never come looking for you, and you would never know how much we loved you."

All around the table, people and howler monkeys were sobbing into their napkins. But not Max. He was still trying to get his head around the details. "Will someone stop crying and tell me how Zia ended up in our house in Boston?"

"Our marriage could not survive the pain of losing a child," Zia explained. "There were too many recriminations, too much sorrow. I even blamed Teo for going to the forest that night and trying to be a hero. Our lives were in ruins. I had to get away. Frank and Carla offered me a place in Boston, so I went. And Teo turned to his life of crime."

"But that's awful," said Max. "You're like family. And Mom and Dad made you our housekeeper? They enslaved you?"

"No, no, it wasn't like that, Max. The job was my idea. I wanted to be helpful. And I wanted to earn my keep. And I wanted never to have to talk to anyone ever again. Your parents threw me a lifeline at a time when I hated the entire human race."

That explains Zia's lethal tamales, thought Max, but he didn't say it. And then another thought occurred to him. He looked confusedly at Uncle Ted. "I'm sorry, but Lola's Maya. She can't be your daughter."

Uncle Ted laughed. "You should have seen her when she was born! Her hair was redder than yours. She looked like a Murphy all right. There's a photo on my office wall—remind me to show you sometime."

"I've seen it! That's Lola? I thought that was me!"

Zia stroked Lola's hair. "It turned dark almost straightaway."

Lola clapped a hand over her mouth. "Hoop—we're cousins!"

"We are?" Max wasn't sure how he felt about that.

"Your parents are my aunt and uncle! And my parents are your aunt and uncle!"

Max looked at his former housekeeper, bewildered. "Should I call you Aunt Zia?"

"You already call me Aunt. Zia is the Italian word. Your mother came up with it because I never liked my Mayan name."

"Tooki? What was that short for?" asked Lola.

"Ix Took' Hool."

Lola burst out laughing. "Lady Flint Skull?"

"Exactly. Chan Kan wanted to give me a name worthy of a Maya queen. He hoped his baby daughter would grow up to lead Utsal to a bright new future. I'm afraid I failed him."

Uncle Ted squeezed her shoulder. "No, Tooki, he failed you."

"Please, please," begged Max, "can I call you Aunt Flint Skull?"

"No." Zia threw a breadstick at him.

"What's my name?" asked Lola suddenly.

"Lily Theodora Murphy." Uncle Ted's voice cracked. "It's the most beautiful name in the world."

"I didn't give you a Maya name because I was so angry at Chan Kan," added Zia. "But I think Ix Sak Lol is beautiful, too."

"Lily Theodora Murphy." Lola repeated it to herself a few times. "I like it. But I guess I'll stick with Lola for a while, till we all get used to things." Her eyes were shining with happiness. "So how old am I, exactly?"

"You're sixteen. You'll be seventeen on 8-Crocodile," replied Zia instantly.

"You keep the days?"

"Then who would knock at this time of night?" mused Uncle Ted.

When Raul walked back in, he didn't look like Raul anymore.

His face was white as chalk dust. His hair had gone completely gray.

"It was the man who looks like an owl," he said. "He brought us mail."

With shaking hands, he passed around the envelopes.

There was one for everyone, except for Max.

And the reason for that became obvious when they opened them:

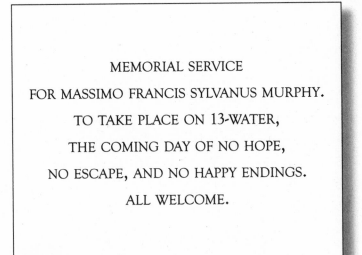

MEMORIAL SERVICE

FOR MASSIMO FRANCIS SYLVANUS MURPHY.

TO TAKE PLACE ON 13-WATER,

THE COMING DAY OF NO HOPE,

NO ESCAPE, AND NO HAPPY ENDINGS.

ALL WELCOME.

To be continued . . .

You probably have a lot of questions
about Max and Lola,
and what will happen next in the story
of the Jaguar Stones.
But honestly, when all is said and done,
only one question really matters:

WHAT WILL BECOME
OF ALL OF US WHO LIVE IN
MIDDLEWORLD,
NOW THAT AH PUKUH HAS
FINALLY FULFILLED
HIS EVIL PLAN
AND GOT HIS
GRASPING HANDS ON
ALL FIVE JAGUAR STONES?

You'll find the answer in
THE JAGUAR STONES,
BOOK FOUR!

Meanwhile, for signed
bookplates and bookmarks, or
free lesson-plan CDs for teachers,
please visit www.jaguarstones.com.

GLOSSARY

AH PUKUH (*awe-poo-coo*): God of violent and unnatural death, depicted in Maya art as a bloated, decomposing corpse or a cigar-smoking skeleton. Ah Pukuh rules over Mitnal, the ninth and most terrible layer of XIBALBA, the Maya underworld.

CENOTE (*say-no-tay*): A deep, water-filled sinkhole. Cenotes are unique to the Yucatan peninsula, where there are around three thousand of them. (The name is a Spanish corruption of the Mayan word *tz'onot*.) Some cenotes are underground lakes in cave systems, while others are pools in open shafts. The ancient Maya thought they were gateways to the watery underworld.

COSMIC CROCODILE: The two-headed Cosmic Crocodile, also known as the Celestial Monster, is a Maya representation of the Milky Way. Its two heads represent the duality of life and death, as the sun moves through the northern sky in the life-giving rainy season and through the southern sky in the dry season.

GLYPHS: The name given to more than eight hundred different signs in the ancient Maya writing system.

HERO TWINS: Twin brothers Xbalanke (*sh-ball-on-kay*) and Hunahpu (*who-gnaw-poo*) are the main characters in the Maya creation story, as told in the POPOL VUH. Challenged to a ballgame by the LORDS OF DEATH, the twins outwit their underworld opponents and take their places in the heavens as the sun and the moon.

IXCHEL (*eesh-shell*): Controversy reigns over the goddess named "Lady Rainbow." Traditionally, she has been viewed as one deity with multiple personalities. As the malevolent Goddess of the Old Moon, she is shown with a snake headband and a skirt embroidered with crossbones; as Goddess of the New Moon, she is a beautiful young woman who reclines inside the crescent moon, holding her pet rabbit. Recently, scholars have made a case for two separate deities: Chak Chel "Great Rainbow" and Ix Uh "Lady Moon."

JAGUAR STONES (in Mayan, *bahlamtuuno'ob*): A literary invention of the Jaguar Stones trilogy. Along with the five (fictional) sacred pyramids, these five stone carvings embody the five pillars of ancient Maya society: agriculture, astronomy, creativity, military prowess, and kingship. As far as we know, no such stones ever existed—nor did the Maya ever relax their warlike ways enough to forge an equal alliance of five great cities.

LANDA, DIEGO DE (1524–1579): The overzealous Franciscan friar who piled Maya books and religious artworks into one big bonfire and burned them all on July 12, 1549.

LORDS OF DEATH: In Maya mythology, the underworld (XIBALBA) is ruled by twelve Lords of Death: One Death, Seven Death, Scab Stripper, Blood Gatherer, Wing, Demon of Pus, Demon of Jaundice, Bone Scepter, Skull Scepter, Demon of Filth, Demon of Woe, and Packstrap. It is their job to inflict sickness, pain, starvation, fear, and death on the citizens of MIDDLEWORLD. Fortunately, they're usually far too busy gambling and playing jokes on one another to get much work done.

339

MAYA: Maya civilization began on the Yucatán peninsula sometime before 1500 BCE and entered its Classic Period around 250 CE, when the Maya established a series of city-states across what is now Mexico, Guatemala, Belize, Honduras, and El Salvador. Building on the accomplishments of earlier civilizations such as the Olmec, the Maya developed astronomy, calendrical systems, and hieroglyphic writing. Although most famous for their soaring pyramids and palaces (built without metal tools, wheels, or beasts of burden), they were also skilled farmers, weavers, and potters, and they established extensive trade networks. Wracked by overpopulation, drought, and soil erosion, Maya power began to decline around 800 CE, when the southern cities were abandoned. By the time of the Spanish Conquest, only a few kingdoms still thrived, and most Maya had gone back to farming their individual family plots. There are still six million Maya living in Mexico, Guatemala, Belize, Honduras, and El Salvador.

MAYAN: The family of thirty-one different and mutually unintelligible languages spoken by Maya groups in Central America.

MIDDLEWORLD: Like the Vikings, the Egyptians, and other ancient cultures, the Maya believed that humankind inhabited a middle world between heaven and hell. The Maya Middleworld (*yok'ol kab*) was sandwiched between the nine dark and watery layers of XIBALBA and the thirteen leafy layers of the heavens (*ka'anal naah*).

MORLEY, SYLVANUS GRISWOLD (1883–1948): Thought by some to have inspired the character of Indiana Jones, Morley was a Harvard-trained archaeologist most famous for his excavations at Chichen Itza and his work as an American spy during World War One.

PITZ: The Mesoamerican ballgame was the first team sport in recorded history and most Maya sites have ball courts. Although no one knows for sure, it seems that the game was played along the lines of tennis or volleyball, but without a net. Using only hips, knees, or elbows, the heavily padded players tried to keep the large rubber ball in play, scoring points if the opposing team made an error or failed to return it. It is now thought that the stone hoops often seen on ball courts served as markers. The game had great religious significance, and it is believed that the losing team, or a team of captive "stunt doubles," was often sacrificed. A version of the game called *ulama* is still played in modern Mexico.

SAN XAVIER: The setting of the Jaguar Stones books, this is a fictional country in Central America based on modern-day Belize.

VISION SERPENT: When a Maya king wished to communicate with an ancestor, he would hold a bloodletting ceremony to summon the Vision Serpent: a hybrid monster depicted as part snake and part giant centipede. In Maya art, this creature is often seen rising out of the smoke, with the ancestor emerging from its mouth.

XIBALBA (*she-ball-buh*): The K'iche' Maya name for the underworld, meaning "Well of Fear." Only kings and those who died a violent death (battle, sacrifice, suicide) or women who died in childbirth could look forward to the leafy shade of heaven. All other souls, good or bad, were headed across rivers of scorpions, blood, and pus to Xibalba. Unlike the Christian hell with its fire and brimstone, the Maya underworld was cold and damp—its inhabitants condemned to an eternity of bone-chilling misery and hunger.

SLOTH (*uch*): These slow-moving animals stay years in the same tree, spending most of their time sleeping. They come down once a week to poop at the base, thus fertilizing the tree that sustains them. Algae grows in their fur, giving them a greenish tinge.

A MIDDLEWORLD BESTIARY

CAVE SPIDER (*am*): With their powerful from pincers, cave spiders look like tailless scorpions.

TOUCAN (*pam*): The toucan's huge and colorful bill is designed for picking fruit and peeling it.

FER-DE-LANCE (*och chan*): This highly venomous pit viper causes more human deaths than any other snake in the Americas.

JAGUAR (*bahlam*): Revered by the Maya as a fearsome warrior, the largest cat in the Americas is now in danger of extinction.

COCKROACH (*xk'uruch*): These ultimate survivors can see in all directions at once.

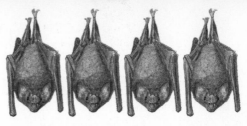

BLACK VULTURE (*usih*): This bald-headed scavenger uses its short, hooked beak to feed on carrion.

VAMPIRE BAT (*suutz'*): Unusual among mammals, this bat is a parasite that lives off the blood of other animals.

HOWLER MONKEY (*baatz'*): With enormous voice boxes that amplify their calls, howlers are the loudest land animals on the planet.

RESPLENDENT QUETZAL (*k'uk'*): The tail feathers of the quetzal were plucked to make headdresses for Maya kings. In those days, it was a crime to kill a quetzal. Today, this shy resident of the cloud forest is an endangered species.

'ILL BUG (*kuklin*): These cave-dwelling crustaceans excrete ammonia.

SCOLOPENDRA (*chapaht*): This giant cave centipede squirts a toxic venom to catch bats and small animals.

TAPIR (*tihl*): It looks like a cross between a hippo and an anteater, but the tapir's closest relatives are the horse and the rhino.

MORELET'S CROCODILE (*ahiin*): This smaller species is found only in Central America.

POISON DART FROG (*muuch*): One of the most toxic creatures on earth, some species carry enough poison to kill ten people.

A SIDE TRIP TO VENICE

In this book, we take the Maya Death Lords to Venice, Italy. It seems like the ideal vacation spot for them because it has a lot in common with Xibalba, the Maya underworld.

Of course, Venice is a beautiful city. But there's no denying that it's watery and misty, sometimes smelly, and sometimes bitterly cold. Most importantly, as Lord Kuy explains to Max, it's a liminal place, and the ancient Maya were fascinated by liminality. It's a concept that comes from the Latin word *limen*, meaning "threshold," and it describes something that's between two states of being. For example, the ancient Maya revered jaguars because they hunt on land and in water, by night and by day; similarly, mountains were sacred because they are half on earth and half in the sky. So we think Venice would have delighted the Death Lords because it's not quite land and not quite water.

Tradition has it that Venice was founded in the fifth century CE (at about the same time the Maya were building Chichen Itza) by refugees fleeing from barbarian invasions of northern Italy. At first, it was just a collection of swampy islands in a tidal lagoon, but the settlers gradually reinforced the mud with millions of wooden pilings.

Today, as the weight of buildings pushes the pilings ever deeper and sea levels rise with climate change, Venice is slowly sinking. At particularly high tides, water floods the city and gushes up through marble floors.

In the beginning, the Venetians relished their isolation in the lagoon. Like a Maya city-state, they formed an independent republic (ruled over by a doge), and established an extensive trading network. But just as smallpox brought over from Europe devastated the Maya, successive waves of plague carried in from other ports ravaged the Venetians. In the 1629–31 epidemic, a third of the Venetian population died. On that occasion, the small island of Poveglia (the inspiration for our Plague Island) was used as a quarantine and plague pit.

Another consequence of the plague was the appearance of the *medico della peste*, or plague doctor. Members of this perilous profession wore beaked masks and head-to-toe robes to protect themselves from disease. Today, the plague doctor costume is a popular choice for revelers at the Venetian *carnevale*.

And that's another reason why the ancient Maya Death Lords would feel at home in Venice: because for all its grim history and ghosts and four rats to every human, it's a fun-loving city that thrives on masked balls and glittering social events. And as you know if you've read the Jaguar Stones books, the Death Lords are just twelve fun-loving guys . . . on a mission to destroy the world.

ANCIENT MAYA BEAUTY SECRETS

When Max visits Salon on Six in the Grand Hotel Xibalba, he's surprised by the array of ancient Maya beauty treatments—many of them extremely painful. So let's look at what this Maya queen (Lady Xook, principal wife of Shield Jaguar, king of Yaxchilan) has endured to look her best for a bloodletting ceremony.

Sloping forehead and tapered skull—molded into a corncob shape when she was born, in tribute to the Maize God.

Crossed eyes—trained to look inward by tying a ball of wax between them when she was a child.

Flamboyant headdress—probably made of jade, woven fabric, wood, feathers, and animal hide.

False nose bridge made of clay or plaster—to streamline her profile.

Cosmetic dentistry—Maya nobility had their teeth filed into various pointed shapes and inlaid with jewels.

Elaborate hairdo—adorned with feathers, shells, and beads.

Pierced ears—with huge jade earspools.

Facial scarification and tattoos. She may also have used body paint.

Heavy jewelry—made of jade and precious stones. (Unlike the Aztecs, the Maya had no gold.) The face badge is probably a god from whom Lady Xook, meaning Lady Shark, claimed ancestry.

THE MAYA CALENDAR

Ancient Maya astronomers devised many different calendars to mark the passage of time. Most of them—including the Long Count calendar, a misinterpretation of which gave rise to all the hokum about 2012—are not in use anymore. But Maya daykeepers still follow a 260-day ritual calendar, the Tzolk'in, to track ceremonial days and indicate the best timing for life events such as weddings and journeys. Like Lord 6-Dog, Maya children were sometimes given their birthday as a nickname. (By this reckoning, the Jaguar Stones books are written by Lord 9-Thunder and Lady 7-Monkey.) To find out your Maya birth sign, just e-mail the day/month/year you were born (*spell out month*) to birthdays@jaguarstones.com.

Here are the twenty day names—which one will be yours?

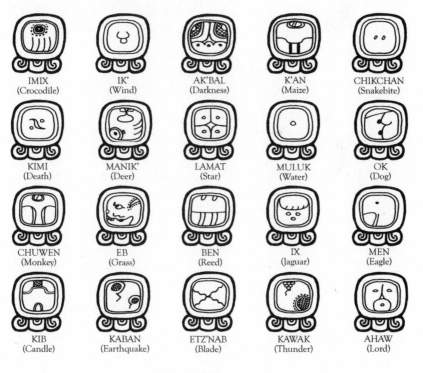

IMIX (Crocodile)	IK' (Wind)	AK'BAL (Darkness)	K'AN (Maize)	CHIKCHAN (Snakebite)
KIMI (Death)	MANIK' (Deer)	LAMAT (Star)	MULUK (Water)	OK (Dog)
CHUWEN (Monkey)	EB (Grass)	BEN (Reed)	IX (Jaguar)	MEN (Eagle)
KIB (Candle)	KABAN (Earthquake)	ETZ'NAB (Blade)	KAWAK (Thunder)	AHAW (Lord)

PIZZA GELATO
(Requires ice-cream maker)

INGREDIENTS:
- 8 oz. finely grated Parmesan cheese
- 5 cups heavy cream
- 1 tablespoon fresh basil & oregano, finely chopped
- 1 small Pizza Margherita, cooked and sliced into half-inch squares
- 1/4 cup chilled tomato puree
- Pepper

PREPARATION:
1) Pour cream into a saucepan and heat to a simmer. Add all the Parmesan and a dash of pepper, stirring until smooth.
2) Push mixture through strainer to extract as much liquid as possible, cool to room temperature, then pour into ice-cream maker.
3) When nearly ready, add chopped herbs.
4) Mix ice cream with slices of pizza and top with tomato puree.
5) THROW OUT IMMEDIATELY AS IT IS DISGUSTING.

The following variations were also tried and are strongly *not* recommended:

- Cheese ice cream, topped with bacon and carbonara sauce.
- Tomato ice cream swirled in cheese ice cream, sprinkled with herbs.

We attempted many ways to re-create Carla Murphy's concept for a savory dessert and, every time, the results were inedible. If you have your own recipe for Pizza Gelato to share on the Jaguar Stones website, please email it (with photos if possible) to recipes@jaguarstones.com *Buon appetito!*

ACKNOWLEDGMENTS

Originally planned as the third and final volume in the Jaguar Stones series, the first draft of this book was as thick as a pyramid step and as heavy as a Maya king's headdress. So, for giving us the freedom to start over and go beyond a trilogy, huge thanks to the most perceptive, most inspiring, most supportive, most fun-to-work-with editor in the world, Elizabeth Law at Egmont USA.

Thank you to everyone else at Egmont for your passion for children's books and your commitment to saving the rainforests by using only paper from sustainable sources; especially to the wonderful Mary Albi, and to Katie Halata, Bonnie Cutler, and Rob Guzman—we love you guys. That goes for you too, Daniel Lazar of Writers House.

Thank you to Arlene Goldberg (who doesn't usually have to work around cockroaches on the page) for making it all fit with such care and precision, Becky Terhune for book design, Cliff Nielsen for the cover illustration. And thank you once again to Katherine Hinds for an amazing job of proofreading a text that includes English, Italian, Spanish, Yucatec Maya, and ancient Maya hieroglyphs.

Massive thanks to our redoubtable advisor-in-chief, Marc Zender, and to all the other real-life Indiana Joneses who have shared their knowledge and experiences with us: Gerardo Aldana, Armando Anaya H., Anthony F. Aveni, Jaime Awe (Director, Belize Institute of Archaeology), Ramzy Barrois, Mary Clarke, Allan Cobb, Stanley Guenter, Norman Hammond, Amanda Harvey, Julie Hoggarth, Patsy Holden, Gyles Iannone, Harri Kettunen, S. Ashley Kistler, Maxime Lamoureux-St Hilaire, David Lee, Bruce Love, Heather McKillop, Meaghan Peuramäki-Brown, Christy Pritchard, Jim Pritchard, Mat Saunders, Priscilla Saunders, James Stemp, Mark Van Stone, George Stuart, Gabrielle Vail, and Belizean chef/storyteller Patricio Balona.

Thank you to the following people for helping with our research: In Mexico, Denis Larsen, proprietor of Casa Hamaca in Valladolid—the best guesthouse in Yucatán; Serviliano Petil Urtcil (Don Carlos), Sofia Pat Balam, Lorenzo Antonio Petul Balam, Lorena Letiticia Petul Balam, and Genny Magaly Petul Balam in Yalcobá; the students of Escuela Primaria Sor Juana Inés de la Cruz—and in respectful memory of their gracious principal, Mauricio Eustaquio Acosta Balam; Allan Brookstone and neighbors in Santa Eléuteria; Alex Aranda in San Cristobal de Las Casas. In Italy, Signor Dino Padovan on Guidecca island, Signorina Giovanna at Grandi Vedute, and Marco Penazzi for recreating Venice in Vermont and correcting our Italian. At the NASA Calendar in the Sky workshop, Brian Mendez of the Space Sciences Lab at UC Berkeley and Marco Antonio Pacheco, President of Casa de la Cultura Maya in Los Angeles.

To Sarah Nasif and Nicole Dufort of Random House: thank you for connecting us with so many wonderful bookstores. And a big thank you to all the booksellers we've had the honor of working with, especially: Pat at Black Forest Books & Toys; Tina, Peter, and Dave at Blue Marble; Cindy at Cardinal Lane Book Fairs; Kenny at DDG; Judith and Tom at Octavia; Brandi, Stephanie, and Eddie at Changing Hands; Emily at Lemuria; Jill at Square Books Junior; Carol at Eight Cousins; Vicky at Titcombs; Gussie at Politics and Prose; Jennifer at Barnes & Noble, Upper East Side; Sarah at Flyleaf; Vicki at Quail Ridge; Rachel at Kings English; Margot at Watchung Booksellers; Nikki and Melissa at Pudd'nhead; Betsy at The Bookshelf; Angie at The Book Carriage; Cathy at Blue Willow; Liesl and the team at Boulder Bookstore; everyone at Tattered Cover; everyone at Anderson's; Keebe (and Christie) at McIntyre's; Linda and Mona at Jabberwocky; Tiffany at bbgb; Trish at Hooray for Books!; Angie at The Country Bookshop; Lisa at Nightbird; Michael and Scott at Joseph Beth; Heather at Children's Book World; Penny and Liza at The Norwich Bookstore; Liz Duffy at Baker & Taylor.

For their hard work behind the scenes, we'd like to thank all the educators, librarians, and parents around the country who've helped make our author visits happen. In particular: Carla Duff at Oelwein Middle School; Elizabeth Kahn at Patrick F. Taylor Science & Technology Academy; Guusje Moore and Maryanna Johnson at Housman Elementary; Monica Campana at Indian Trails Middle School; Tony Novak at Hull Elementary; Paul Hankins at Silver Creek; Donalyn Miller at Trinity Meadows Elementary; Lindy Sargent at Newport Elementary; Nathan Sekinger at Gayle Middle School; Freddie Moore and her students at Mannion Middle School; Ally in Utah; Christie Kimsey at Chatham Community Library; Claudia and Angie at the Missouri River Regional Library; Julia Chang at The New York Public Library; Jennifer Ripstra at The Penn Museum; Joel Smeltzer of The Mint Museum; Kelly Lindberg and Ben Thomas of the AIA; Mike Adams of the Boston Museum of Science; Ann Abadie of the Oxford Conference for the Book; Beth Reynolds of the Norwich Public Library; Cammie Backus of RIF.

For their excellent advice, incisive comments, and eagle-eyed proofreading, thanks to our panel of young readers: Billy Bender, Trevor Cigogna, Brett Clouse, Zea Eanet, Devon Ewing, Mateo Ellerson, Amy Fightmaster, Jennifer Funderburk, Aidan Grant, Lucille Inglis, Meredith Mackall, Sam Pocock, Alexandra Pritchard, Tobias Reynolds, Siobhan Seigne, Stefan Suazo, Parker Thurston, and special consultant, Bill Hodgkinson.

Thank you to our own three children for driving all those miles with us over bumpy dirt roads, and for being such good sports about termites for breakfast, howlers on the roof, and frogs in the bath. Thanks to family and friends for all that love, support, and unpaid labor: the amazing Captain Doctor Dre; Jack and Mary Anne; Trina; Hetty and Peter; Christy and Alan; Lisa, Juanga, and Julie; Max, Nicole, Heather, Dustin; Uncle Ted; Graham. Also to Don, Jenn, Rose, Felix, Brittany; Yaniris Sotelo; Cee, Paul, and Big Guy; Wendy Thompson.

Finally, to the person who did more than anyone else to make sure that 2012 was not the end of the world: eternal thanks to Kari Rosenkranz.